Stories Worth Re-reading

iBoo Press
London

Stories Worth Re-reading

Layout & Cover © Copyright 2019 iBooPress, London

Published by

iBoo Press

86-90 Paul Street
London, EC2A4NE UK

t: +44 20 3695 0809
info@iboo.com II iBoo.com

ISBNs
978-1-64181-662-5 (h)
978-1-64181-663-2 (p)

Printed in the United States

Stories Worth
Re-reading

Contents

THEIR WORD OF HONOR

The president of the Great B. railway system laid down the letter he had just reread three times, and turned about in his chair with an expression of extreme annoyance.

"I wish it were possible," he said, slowly, "to find one boy or man in a thousand who would receive instructions and carry them out to the letter without a single variation from the course laid down. Cornelius," he looked up sharply at his son, who sat at a desk close by, "I hope you are carrying out my ideas with regard to your sons. I have not seen much of them lately. The lad Cyrus seems to me a promising fellow, but I am not so sure of Cornelius. He appears to be acquiring a sense of his own importance as Cornelius Woodbridge, Third, which is not desirable, sir,—not desirable. By the way, Cornelius, have you yet applied the Hezekiah Woodbridge test to your boys?"

Cornelius Woodbridge, Junior, looked up from his work with a smile. "No, I have not, father," he said.

"It's a family tradition; and if the proper care has been taken that the boys should not learn of it, it will be as much a test for them as it was for you and for me and for my father. You have not forgotten the day I gave it to you, Cornelius?"

"That would be impossible," said his son, still smiling.

The elder man's somewhat stern features relaxed, and he sat back in his chair with a chuckle. "Do it at once," he requested, "and make it a stiff one. You know their characteristics; give it to them hard. I feel pretty sure of Cyrus, but Cornelius—" He shook his head doubtfully, and returned to his letter. Suddenly he wheeled about again.

"Do it Thursday, Cornelius," he said, in his peremptory way, "and whichever one of them stands it shall go with us on the tour of inspection. That will be reward enough, I fancy."

"Very well, sir," replied his son, and the two men went on with their work without further words. They were in the habit of despatching important business with the smallest possible waste of breath.

On Thursday morning, immediately after breakfast, Cyrus Woodbridge found himself summoned to his father's library. He presented himself at once, a round-cheeked, bright-eyed lad of fifteen, with an air of alertness in every line of him.

"Cyrus," said his father, "I have a commission for you to undertake, of a character which I cannot now explain to you. I want you to take this envelope"—he held out a large and bulky packet—"and, without saying anything to any one, follow its instructions to the letter. I ask of you your word of honor that you will do so."

The two pairs of eyes looked into each other for a moment, singularly alike in a certain intent expression, developed into great keenness in the man, but showing as yet only an extreme wide-awakeness in the boy. Cyrus Woodbridge had an engagement with a young friend in half an hour, but he responded, firmly:—

"I will, sir."

"On your honor?"

"Yes, sir."

"That is all I want. Go to your room, and read your instructions. Then start at once."

Mr. Woodbridge turned back to his desk with the nod and smile of dismissal to which Cyrus was accustomed. The boy went to his room, opening the envelope as soon as he had closed the door. It was filled with smaller envelopes, numbered in regular order. Infolding these was a typewritten paper, which read as follows:—

"Go to the reading-room of the Westchester Library. There open envelope No. 1. Remember to hold all instructions secret. C.W., Jr."

8

Cyrus whistled. "That's funny! It means my date with Harold is off. Well, here goes!"

He stopped on his way out to telephone his friend of his detention, took a Westchester Avenue car at the nearest point, and in twenty minutes was at the library. He found an obscure corner and opened envelope No. 1.

"Go to office of W.K. Newton, room 703, tenth floor, Norfolk Building, X
Street, reaching there by 9:30 A.M. Ask for letter addressed to Cornelius
Woodbridge, Jr. On way down elevator open envelope No. 2."

Cyrus began to laugh. At the same time he felt a trifle irritated. "What's father at?" he questioned, in perplexity. "Here I am away up-town, and he orders me back to the Norfolk Building. I passed it on my way up. Must be he made a mistake. Told me to obey instructions, though. He usually knows just about why he does things."

Meanwhile Mr. Woodbridge had sent for his elder son, Cornelius. A tall youth of seventeen, with the strong family features, varied by a droop in the eyelids and a slight drawl in his speech, lounged to the door of the library. Before entering he straightened his shoulders; he did not, however, quicken his pace.

"Cornelius," said his father, promptly, "I wish to send you upon an errand of some importance, but of possible inconvenience to you. I have not time to give you instructions, but you will find them in this envelope. I ask you to keep the matter and your movements strictly to yourself. May I have from you your word of honor that I can trust you to follow the orders to the smallest detail?"

Cornelius put on a pair of eye-glasses, and held out his hand for the envelope. His manner was almost indifferent. Mr. Woodbridge withheld the packet, and spoke with decision: "I cannot allow you to look at the instructions until I have your word of honor that you will fulfil them."

"Is not that asking a good deal, sir?"

9

"Perhaps so," said Mr. Woodbridge, "but no more than is asked of trusted messengers every day. I will assure you that the instructions are mine and represent my wishes."

"How long will it take?" inquired Cornelius, stooping to flick an imperceptible spot of dust from his trousers.

"I do not find it necessary to tell you."

Something in his father's voice sent the languid Cornelius to an erect position, and quickened his speech.

"Of course I will go," he said, but he did not speak with enthusiasm.

"And—your word of honor?"

"Certainly, sir." The hesitation before the promise was only momentary.

"Very well. I will trust you. Go to your room before opening your instructions."

And the second somewhat mystified boy went out of the library on that memorable Thursday morning, to find his first order one which sent him to a remote district of the city, with the direction to arrive there within three quarters of an hour.

Out on an electric car Cyrus was speeding to another suburb. After getting the letter from the tenth floor of the Norfolk Building, he had read:—

"Take cross-town car on L Street, transfer to Louisville Avenue, and go out to Kingston Heights. Find corner West and Dwight Streets, and open envelope No. 3."

Cyrus was growing more and more puzzled, but he was also getting interested. At the corner specified he hurriedly tore open No. 3, but found, to his amazement, only the singular direction:—

"Take Suburban Underground Road for Duane Street Station. From there go to Sentinel office, and secure third edition of yesterday's paper. Open envelope No. 4."

"Well, what under the sun, moon, and stars did he send me out to Kingston Heights for!" cried Cyrus aloud. He caught the next train, thinking longingly of his broken engagement with Harold Dunning, and of certain plans for the afternoon which he was beginning to fear might be thwarted if this seemingly endless and aimless excursion continued. He looked at the packet of un-opened envelopes.

"It would be easy to break open the whole outfit, and see what this game is," he thought. "Never knew father to do a thing like this before. If it's a joke,"—his fingers felt the seal of envelope No. 4,—"I might as well find it out at once. Still, father never would joke with a fellow's promise the way he asked it of me. 'My word of honor'—that's putting it pretty strong. I'll see it through, of course. My, but I'm getting hungry! It must be near luncheon-time."

It was not; but by the time Cyrus had been ordered twice across the city and once up a sixteen-story building in which the eleva-tor service was out of order, it was past noon, and he was in a condition to find envelope No. 7 a very satisfactory one:—

"Go to Cafe Reynaud on Westchester Square. Take a seat at table in left alcove. Ask waiter for card of Cornelius Woodbridge, Jun-ior. Before ordering luncheon read envelope No. 8."

The boy lost no time in obeying this command, and sank into his chair in the designated alcove with a sigh of relief. He mopped his brow, and drank a glass of ice-water at a gulp. It was a warm October day, and the sixteen flights had been somewhat trying. He asked for his father's card, and then sat studying the attractive menu.

"I think I'll have—" He mused for a moment, then said, with a laugh,
"Well, I'm about hungry enough to eat the whole thing. Bring me the—"

Then he recollected, paused, and reluctantly pulled out enve-lope No. 8, and broke the seal. "Just a minute," he murmured to the waiter. Then his face turned scarlet, and he stammered, under his breath, "Why—why—this can't be—"

Envelope No. 8 ought to have been bordered with black, judging by the dismay its order to a lecture hall to hear a famous electrician, caused. But the Woodbridge blood was up now, and it was with an expression resembling that of his grandfather Cornelius under strong indignation that Cyrus stalked out of that charming place to proceed grimly to the lecture hall.

"Who wants to hear a lecture on an empty stomach?" he groaned. "I suppose I'll be ordered out, anyway, the minute I sit down and stretch my legs. Wonder if father can be exactly right in his mind. He doesn't believe in wasting time, but I'm wasting it today by the bucketful. Suppose he's doing this to size me up some way; he isn't going to tire me out so quick as he thinks. I'll keep going till I drop."

Nevertheless, when, just as he was getting interested, he was ordered to go three miles to a football field, and then ordered away again without a sight of the game he had planned for a week to see, his disgust was intense.

All through that long, warm afternoon he raced about the city and suburbs, growing wearier and more empty with every step. The worst of it was, the orders were beginning to assume the form of a schedule, and commanded that he be here at 3:15, and there at 4:05; and so on, which forbade loitering, had he been inclined to loiter. In it all he could see no purpose, except the possible one of trying his physical endurance. He was a strong boy, or he would have been quite exhausted long before he reached envelope No. 17, which was the last but three of the packet. This read:—

"Reach home at 6:20 P.M. Before entering house, read No. 18."

Leaning against one of the big white stone pillars of the porch of his home, Cyrus wearily tore open envelope No. 18, and the words fairly swam before his eyes. He had to rub them hard to make sure that he was not mistaken:—

"Go again to Kingston Heights, corner West and Dwight Streets, reaching there by 6:50. Read No. 19."

The boy looked up at the windows, desperately angry at last. If his pride and his sense of the meaning of that phrase, "My word of honor," as the men of the Woodbridge family were in the habit of teaching their sons, had not both been of the strongest sort, he would have rebelled, and gone defiantly and stormily in. As it was, he stood for one long minute with his hands clenched and his teeth set; then he turned and walked down the steps away from the longed-for dinner, and out toward L Street and the car for Kingston Heights.

As he did so, inside the house, on the other side of the curtains, from behind which he had been anxiously peering, Cornelius Woodbridge, Senior, turned about and struck his hands together, rubbing them in a satisfied way.

"He's come—and gone," he cried, softly, "and he's on time to the minute!"

Cornelius, Junior, did not so much as lift his eyes from the evening paper, as he quietly answered, "Is he?" But the corners of his mouth slightly relaxed.

The car seemed to crawl out to Kingston Heights. As it at last neared its terminus, a strong temptation seized the boy Cyrus. He had been on a purposeless errand to this place once that day. The corner of West and Dwight Streets lay more than half a mile from the end of the car route, and it was an almost untenanted district. His legs were very tired; his stomach ached with emptiness. Why not wait out the interval which it would take to walk to the corner and back in a little suburban station, read envelope No. 19, and spare himself? He had certainly done enough to prove that he was a faithful messenger.

Had he? Certain old and well-worn words came into his mind; they had been in his writing-book in the early school-days: "A chain is no stronger than its weakest link." Cyrus jumped off the car before it fairly stopped, and started at a hot pace for the corner of West and Dwight Streets. There must be no weak places in his word of honor.

Doggedly he went to the extreme limit of the indicated route, even taking the longest way round to make the turn. As he started back, beneath the arc light at the corner there suddenly appeared a city messenger boy. He approached Cyrus, and, grinning, held

13

out an envelope.

"Ordered to give you this," he said, "if you made connections. If you'd been later than five minutes past seven, I was to keep dark. You've got seven minutes and a half to spare. Queer orders, but the big railroad boss, Woodbridge, gave 'em to me."

Cyrus made his way back to the car with some self-congratulations that served to brace up the muscles behind his knees. This last incident showed him plainly that his father was putting him to a severe test of some sort, and he could have no doubt that it was for a purpose. His father was the sort of man who does things with a very definite purpose indeed. Cyrus looked back over the day with an anxious searching of his memory to be sure that no detail of the singular service required of him had been slighted.

As he once more ascended the steps of his own home, he was so confident that his labors were now ended that he almost forgot about envelope No. 20, which he had been directed to read in the vestibule before entering the house. With his thumb on the bell button he recollected, and with a sigh broke open the final seal:—

"Turn about, and go to Lenox Street Station, B. Railroad, reaching there by 8:05. Wait for messenger in west end of station, by telegraph office."

It was a blow, but Cyrus had his second wind now. He felt like a machine—a hollow one—which could keep on going indefinitely.

The Lenox Street Station was easily reached on time. The hands of the big clock were only at one minute past eight when Cyrus entered. At the designated spot the messenger met him. Cyrus recognized him as the porter on one of the trains of the road of which his grandfather and father were officers. Why, yes, he was the porter of the Woodbridge special car! He brought the boy a card which ran thus:—

"Give porter the letter from Norfolk Building, the card received at restaurant, the lecture coupon, yesterday evening's Sentinel, and the envelope received at Kingston Heights."

Cyrus silently delivered up these articles, feeling a sense of thankfulness that not one was missing. The porter went away with them, but was back in three minutes.

"This way, sir," he said, and Cyrus followed, his heart beating fast. Down the track he recognized the "Fleetwing," President Woodbridge's private car. And Grandfather Cornelius he knew to be just starting on a tour of his own and other roads, which included a flying trip to Mexico. Could it be possible—

In the car his father and grandfather rose to meet him. Cornelius Woodbridge, Senior, was holding out his hand.

"Cyrus, lad," he said, his face one broad, triumphant smile, "you have stood the test, the Hezekiah Woodbridge test, sir, and you may be proud of it. Your word of honor can be depended upon. You are going with us through nineteen States and Mexico. Is that reward enough for one day's hardships?"

"I think it is, sir," agreed Cyrus, his round face reflecting his grandfather's smile, intensified.

"Was it a hard pull, Cyrus?" questioned the senior Woodbridge with interest.

Cyrus looked at his father. "I don't think so—now, sir," he said. Both gentlemen laughed.

"Are you hungry?"

"Well, just a little, grandfather."

"Dinner will be served the moment we are off. We have only six minutes to wait. I am afraid—I am very much afraid "—the old gentleman turned to gaze searchingly out of the car window into the station—"that another boy's word of honor, is not—"

He stood, watch in hand. The conductor came in and remained, awaiting orders. "Two minutes more, Mr. Jefferson," he said. "One and a half—one—half a minute." He spoke sternly: "Pull out at 8:14 on the second, sir. Ah——"

The porter entered hurriedly, and delivered a handful of envelopes into
Grandfather Cornelius's grasp. The old gentleman scanned

15

them at a glance.

"Yes, yes—all right!" he cried, with the strongest evidences of excitement Cyrus had ever seen in his usually quiet manner. As the train made its first gentle motion of departure, a figure appeared in the doorway. Quietly, and not at all out of breath, Cornelius Woodbridge, Third, walked into the car.

Then Grandfather Woodbridge grew impressive. He advanced, and shook hands with his grandson as if he were greeting a distinguished member of the board of directors. Then he turned to his son, and shook hands with him also, solemnly. His eyes shone through his gold-rimmed spectacles, but his voice was grave with feeling.

"I congratulate you, Cornelius," he said, "on possessing two sons whose word of honor is above reproach. The smallest deviation from the outlined schedule would have resulted disastrously. Ten minutes' tardiness at the different points would have failed to obtain the requisite documents. Your sons did not fail. They can be depended upon. The world is in search of men built on those lines. I congratulate you, sir."

Cyrus was glad presently to escape to his stateroom with Cornelius. "Say, what did you have to do?" he asked, eagerly. "Did you trot your legs off all over town?"

"Not much, I didn't!" said Cornelius, grimly, from the depths of a big towel. "I spent the whole day in a little hole of a room at the top of an empty building, with just ten trips down the stairs to the ground floor to get envelopes at certain minutes. I had not a crumb to eat nor a thing to do, and could not even snatch a nap for fear I'd oversleep one of my dates at the bottom."

"I believe that was worse than mine," commented Cyrus, reflectively.

"I should say it was. If you don't think so, try it."

"Dinner, boys," said their father's voice at the door, and they lost no time in responding.—Grace S. Richmond, in Youth's Companion.

Heroism

A tone of pride or petulance repressed,
A selfish inclination firmly fought,
A shadow of annoyance set at naught,
A measure of disquietude suppressed,
A peace in importunity possessed,
A reconcilement generously sought,
A purpose put aside, a banished thought,
A word of self-explaining unexpressed,—
Trifles they seem, these petty soul-restraints;
Yet he who proves them so must needs possess
A constancy and courage grand and bold.
They are the trifles that have made the saints.
Give me to practise them in humbleness,
And nobler power than mine doth no man hold.
—Selected.

𝑀URIEL'S BRIGHT IDEA

My friend Muriel is the youngest daughter in a large family of busy people. They are in moderate circumstances, and the original breadwinner has been long gone; so in order to enjoy many of the comforts and a few of the luxuries of life the young people have to be wage-earners. I am not sure that they would enjoy life any better than they do now if such were not the case, though there are doubtless times when they would like to be less busy. Still, even this condition has its compensations.

"Other people do not know how lovely vacations are," was the way Esther expressed it as she sat one day on the side porch, hands folded lightly in her lap, and an air of delicious idleness about her entire person. It was her week of absolute leisure, which she had earned by a season of hard work. She is a public-school teacher, belonging to a section and grade where they work their teachers fourteen hours of the twenty-four.

Alice is a music-teacher, and goes all day from house to house in town, and from school to school, with her music-roll in hand. Ben, a young brother, is studying medicine in a doctor's office, also in town, and serving the doctor between times to pay for his opportunities. There are two others, an older brother just started in business for himself, and a sister in a training-school for nurses.

So it was that this large family scattered each morning to their duties in the city ten miles away, and gathered at night, like chickens, to the home nest, which was mothered by the dearest little woman, who gave much of her time and strength to the preparation of favorite dishes with which to greet the wage-earners as they gathered at night around the home table. It is a very happy family, but it was not about any of them that I set out to tell you. In truth, it was Muriel's apron that I wanted to talk about; but it seemed necessary to describe the family in order to secure full appreciation of the apron.

Muriel, I should tell you, is still a high-school girl, hoping to be graduated next year, though at times a little anxious lest she may not pass, and with ambitions to enter college as soon as possible.

The entire family have ambitions for Muriel, and I believe that she will get to college in another year. But about her apron. I saw it first one morning when I crossed the street to my neighbor's side door that opens directly into the large living-room, and met Muriel in the doorway, as pretty a picture as a fair-haired, bright-eyed girl of seventeen can make. She was in what she called her uniform, a short dress made of dark print, cut lower in the neck than a street dress. It had elbow sleeves, and a bit of white braid stitched on their bands and around the square neck set off the little costume charmingly.

Her apron was of strong dark-green denim, wide enough to cover her dress completely; it had a bib waist held in place by shoulder straps; and the garment fastened behind with a single button, making it adjustable in a second. But its distinctive feature was a row of pockets—or rather several rows of them—extending across the front breadth; they were of varying sizes, and all bulged out as if well filled.

"What in the world?" I began, and stared at the pockets. Muriel's merry laugh rang out.

"Haven't you seen my pockets before?" she asked. "They astonish you, of course; everybody laughs at them; but I am proud of them; they are my own invention. You see, we are such a busy family all day long, and so tired when we get home at night, that we have a bad habit of dropping things just where they happen to land, and leaving them. By the last of the week this big living-room is a sight to behold. It used to take half my morning to pick up the thousand and one things that did not belong here, and carry them to their places. You do not know how many journeys I had to make, because I was always overlooking something. So I invented this apron with a pocket in it for every member of the family, and it works like a charm.

"Look at this big one with a B on it; that is for Ben, of course, and it is always full. Ben is a great boy to leave his pencils, and his handkerchiefs, and everything else about. Last night he even discarded his necktie because it felt choky.

"This pocket is Esther's. She leaves her letters and her discarded handkerchiefs, as well as her gloves. And Kate sheds hair ribbons and hatpins wherever she goes. Just think how lovely it is to have a pocket for each, and drop things in as fast as I find them. When I am all through dusting, I have simply to travel once around the house and unpack my load. I cannot tell you how much time and trouble and temper my invention has saved me."

"It is a bright idea," I said, "and I mean to pass it on. There are other living-rooms and busy girls. Whose is that largest pocket, marked M?"

"Why, I made it for mother; but, do you know, I have found out just in this very way that mothers do not leave things lying around. It is queer, isn't it, when they have so many cares? It seems to be natural for mothers to think about other people. So I made the M stand for 'miscellaneous,' and I put into that pocket articles which will not classify, and that belong to all of us. There are hosts of things for which no particular one seems to be responsible. Is it not a pity that I did not think of pockets last winter, when we all had special cares and were so dreadfully busy? It is such a simple idea you would have supposed that any person would have thought of it, but it took me two years. I just had to do it this spring, because there simply was not time to run up- and down-stairs so much."

"You have proved once more the truth of the old proverb, 'Necessity is the mother of invention,'" I said. "And, besides, you have given me a new idea. I am going home to work it out. When it is finished, I will show it to you." Then I went home, and made rows and rows of strong pockets to sew on a folding screen I was making for my work-room.—Pansy, in Christian Endeavor World. By permission of Lothrop, Lee & Shepard Co.

* * * * *

Just Do Your Best

Just do your best. It matters not how small,
    How little heard of;
Just do your best—that's all.
Just do your best. God knows it all,
And in his great plan you count as one;

Just do your best until the work is done.

Just do your best. Reward will come
  To those who stand the test;
God does not forget. Press on,
  Nor doubt, nor fear. Just do your best.

ERNEST LLOYD.

THE STRENGTH OF CLINTON

When Clinton Stevens was eleven years old, he was taken very sick with pneumonia. During convalescence, he suffered an unexpected relapse, and his mother and the doctor worked hard to keep him alive.

"It is ten to one if he gets well," said Dr. Bemis, shaking his head. "If he does, he will never be very strong."

Mrs. Stevens smoothed Clinton's pillow even more tenderly than before. Poor Clinton! who had always been such a rollicking, rosy-cheeked lad. Surely it was hard to bear.

The long March days dragged slowly along, and April was well advanced before Clinton could sit at the window, and watch the grass grow green on the slope of the lawn. He looked frail and delicate. He had a cough, too, a troublesome "bark," that he always kept back as long as he could.

The bright sunlight poured steadily in through the window, and Clinton held up his hand to shield his eyes. "Why, Ma Stevens!" he said, after a moment, "just look at my hands! They are as thin and white as a girl's, and they used to be regular paws. It does not look as if I would pull many weeds for Mr. Carter this summer, does it?"

Mrs. Stevens took his thin hands in her own patient ones. "Never mind, dearie," she said, "they will grow plump and brown again, I hope." A group of school-children were passing by, shouting and frolicking. Clinton leaned forward and watched them till the last one was gone. Some of them waved their caps, but he did not seem elated. "Mother," he said, presently, "I believe I will go to bed if you will help me. I—I guess I am not quite so—strong— now as I used to be."

Clinton did not pull weeds for Mr. Carter that summer, but he rode around with the milkman, and did a little outdoor work for his mother, which helped him to mend. One morning in July he surprised the village by riding out on his bicycle; but he overdid the matter, and it was several weeks before he again appeared. His cough still continued, though not so severe as in the spring, and it was decided to let him go to school in the fall.

Dr. Bemis told Mrs. Stevens that the schoolroom would be a good place to test Clinton's strength. And he was right. In no other place does a young person's strength develop or debase itself so readily, for honor or dishonor. Of course the doctor had referred to physical strength; but moral strength is much more important.

Clinton was a bright lad for his years; and, although he had not looked into his books during the summer, he was placed in the same grade he had left when taken sick. He did not find much difficulty in keeping up with any of his studies except spelling. Whenever he received a perfect mark on that subject, he felt that a real victory had been won.

About Christmas-time the regular examinations were held. The teacher offered a prize to each grade, the pupil receiving the highest average in all studies to receive the prize. Much excitement, no little speculation, and a great deal of studying ensued. Clinton felt fairly confident over all his studies except spelling. So he carried his spelling-book home every night, and he and his mother spent the evenings in wrestling with the long and difficult words.

Examination day came at length, and the afternoon for the seventh grade spelling was at hand. The words were to be written, and handed in. Across the aisle from Clinton sat Harry Meyers. Several times when teacher pronounced a word, Harry looked slyly into the palm of his hand. Clinton watched him, his cheeks growing pink with shame. Then he looked around at the others. Many of them had some dishonest device for copying the words. Clinton swallowed something in his throat, and looked across at Matthews, who pursed up his lips and nodded, if to say that he understood.

The papers were handed in, and school was dismissed. On Monday, after the morning exercises, Miss Brooks gave out the prizes to the three grades under her care. "I have now to award the prize for the highest average to the seventh grade," she said. "But first I wish to say a few words on your conduct during the recent examination in spelling. I shall censure no one in particular, although there is one boy who must set no more bad examples. No one spelled the words correctly—Clinton Stevens the least of any—making his average quite low; yet the prize goes to him. I will tell you why—" as a chorus of O! O's! greeted her ears. "Spelling is Clinton's hardest subject, but he could easily have spelled more words right had he not possessed sufficient strength to prevent him from falling into the way followed by some of you."

As Clinton went up the aisle for his prize, he felt like crying, but he managed to smile instead. A few days before, Harry Meyers had ridiculed him because he was not strong enough to throw a snowball from the schoolhouse to the road; now the teacher had said he was strong!

Clinton's Aunt Jennie came to visit the family in December, bringing her little daughter Grace with her. Now Grace had a mania for pulling other people's hair, but there was no one in the Stevens family upon whom she dared operate except Clinton. She began on him cautiously, then aggressively. Clinton stood it for a while, and then asked her, politely but firmly, to stop. She stopped for half a day.

One night Clinton came home from school pale and tired. Some of the boys had been taunting him on his spare frame, and imitating his cough, which had grown worse as the winter advanced. Sitting down by the window, he looked out at the falling snow. Grace slipped up behind him, and gave his hair a sharp tweak. He struck out, hastily, and hit her. She was not hurt,—only very much surprised,—but she began to cry lustily, and Aunt Jennie came hurrying in, and took the child in her arms.

That night after supper Clinton went into the sitting-room, and called Grace to him. "I want to tell you something," he said. "I am sorry that I hit you, and I ask your pardon. Will you forgive me, dear?" Grace agreed quickly, and said, shyly, "Next time I want to pull any one's hair, I will pull my own."

Aunt Jennie was in the next room and overheard the conversation. "It strikes me, Sarah," she said to Mrs. Stevens, later, "that Clinton is a remarkably strong boy for one who is not strong. Most boys would not have taken the trouble to ask a small girl to forgive them, even if they were very much in the wrong. But

Clinton has a strong character."

The year Clinton was thirteen, the boys planned to have a corn roast, one
August night. "We will get the corn in old Carter's lot," said Harry
Meyers. "He has just acres of it, and can spare a bushel or so as well as
not. I suppose you will go with us, Clint?"

Clinton hesitated. "No," said he. "I guess not; and I should think if you want to roast corn, you could get it out of your own gardens. But if Mr. Carter's corn is better than any other, why can you not ask him——"

"O, come, now," retorted Harry, "do not let it worry you! Half the fun of roasting corn is in—in taking it. And don't you come, Clinton—don't. We would not have you for the world. You are too nice, Mr. Coughin."

Clinton's cheeks flushed red, but he turned away without a word. When Mr. Carter quizzed Billy Matthews, and found out all about it, Clinton was made very happy by the old man's words: "It is not every chap that will take the stand you took. You ought to be thankful that you have the strength to say No."

In the fall, when Clinton was fifteen, his health began to fail noticeably, and Dr. Bemis advised a little wine "to build him up."

"Mother," said the boy, after thinking it over, "I am not going to touch any wine. I can get well without it, I know I can. I do not want liquor," he continued. "'Wine is a mocker,' you know. Did you not tell me once that Zike Hastings, over in East Bloomfield, became a drunkard by drinking wine when he was sick?"

"Yes, Clinton, I believe I told you so."

"Well, then, I do not want any wine. I have seen Zike Hastings too many times."

In December Aunt Jennie and Grace made their annual visit. With them came
Uncle Jonathan, who took a great liking to Clinton.

"My boy," said he one day, placing a big hand on the lad's shoulder, "early in the new year Aunt Jennie and I start for the Pacific Coast. Should you like to go with us?"

"Well, I rather guess I should!" gasped the surprised boy, clasping his hands joyfully. "Very well, then, you shall go," returned Uncle Jonathan, "and your mother, too."

Clinton began to feel better before they were outside of Pennsylvania. When they had crossed the Mississippi and reached the prairies, his eyes were sparkling with excitement. The mountains fairly put new life in him. Uncle Jonathan watched him with pleasure. "Tell me," he said one day, when they were winding in and out among the Rockies, "what has given you so much strength of character?"

"Why, it was this way," said Clinton, bringing his eyes in from a chasm some hundreds of feet below: "one day when I was beginning to recover from that attack of pneumonia, I saw a lot of the boys romping along, and I felt pretty bad because I could not romp and play, too; then I thought that if I could not be strong that way, I could have the strength to do right; so I began to try, and——"

"Succeeded admirably," said Uncle Jonathan, approvingly. "And, really, my boy, I see no reason why you should not shout and play to your heart's content in a few months."

And Uncle Jonathan's words proved true; for Clinton, in a sun-kissed California valley, grew well and strong in a few months. But through all his life he will have cause to be glad that he learned the value of the strength that is gained by resisting temptation, controlling one's spirit, and obeying the Lord's commands.

BENJAMIN KEECH

THE DOCTOR'S COW

"I am afraid she is done for," said the veterinary surgeon as he came out of the barn with Dr. Layton, after working for an hour over Brindle, who had broken into the feed bins, and devoured bran and middlings until she could eat no more. "But keep up the treatment faithfully, and if she lives through the night, she will stand some show of getting well."

The doctor walked down the driveway with the surgeon, and stood for a few minutes at the gate under the maple-trees that lined the sidewalk, talking earnestly. Then he went back into the house by the kitchen door. His wife met him, with the oft-repeated words, "I told you so; I said that boy would turn out of no earthly account."

"But he has turned out of some account," contradicted the doctor mildly. "In spite of this carelessness, he has been a great help to me during the last month. It was boyish ignorance more than mere carelessness that brought about this disaster. To be sure, I have cautioned him not to leave the door of the feed-room unfastened. But he had no idea how a cow would make a glutton of herself if she had a chance at the bins. You cannot expect a boy who was reared in a city tenement to learn all about the country, and the habits and weaknesses of cattle, in one short month. No, I shall not send him adrift again—not even if poor Brindle dies."

"You mean to say you are going to keep him just the same, John Layton?" cried the doctor's wife. "Well, if you are not the meekest man! Moses was not anything to you! He did lose his temper once."

The doctor smiled, and said quietly: "Yes, and missed entering the promised land on account of it. Perhaps I should have done the same thing in his place; but I am sure that Moses, if he were in my place today, would feel just as I do about discharging Harry. It is pretty safe to assume that he, even if he did lose his temper at the continual grumbling of the croakers who were sighing for the flesh-pots of Egypt, never ordered a young Israelite boy whose father and mother had been bitten by the fiery serpents and died in the wilderness, to clear out of camp for not putting a halter on one of the cows."

"John Layton, you are talking Scripture!" remonstrated the perturbed housewife, looking up reprovingly as she sadly skimmed the cream from the very last pan of milk poor Brindle would ever give her.

"I certainly am, and I am going to act Scripture, too," declared the doctor, with the air of gentle firmness that always ended any controversy between him and his excellent, though somewhat exacting, wife. "Harry is a good boy, and he had a good mother, too, he says, but he has had a hard life, ill-treated by a father who was bitten by the fiery serpent of drink. Now because of his first act of negligence I am not going to send him adrift in the world again."

"Not if it costs you a cow!" remarked the woman.

"No, my dear, not if it costs me two cows," reasserted the doctor. "A cow is less than a boy, and it might cost the world a man if I sent Harry away in a fit of displeasure, disgraced by my discharge so that he could not find another place in town to work for his board, and go to school. Besides, Brindle will die anyway, and discharging the boy will not save her."

"No, of course not. But it was your taking the boy in, a penniless, unknown fellow, that has cost you a cow," persisted the wife. "I told you at the time you would be sorry for it."

"I have not intimated that I am sorry I took the boy in," remarked the doctor, not perversely, but with steadfast kindness. "If our own little boy had lived, and had done this thing accidentally, would I have been sorry he had ever been born? Or if little Ted had grown to be thirteen, and you and I had died in the wilderness of poverty, leaving him to wander out of the city to seek for a home in God's fair country, where his little peaked face could fill out and grow rosy, as Harry's has, would you think it just to have him sent away because he had made a boyish mistake? Of course you would not, mother. Your heart is in the right place, even if it does get covered up sometimes. And I guess, to come right down to it, you would not send Harry away any more

28

than I would, when the poor boy is almost heart-broken over this unfortunate affair. Now, let us have supper, for I must be off. We cannot neglect sick people for a poor, dying cow. Harry will look after Brindle. He will not eat a bite, I am afraid, so it is no use to call him in now. By and by you would better take a plate of something out to him; but do not say a harsh word to the poor fellow, to make it any harder for him than it is."

The doctor ate his supper hurriedly; for the sick cow had engaged every moment of his spare hours that day, and he had postponed until his evening round of visits a number of calls that were not pressing. When he came out to his buggy, Harry Aldis stood at the horse's head, at the carriage steps beside the driveway, his chin sunk on his breast, in an attitude of hopeless misery.

"Keep up the treatment, Harry, and make her as easy as possible," said the doctor as he stepped into his buggy.

"Yes, sir; I'll sit up all night with her, Dr. Layton, if I can only save her," was the choking answer, as the boy carefully spread the lap robe over the doctor's knees.

"I know you will, Harry; but I am afraid nothing can save the poor creature. About all we can do is to relieve her suffering until morning, giving her a last chance; and if she is no better then, the veterinary surgeon says we would better shoot her, and put her out of her misery."

The boy groaned. "O Dr. Layton, why do you not scold me? I could bear it better if you would say just one cross word," he sobbed. "You have been kinder to me than my own father ever was, and I have tried so hard to be useful to you. Now this dreadful thing has taken place, all because of my carelessness. I wish you would take that buggy whip to me; I deserve it."

The doctor took the whip, and gently dropped its lash across the drooping shoulders bowed on the horse's neck as the boy hid his face in the silken mane he loved to comb. Indeed, Dandy's black satin coat had never shone with such a luster from excessive currying as in the month past, since the advent of this new little groom, who slept in the little back bedroom of the doctor's big white house, and thought it a nook in paradise.

"There's no use in scolding or thrashing a fellow who is all broken up, anyway, over an accident, as you are," the doctor said, kindly. "Of course, it is a pretty costly accident for me, but I think I know where I can get a heifer—one of Brindle's own calves, that I sold to a farmer two years ago—that will make as fine a cow as her mother."

"But the money, Dr. Layton! How can I ever earn that to make good your loss?" implored the boy, looking up.

"The money? O, well, some day when you are a rich man, you can pay me for the cow!" laughed the doctor, taking up the reins. "In the meantime, make a good, trustworthy, honest man of yourself, no matter whether you get rich or not, and keep your 'thinking cap' on a little better."

"You had better eat some supper," said a voice in the doorway a little later, as Mrs. Layton came noiselessly to the barn, and surprised the boy kneeling on the hay in the horse's stall adjoining the one where Brindle lay groaning, his face buried in his arms, which were flung out over the manger.

The lad scrambled to his feet in deep confusion.

"O, thank you, Mrs. Layton, but I cannot eat a bite!" he protested. "It is ever so good of you to think of me, but I cannot eat anything."

"You must," said the doctor's wife, firmly. "Come outside and wash in the trough if you do not want to leave Brindle. You can sit near by and watch her, if you think you must, though it will not do a particle of good, for she is bound to die anyway. What were you doing in there on your knees—praying?"

The woman's voice softened perceptibly as the question passed her lips, and she looked half-pityingly into the pale, haggard young face, thinking of little Ted's, and wondering how it would have looked at thirteen if he had done this thing.

"Yes," muttered Harry, plunging his hands into the water of the trough, and splashing it over the red flame of a sudden burning blush that kindled in his ash-pale cheeks. "Isn't it all right to pray for a cow to get well? It 'most kills me to see her suffer so."

Mrs. Layton smiled unwillingly; for the value of her pet cow's products touched her more deeply than a boy's penitent tears, particularly when that boy was not her own. "There is no use of your staying in there and watching her suffer, you cannot do her any good," she insisted. "Stay out here in the fresh air. Do you hear?"

"Yes, ma'am," choked Harry, drying his face on the sleeve of his gingham shirt. He sat down on a box before the door, the plate of food in his lap, and made an attempt to eat the daintily cooked meal, but every mouthful almost choked him.

At about midnight, the sleepless young watcher, lying on the edge of the hay just above the empty manger over which a lantern swung, lifted himself on his elbow at the sound of a long, low, shuddering groan, and in another moment, Harry knew that poor Brindle had ceased to suffer the effects of her gluttonous appetite. Creeping down into the stall, he saw at a glance that the cow was dead, and for a moment, alone there in the stillness and darkness of the spring night, he felt as if he were the principal actor in some terrible crime.

"Poor old boss!" he sobbed, kneeling down, and putting his arm over the still warm neck. "I—I have killed you—after all the rich milk and butter you have given me, that have made me grow strong and fat—just by my carelessness!"

In after-years the memory of that hour came back to Harry Aldis as the dominant note in some real tragedy, and he never again smelled the fragrance of new hay, mingled with the warm breath of sleeping cattle, without recalling the misery and self-condemnation of that long night's watch.

In the early dawn, Dr. Layton found the boy lying beside the quiet form in the stall, fast asleep from exhaustion and grief, his head pillowed on the soft, tawny coat he had loved to brush until it gleamed like silk.

"Child alive!" he gasped, bending over and taking the lad in his arms, and carrying him out into the sweet morning air. "Harry, why did you not come and tell me, and then go to bed?" he cried, setting the bewildered boy on his feet, and leading him to the

31

house. "Now, my boy, no more of this grieving. The thing is done, and you cannot help it now. There is no more use in crying for a dead cow than for spilled milk. Now come in and go to bed, and stay there until tonight; and when you wake up, the new heifer, Brindle's daughter, will be in the barn waiting for you to milk her. I am going to buy her this morning."

* * * * *

Five years after that eventful night, Harry Aldis stood on the doctor's front porch, a youth of eighteen, bidding good-by to the two who had been more to him than father and mother. He was going to college in the West, where he could work his way, and in his trunk was a high-school diploma, and in his pocket a "gilt-edge recommendation" from Dr. Layton.

"God bless you, my boy! Don't forget us," said the doctor, his voice husky with unshed tears as he wrung the strong young hand that had been so helpful to him in the busy years flown by.

"Forget you, my more than father!" murmured the young man, not even trying to keep the tears out of his eyes. "No matter how many years it may be before I see you again, I shall always remember your unfailing kindness to me. And can I ever forget how you saved me for a higher life than I could possibly have lived if you had set me adrift in the world again for leaving that barn door unfastened, and killing your cow? As long as I live, I shall remember that great kindness, and shall try to deserve it by my life."

"Pshaw, Harry," said the doctor, "that was nothing but common humanity!"

"Uncommon humanity," corrected the youth. "Good-by, Mrs. Layton. I shall always remember your kindness, too, and that you never gave me any less butter or cream from poor Brindle's daughter for my grave offense. You have been like an own mother to me."

"You have deserved it all, Harry," said the doctor's wife, and there was a tear in her eye, too, which was an unusual sight, for she was not an emotional woman. "I do not know as it was such a great calamity, after all, to lose Brindle just as we did, for Daisy is a finer cow than her mother was, and there has not been another chance since to get as good a heifer."

"So it was a blessing in disguise, after all, Harry," laughed the doctor.

"As for you, you have been a blessing undisguised from that day to this.

May the Lord bless and prosper you! Write to us often."

* * * * *

Four years passed, and in one of the Western States a young college graduate stepped from his pedestal of oratorical honors to take a place among the rising young lawyers of a prosperous new town that was fast developing into a commercial center.

"I am doing well, splendidly," he wrote Dr. Layton after two years of hard work, "and one of these days I am coming back to make that promised visit."

But the years came and went, and still the West held him in its powerful clutch. Success smiled upon his pathway, and into his life entered the sweet, new joy of a woman's love and devotion, and into his home came the happy music of children's voices. When his eldest boy was eight years old, his district elected him to the State senate, and four years later sent him to Congress,—an honest, uncompromising adherent to principle and duty.

"And now, at last," he wrote Dr. Layton, "I am coming East, and I shall run down from Washington for that long-promised visit. Why do you write so seldom, when I have never yet failed to inform you of my pyrotechnic advancement into the world of politics? It is not fair. And how is the family cow? Surely Madam Daisy sleeps with her poor mother ere this, or has been cut up into roasts and steaks."

And to this letter the doctor replied briefly but gladly:—

"So you are coming at last, my boy! Well, you will find us in the same old house,—a little the worse for wear, perhaps,—and leading the same quiet life. No, not the same, though it is quiet enough, for I am growing old, and the town is running after the new young doctors, leaving us old ones in the rear, to trudge along as best we can. There isn't any 'family cow' now, Harry. Daisy was sold long ago for beef, poor thing! We never got another, for I am getting too old to milk, and there never seemed to come along another boy like the old Harry, who would take all the barn-yard responsibility on his shoulders. Besides, mother is crippled with rheumatism, and can hardly get around to do her housework, let alone to make butter. We are not any too well off since the Union Bank failed; for, besides losing all my stock, I have had to help pay the depositors' claims. But we have enough to keep us comfortable, and much to be thankful for, most of all that our famous son is coming home for a visit. Bring your wife, too, Harry, if she thinks it will not be too much of a drop from Washington society to our humble home; and the children, all five of those bright boys and girls,—bring them all! I want to show them the old stall in the barn, where, twenty-five years ago, I picked their father up in my arms early one spring morning as he lay fast asleep on the neck of the old cow over whose expiring breath he had nearly broken his poor little heart."

* * * * *

"Yes, father, of course it has paid to come down here. I would not have missed it for all the unanimous votes of the third ballot that sent me East," declared the United States senator at the end of his three days' visit. Long ago, the Hon. Henry Aldis had fallen into the habit of addressing Dr. Layton, in his letters, by the paternal title.

"It does not seem possible that it is twenty years since I stood here, saying good-by when I started West. By the way, do you remember what you told me that memorable night when the lamented Brindle laid down her life because of my carelessness, and her own gluttony? I was standing at the horse's head, and you were sitting in your buggy, there at the carriage steps, and I said I wished you would horsewhip me, instead of treating me so kindly. I remember you reached over and tickled my neck with the lash playfully, and told me there was no use in thrashing a fellow who was all broken up, anyway, over an accident."

The doctor laughed as he held his arms more closely about the shoulders of
Senator Aldis's two eldest boys; while "Grandmother Layton," with little

Ted in her lap, was dreaming again of the little form that had long, long
ago been laid in the graveyard on the hillside.

"Yes, yes," said the doctor, "I remember. What a blessed thing it was I did not send you off that day to the tune the old cow died on," and he laughed through his tears.

"Blessed!" echoed Mrs. Layton, putting down the wriggling Ted. "It was providential. You know, Harry, I was not so kind-hearted as John in those days and I thought he ought to send you off. But he declared he would not, even if you had cost him two cows. He said that if he did it might cost the world a man. And so it would have, if all they say you are doing out West for clean government is true."

Senator Aldis laughed, and kissed the old lady.

"I do not know about that," he said modestly. "I am of the opinion that he might have saved more of a man for the world; but certain it is, he saved whatever manhood there was in that boy from going to waste by his noble act of kindness. But what I remember most, father, is what you told me, there at the carriage step, that when I became a rich man, I could pay you for that cow. Well, I am not exactly a rich man, for I am not in politics for all the money I can get out of it, but I am getting a better income than my leaving that barn door open would justify any one in believing I ever could get by my brains; so now I can pay that long-standing debt without inconvenience. It may come handy for you to have a little fund laid by, since the Union Bank went to smash, and all your stock with it, and so much of your other funds went to pay the poor depositors of that defunct institution. It was just like you, father, not to dodge the assessments, as so many of the stockholders did, by putting all your property in your wife's name. So, since you made one investment twenty-five years ago that has not seemed to depreciate in value very much,—an investment in a raw young boy who did not have enough gumption to fasten a barn door,—here is the interest on what the investment was worth to the boy, at least a little of it; for I can never begin to pay it all. Good-by, both of you, and may God bless you! Here comes our carriage, Helen."

When the dust of the departing hack had filtered through the morning sunlight, two pairs of tear-dimmed eyes gazed at the slip of blue paper in Dr. Layton's hand,—a check for five thousand dollars.

"We saved a man that time, sure enough!" murmured the old doctor softly.—Emma S. Allen in the Wellspring.

* * * * *

Brotherly Kindness

A man may make a few mistakes,
  Regardless of his aim.
But never, never criticize
  And cloud him o'er with blame;
For all have failed in many things
And keenly feel the smarting stings,
Which haunt the mind by day and night
Till they have made offenses right.

So liberal be with those you meet
  E'en though they may offend,
And wish them well as on they go
  Till all the journey end.
Sometimes we think our honor's hurt
When some one speaks a little pert;
But never mind, just hear the good,
And ever stand where Patience stood.

Look for the good, the true, the grand
  In those you wish to shun,
And you will be surprised to find
  Some good in every one;
Then help the man who makes mistakes
To rise above his little quakes,
To build anew with courage strong,
And fit himself to battle wrong.

JOHN FRANCIS OLMSTED

36

HONEY AT THE PHONE

Honey's mama had gone to market, leaving her home with nurse. Nurse was up-stairs making beds, while little Honey, with hands behind her, was trudging about the sitting-room looking for something to do.

There was a phone in the house, which was a great mystery to Honey when it first came. She could hear voices talking back to mama, yet could not see a person. Was some one hidden away in the horn her mother put to her ear, or was it in the machine itself?

Honey never failed to be on hand when the bell rang, and found that her mother generally talked to her best and dearest friends, ladies who were such frequent callers that Honey knew them all by name.

Her mama wrote down the names of her friends, with the number of their phones, and, because the child was so inquisitive about it, she very carefully explained to her just how the whole thing worked, never thinking that Honey would sometime try it for herself; and, indeed, for a while Honey satisfied herself by playing phone. She would roll up a piece of paper, and call out through it, "Hullo!" asking and answering all the questions herself.

One day, on finding herself alone, she took down the receiver and tried to talk to one of her mama's friends, but it was a failure. She watched mama still more closely after that. On this particular morning, while mama was at market, she tried again, commencing with the first number on her mama's list.

Taking down the receiver, she called out, "Hullo!" the answer came back,
"Hullo!" "I wants A 215," said Honey, holding the receiver to her ear.

"Yes," came the reply.

"Are you Miss Samor?" asked Honey.

"Yes," was the reply.

"We wants you to come to our house tonight to supper, mama and me."

"Who's mama and me?" asked the voice.

"Honey," was the reply.

"Honey, through the phone, eh?" laughed the voice. "Tell mama I will come with pleasure."

Honey was not only delighted, but greatly excited. She used every number on her mother's list, inviting them all to supper.

About four o'clock in the afternoon the guests began to arrive, much to mama's amazement and consternation, especially when they divested themselves of their wraps, and proceeded to make themselves comfortable. What could it mean? She would think she was having a surprise party if every one had not come empty-handed. Perhaps it was a joke on her. If so, they would find she would take it pleasantly.

There was not enough in the house to feed half that crowd, but she had the phone, and she fairly made the orders fly for a while.

When her husband came home from his office, he was surprised to find the parlors filled with company. While helping the guests, he turned to his wife, saying, "Why, this is a sort of surprise, is it not?"

Mama's face flamed, and she looked right down to her nose without saying a word.

"Why did you not tell me you were going to invite them, and I would have brought home some flowers?" said Honey's papa.

Honey, who sat next to her papa, resplendent in a white dress and flowing curls, clutched his sleeve, and said: "It's my party papa. I 'wited 'em frew the phone. Honey likes to have c'ean c'o'es on, and have comp'ny."

It was the visitors' turn now to blush, but Honey's papa and mama laughed so heartily it made them feel that it was all right even if Honey had sent out the invitations. And not one went home without extending an invitation to her host and hostess to another dinner or supper, and in every one Honey was included.

"Just what she wanted," said her papa, as he tossed her up in his arms and kissed her. Then, turning to his wife, he said, "Never mind, mother, she will learn better as she grows older."—Mrs. A. E. C. Maskell.

ONE OF FATHER'S STORIES

When children, nothing pleased us more than to listen to father's stories. Mother Goose melodies were nothing beside them. In fact, we never heard fairy stories at home; and when father told of his boyhood days, the stories had a charm which only truth can give. I can hear him now, as he would reply to our request for a story by asking if he had ever told us how his father tried to have a "raising" without rum. Of course we had heard about it many times, but we were sure to want our memories refreshed; so we would sit on a stool at his feet or climb upon his knee, while he told us this story:—

"My grandfather, George Hobbs, was one of the pioneers of the Kennebec Valley. He had an indomitable will, and was the kind of man needed to subdue a wilderness and tame it into a home. He was a Revolutionary pensioner, having enlisted when only twelve years of age. He was too young to be put in the ranks, and was made a waiter in camp. When I was a boy, I can remember that he drove twenty miles, once a year, to Augusta, Maine's capital, to draw his pension. Snugly tucked under the seat of his sleigh was a four-gallon keg and a box. The keg was to be filled with Medford rum for himself, and the box with nuts and candy for his grandchildren. After each meal, as far back as father could remember, grandfather had mixed his rum and water in a pewter tumbler, stirred in some brown sugar with a wooden spoon, and drunk it with the air of one who was performing an unquestionable duty.

"Grandfather was a ship-carpenter by trade, and therefore in this new country was often employed to frame and raise buildings. Raisings were great social events. The whole neighborhood went, and neighbors covered more territory than they do now. The raising of a medium-sized building required about one hundred and fifty men, and their good wives went along to help in the preparation of the dinner. The first thing on the day's program was the raising, and not a stroke of work was done until all had been treated to a drink of rum, the common liquor of the day. After the frame was erected, one or two men, whose courage fitted them for the feat, had the honor of standing erect on the ridge-pole and repeating this rhyme:—

'Here is a fine frame,
  Stands on a fine spot;
May God bless the owner,
  And all that he's got.'

Men would sometimes walk the ridge-pole, and sometimes one, more daring than the others, would balance himself on his head upon it.

"Then followed a bountiful dinner, in which meat and potatoes, baked beans, boiled and fried eggs, Indian pudding, and pumpkin pies figured prominently. Often as many as one hundred and twenty-five eggs were eaten. After dinner came wrestling, boxing, and rough-and-tumble contests, in which defeat was not always taken with the best of grace.

"This was before the subject of temperance was agitated much in the good old State of Maine. The spirit of it, however, was awakening in the younger generation. My father was enthusiastic over it, and announced his intention of raising his new house without the aid of rum. To grandfather this was no trifling matter. It was the encroachment of new ideas upon old ones—a pitting of the strength of the coming generation against his own. To his mind, no less than to father's, a principle was involved, and the old soldier prepared to fight his battle. With some spirit he said to father, 'It cannot be done, Jotham; it cannot be done.' But father was just as sure that it could. It was grandfather's task to fit the frame. He went industriously to work, and father thought that he had quietly yielded the point.

"The day for the raising came, the first in that part of the country to be conducted on temperance principles. There were no telephones to spread the news, but long before the day arrived, everybody, far and near, knew that Jotham Hobbs was going to raise his new house without rum. The people came, some eager to help to establish the era of temperance, and some secretly hoping that the project would fail. A generous dinner was cooking indoors; for the host intended to refuse his guests nothing that was good. The song of mallets and hammers rang out, and the timbers began to come together; but the master framer was idle. Over by the old house door sat grandfather. He positively refused to lend a hand to the enterprise unless treated to his rum. For a time the work progressed rapidly; then there came a halt. There was a place where the timbers would not fit. After much delay and many vain attempts to go on with the work, father asked grandfather to help; but he only shook his head, and grimly replied that it was ten to one if it ever came together without rum. There were more vain attempts, more delays. Finally, father, seeing that he must yield or give up the work, got some rum and handed it to grandfather. The old man gravely laid aside his pipe, drank the Medford, and walked over to the men. He took a tenon marked ten and placed it in a mortise marked one. The problem was solved. He had purposely marked them in that way, instead of marking them alike, as was customary. With a sly twinkle in his eye he said, 'I told you it was ten to one if it ever came together.'

"But the cause of temperance had come to stay, and grandfather met his Waterloo when Squire Low built his one-hundred-foot barn. Three hundred men were there to see that it went up without rum. Grandfather and a kindred spirit, Old Uncle Benjamin Burrill, stood at a safe distance, hoping to see another failure. But section after section was raised. The rafters went on, and finally the ridge-pole. The old men waited to see no more. They dropped their heads, turned on their heels, and walked away."

These events occurred between 1830 and 1840. Since then the cause of temperance has made rapid progress.

In the State Capitol at Augusta, Maine, is a petition sent to the legislature in 1835 by one hundred and thirty-nine women of Brunswick, Maine. It is a plea for a prohibitory law, and is, probably, the first attempt made to secure a legislative enactment against the liquor traffic. One paragraph, which is characteristic of the whole document, is worth quoting:—

"We remonstrate against this method of making rich men richer and poor men poorer; of making distressed families more distressed; of making a portion of the human family utterly and hopelessly miserable, debasing the moral nature, and thus clouding with despair their temporal and future prospects."

This petition met with no recognition by that legislature. There were many customs to be laid aside, many prejudices to be overcome, and it was not till 1851 that Maine became a prohibition State. Since that time her health and wealth have steadily increased, in greater proportion than other States which have not adopted temperance principles; and public sentiment, which is a powerful ally, is against the liquor traffic.

ETHEL HOBBS WALTERS.

WHAT RUM DOES

I was sitting at my breakfast-table one Sunday morning, when I was called to my door by the ringing of the bell. There stood a boy about fourteen years of age, poorly clad, but tidied up as best he could. He was leaning on crutches; for one leg was off at the knee.

In a voice trembling with emotion, and with tears coursing down his cheeks, he said: "Mr. Hoagland, I am Freddy Brown. I have come to see if you will go to the jail and talk and pray with my father. He is to be hanged tomorrow for the murder of my mother. My father was a good man, but whisky did it. I have three little sisters younger than myself. We are very, very poor, and have no friends. We live in a dark and dingy room. I do the best I can to support my sisters by selling papers, blacking boots, and doing odd jobs; but Mr. Hoagland, we are very poor. Will you come and be with us when father's body is brought home? The governor says we may have his body after he is hanged."

I was deeply moved to pity. I promised, and made haste to the jail, where I found his father.

He acknowledged that he must have murdered his wife, for the circumstances pointed that way, but he had not the slightest remembrance of the deed. He said he was crazed with drink, or he never would have committed the crime. He said: "My wife was a good and faithful mother to my little children. Never did I dream that my hand could be guilty of such a crime."

The man could bravely face the penalty of the law for his deed, but he broke down and cried as if his heart would break when he thought of leaving his children in a destitute and friendless condition. I read and prayed with him, and left him to his fate.

The next morning I made my way to the miserable quarters of the children. I found three little girls upon a bed of straw in one corner of the room. They were clad in rags. They would have been beautiful girls had they had the proper care. They were expecting the body of their dead father, and between their cries and sobs they would say, "Papa was good, but whisky did it."

In a little time two strong officers came bearing the body of the dead father in a rude pine box. They set it down on two old rickety stools. The cries of the children were so heartrending that the officers could not endure it, and made haste out of the room.

In a moment the manly boy nerved himself, and said, "Come, sisters, kiss papa's face before it is cold." They gathered about his face and smoothed it down with kisses, and between their sobs cried out: "Papa was good, but whisky did it! Papa was good, but whisky did it!"

I raised my heart to God and said, "O God, did I fight to save a country that would derive a revenue from a traffic that would make a scene like this possible?"—Youth's Outlook.

$\mathcal{M}$Y MOTHER'S RING

I am living now on borrowed time. The sun of my allotted life-day has set, and with the mellow twilight of old age there come to my memory reflections of a life which, if not well spent, has in it enough of good at least to make these reflections pleasant. And yet, during all the years in which I have responded to the name Carter Brassfield, but a single fortnight of time, it seems to me, is worth recounting.

We were living in Milwaukee, having recently moved there from York State, where I was born. My father, a bookkeeper of some expertness, not securing a position in our newly adopted city as soon as he had expected, became disheartened, and, to while away the time that hung so heavily, took to drinking beer with some newly acquired German friends. The result was that our funds were exhausted much sooner than they should have been, and mother took it upon herself to turn bread-winner for the family by doing some plain sewing.

A small allotment of this money she gave to me one day on my return from school, and sent me to Mr. Blodget, the grocer, to purchase some supplies. After giving my order to one of the clerks I immediately turned my attention to renewing my acquaintance with Tabby, the store cat.

While I was thus engaged, I heard my name repeated by a stranger who was talking with Mr. Blodget, and erelong the man sauntered over, spoke to me, and after some preliminary remarks asked if I was Carter Brassfield. He was dark, had a sweeping mustache, and wore eye-glasses. Upon being assured that I was Carter Brassfield, he took from his pocket a gold ring, and, turning it around carefully in the light, read the inscription on its inner side.

"Is your mother's name Alice?" he asked.

I told him that it was.

"And your father's name Carter?"

"Yes, sir," said I.

Then he showed the ring to me and asked if I had seen it before.

I at once recognized the ring as my mother's. Since I could remember she had worn it, until recently. Of late she had grown so much thinner that the ring would no longer stay on her finger, and she was accustomed, therefore, to keep the circlet in a small drawer of her dresser, secure in an old purse with some heirlooms of coins; and I was greatly surprised that it should be in the possession of this stranger. I told him that it was my mother's ring, and asked him how he came by it.

"Your father put it up in a little game the other day," said he, "and it fell into my possession." He dropped the ring into his purse, which he then closed with a snap. "I have been trying for several days to see your father and give him a chance at the ring before I turned it in to the pawnbroker's. If your mother has any feeling in the matter, tell her she can get the ring for ten dollars," he added as he turned away.

I did not know what to do. I was so ashamed and hurt to think that my father, whom I loved and in whom I had such implicit confidence, should have gambled away my mother's ring, the very ring—I was old enough to appreciate—he had given her in pledging to her his love. My eyes filled with tears, and as I stood, hesitating, Mr. Blodget came forward, admonishing me not to forget my parcels. He evidently observed my tears, although I turned my face the other way, for shame of crying. At any rate, he put his hand on my shoulder and said very kindly:—

"It's pretty tough, Carter, my boy, isn't it?"

He referred, I thought, to my father, for father was uppermost in my thoughts. Then, lowering his voice, he said:—

"But I will help you out, son, I will help you out."

I forgot all about hiding my tears, and faced about, attracted by his kindness.

"I will redeem the ring, and keep it for you until you can get the money. What do you say? You can rest easy then, knowing that it is safe, and you can take your time. What do you say?"

With some awkwardness I acquiesced to his plan. Then he called the stranger, and, leading the way back to his desk, paid to him the ten dollars, requiring him to sign a paper, though I did not understand why. He then placed the ring carefully in his safe.

"There, Carter," said he, rubbing his hands together, "it is safe now, and we need not worry."

I held out my hand to him, then without a word took my parcels and started on a run for home.

That evening father was more restless than usual. He repeatedly lamented his long-enforced idleness. After retiring that night, I lay awake for a long time evolving in my mind plans whereby I might earn ten dollars to redeem the ring. Finally, with my boyish heart full of hope and adventure, I fell asleep in the wee hours of morning.

After breakfast I took my books, as usual, but, instead of going to school, I turned my steps toward a box factory where I knew a boy of about my own age to be working. I confided to him as much of my story as I thought advisable, and he took me to the superintendent's office and introduced me. I was put to work, at five dollars a week, with the privilege of stopping at four each day. Every afternoon I brought my school-books home and studied as usual till bed-time, and took them with me again in the morning.

During the two weeks I was employed at the factory neither father nor mother suspected that I had not been to school each day. In fact, I studied so assiduously at night that I kept up with my classes. But my mother observed that I grew pale and thin.

At the end of two weeks, when I told the manager I wanted to stop work, he seemed somewhat disappointed. He paid me two crisp five-dollar notes, and I went very proudly to Mr. Blodget with the first ten dollars I had ever earned, and received that gentleman's hearty praise, and my mother's ring.

That evening father was out as usual, and I gave the ring to mother, telling her all about it, and what I had done. She kissed me, and, holding me close in her arms for a long time, cried, caressing my hair with her hand, and told me that I was her dear, good boy. Then we had a long talk about father, and agreed to lay nothing to him, at present, about the ring.

The next evening, when I returned from school, father met me at the hall door, and asked if I had been to school. I saw that he had been drinking, and was not in a very amiable mood.

"I met Clarence Stevenson just now," he said, "and he inquired about you.
He thought you were sick, and said you had not been to school for two
weeks, unless you had gone today." I stood for a moment without answering.
"What do you say to that?" he demanded.

"Clarence told the truth, father," I replied.

"He did, eh? What do you mean by running away from school in this manner?" He grew very angry, catching me by the shoulder, gave me such a jerk that my books, which I had under my arm, went flying in all directions. "Why have you not been to school?" he said thickly.

"I was working, but I did not intend to deceive you father."

"Working! Working! Where have you been working?"

"At Mr. Hazleton's box factory."

"At a what factory?"

"Box factory."

"How much did you earn?" he growled, watching me closely to see if I told the truth.

"Five dollars a week," I said timidly, feeling all the time that he was exacting from me a confession that I wished, on his account, to keep secret.

"Five dollars a week! Where is the money? Show me the money!" he persisted incredulously.

49

"I cannot, father. I do not have it."

I was greatly embarrassed and frightened at his conduct.

"Where is it?" he growled.

"I—I—spent it," I said, not thinking what else to say.

A groan escaped through his shut teeth as he reeled across the hall and took down a short rawhide whip that had been mine to play with. Although he had never punished me severely, I was now frightened at his anger.

"Don't whip me, father!" I pleaded, as he came staggering toward me with the whip. "Don't whip me, please!"

I started to make a clean breast of the whole matter, but the cruel lash cut my sentence short. I had on no coat, only my waist, and I am sure a boy never received such a whipping as I did.

I did not cry at first. My heart was filled only with pity for my father. Something lay so heavy in my breast that it seemed to fill up my throat and choke me. I shut my teeth tightly together, and tried to endure the hurt, but the biting lash cut deeper and deeper until I could stand it no longer. Then my spirit broke, and I begged him to stop. This seemed only to anger him the more, if such a thing could be. I cried for mercy, and called for mother, who was out at one of the neighbor's. Had she been at home, I am sure she would have interceded for me. But he kept on and on, his face as white as the wall. I could feel something wet running down my back, and my face was slippery with blood, when I put up my hand to protect it. I thought I should die; everything began to go round and round. The strokes did not hurt any longer; I could not feel them now. The hall suddenly grew dark, and I sank upon the floor. Then I suppose he stopped.

When I returned to consciousness, I was lying on the couch in the dining-room, with a wet cloth about my forehead, and mother was kneeling by me, fanning me and crying. I put my arms about her neck, and begged her not to cry, but my head ached so dreadfully that I could not keep back my own tears. I asked where father was, and she said he went down-town when she came. He did not return at supper-time, nor did we see him again until the following morning.

I could eat no supper that night before going to bed, and mother came and stayed with me. I am sure she did not sleep, for as often as I dropped off from sheer exhaustion, I was wakened by her sobbing. Then I, too, would cry. I tried to be brave, but my wounds hurt me so, and my head ached. I seemed to be thinking all the time of father. My poor father! I felt sorry for him, and kept wondering where he was. All through the night it seemed to me that I could see him drinking and drinking, and betting and betting. My back hurt dreadfully, and mother put some ointment and soft cotton on it.

It was late in the morning when I awoke, and heard mother and father talking down-stairs. With great difficulty, I climbed out of bed and dressed myself. When I went down, mother had a fire in the dining-room stove, and father was sitting, or rather lying, with both arms stretched out upon the table, his face buried between them. By him on a plate were some slices of toast that mother had prepared, and a cup of coffee, which had lost its steam without being touched.

I went over by the stove and stood looking at father. I had remained there but a moment, my heart full of sympathy for him, and wondering if he were ill, when he raised his head and looked at me. I had never before seen him look so haggard and pale. As his eyes rested on me, the tears started down my cheeks.

"Carter, my child," he said hoarsely, "I have done you a great wrong. Can you forgive me?"

In an instant my arms were about his neck—I felt no stiffness nor soreness now. He folded me to his breast, and cried, as I did. After a long time he spoke again:—

"If I had only known—your mother has just told me. It was the beer, Carter, the beer. I will never touch the stuff again, never," he said faintly. Then he stretched out his arms upon the table, and bowed his head upon them. I stood awkwardly by, the tears streaming down my cheeks, but they were tears of joy.

Mother, who was standing in the kitchen doorway with her

apron to her eyes, came and put her arm about him, and said something, very gently, which I did not understand. Then she kissed me several times. I shall never forget the happiness of that hour.

For a long time after that father would not go downtown in the evening unless I could go with him. He lived to a good old age, and was for many years head bookkeeper for Mr. Blodget. He kept his promise always.

Mother is still living, and still wears the ring.—Alva H. Sawins, M.D., in the Union Signal.

* * * * *

The Lad's Answer

Our little lad came in one day
  With dusty shoes and weary feet
His playtime had been hard and long
  Out in the summer's noontide heat.
"I'm glad I'm home," he cried, and hung
  His torn straw hat up in the hall,
While in the corner by the door
  He put away his bat and ball.

"I wonder why," his aunty said,
  "This little lad always comes here,
When there are many other homes
  As nice as this, and quite as near."
He stood a moment deep in thought,
  Then, with the love-light in his eye,
He pointed where his mother sat,
  And said: "Here she lives; that is why '"

With beaming face the mother heard,
  Her mother-heart was very glad.
A true, sweet answer he had given,
  That thoughtful, loving little lad.
And well I know that hosts of lads
  Are just as loving, true, and dear,
That they would answer as did he,
  "Tis home, for mother's living here."

ARTHUR V. FOX.

THE BRIDAL WINE-CUP

"Pledge with wine! Pledge with wine!" cried young and thoughtless Harvey
Wood. "Pledge with wine!" ran through the bridal party.

The beautiful bride grew pale; the decisive hour had come. She pressed her white hands together, and the leaves of the bridal wreath trembled on her brow. Her breath came quicker, and her heart beat wilder.

"Yes, Marian, lay aside your scruples for this once," said the judge in a low tone, going toward his daughter; "the company expects it. Do not so seriously infringe upon the rules of etiquette. In your own home do as you please; but in mine, for this once, please me."

Pouring a brimming cup, they held it, with tempting smiles, toward Marian. She was very pale, though composed; and her hand shook not, as, smiling back, she gracefully accepted the crystal tempter, and raised it to her lips. But scarcely had she done so when every hand was arrested by her piercing exclamation of "O, how terrible!"

"What is it?" cried one and all, thronging together, for she had slowly carried the glass at arm's length and was fixedly regarding it.

"Wait," she answered, while a light, which seemed inspired, shone from her dark eyes—"wait, and I will tell you. I see," she added slowly, pointing one finger at the sparkling ruby liquid, "a sight that beggars all description; and yet, listen! I will paint it for you, if I can. It is a lovely spot. Tall mountains, crowned with verdure, rise in awful sublimity around; a river runs through, and bright flowers grow to the water's edge. But there a group of Indians gather. They flit to and fro, with something like sorrow upon their dark brows. In their midst lies a manly form, but his cheek, how deathly! His eyes are wild with the fitful fire of fever. One friend stands before him—nay, I should say, kneels; for see, he is pillowing that poor head upon his breast.

"O, the high, holy-looking brow! Why should death mark it, and he so young? Look, how he throws back the damp curls! See him clasp his hands! Hear his thrilling shrieks for life! Mark how he clutches at the form of his companion, imploring to be saved! O, hear him call piteously his father's name! See him twine his fingers together as he shrieks for his sister—his only sister, the twin of his soul, weeping for him in his distant native land!

"See!" she exclaimed, while the bridal party shrank back, the untasted wine trembling in their faltering grasp, and the judge fell overpowered upon his seat—"see! his arms are lifted to heaven—he prays—how wildly!—for mercy. Hot fever rushes through his veins. He moves not; his eyes are set in their sockets; dim are their piercing glances. In vain his friend whispers the name of father and sister—death is there. Death—and no soft hand, no gentle voice to soothe him. His head sinks back; one convulsive shudder—he is dead!"

A groan ran through the assembly. So vivid was description, so unearthly her look, so inspired her manner, that what she described seemed actually to have taken place then and there. They noticed, also, that the bridegroom hid his face in his hands, and was weeping.

"Dead!" she repeated again, her lips quivering faster and faster, and her voice more broken. "And there they scoop him a grave; and there, without a shroud, they lay him down in that damp, reeking earth, the only son of a proud father, the only idolized brother of a fond sister. There he lies, my father's son, my own twin brother, a victim to this deadly poison. Father," she exclaimed, turning suddenly, while the tears rained down her beautiful cheeks, "father, shall I drink it now?"

The form of the old judge was convulsed with agony. He raised not his head, but in a smothered voice he faltered:—

"No, no, my child; no!"

She lifted the glittering goblet, and let it suddenly fall to the floor, where it was dashed in a thousand pieces. Many a tearful eye watched her movement, and instantaneously every wine-glass was transferred to the marble table on which it had been prepared. Then, as she looked at the fragments of crystal, she turned to the company, saying: "Let no friend hereafter who loves me tempt me to peril my soul for wine. Not firmer are the ever-lasting hills than my resolve, God helping me, never to touch or taste the poison cup. And he to whom I have given my hand, who watched over my brother's dying form in that last solemn hour, and buried the dear wanderer there by the river in that land of gold, will, I trust, sustain me in that resolve."

His glistening eyes, his sad, sweet smile, were her answer. The judge left the room. When, an hour after, he returned, and with a more subdued manner took part in the entertainment of the bridal guests, no one could fail to read that he had determined to banish the enemy forever from his princely home.—"Touching Incidents and Remarkable Answers to Prayer."

$\mathcal{A}$ MOTHER'S SORROW

A company of Southern ladies, assembled in a parlor, were one day talking about their different troubles. Each had something to say about her own trials. But there was one in the company, pale and sad-looking, who for a while remained silent. Suddenly rousing herself, she said:—

"My friends, you do not any of you know what trouble is."

"Will you please, Mrs. Gray," said the kind voice of one who knew her story, "tell the ladies what you call trouble?"

"I will, if you desire it; for, in the words of the prophet, 'I am the one who hath seen affliction.'

"My parents were very well off; and my girlhood was surrounded by all the comforts of life. Every wish of my heart was gratified, and I was cheerful and happy.

"At the age of nineteen I married one whom I loved more than all the world besides. Our home was retired; but the sun never shone upon a lovelier spot or a happier household. Years rolled on peacefully. Five lovely children sat around our table, and a little curly head still nestled in my bosom.

"One night about sundown one of those fierce, black storms came up, which are so common to our Southern climate. For many hours the rain poured down incessantly. Morning dawned, but still the elements raged. The country around us was overflowed. The little stream near our dwelling became a foaming torrent. Before we were aware of it, our house was surrounded by water. I managed, with my babe, to reach a little elevated spot, where the thick foliage of a few wide-spread trees afforded some protection, while my husband and sons strove to save what they could of our property. At last a fearful surge swept away my husband, and he never rose again. Ladies, no one ever loved a husband more. But that was not trouble.

"Presently my sons saw their danger, and the struggle for life became the only consideration. They were as brave, loving boys as ever blessed a mother's heart; and I watched their efforts to escape, with such an agony as only mothers can feel. They were so far off that I could not speak to them; but I could see them closing nearer and nearer to each other, as their little island grew smaller and smaller.

"The swollen river raged fearfully around the huge trees. Dead branches, upturned trunks, wrecks of houses, drowning cattle, and masses of rubbish, all went floating past us. My boys waved their hands to me, and then pointed upward. I knew it was their farewell signal; and you, mothers, can imagine my anguish. I saw them perish—all perish. Yet that was not trouble.

"I hugged my baby close to my heart; and when the water rose at my feet, I climbed into the low branches of the tree, and so kept retiring before it, till the hand of God stayed the waters, that they should rise no farther. I was saved. All my worldly possessions were swept away; all my earthly hopes were blighted. Yet that was not trouble.

"My baby was all I had left on earth. I labored day and night to support him and myself, and sought to train him in the right way. But, as he grew older, evil companions won him away from me. He ceased to care for his mother's counsels; he sneered at her entreaties and agonizing prayers. He became fond of drink. He left my humble roof, that he might be unrestrained in his evil ways. And at last one night, when heated by wine, he took the life of a fellow creature. He ended his days upon the gallows. God had filled my cup of sorrow before; now it ran over. That was trouble, my friends, such as I hope the Lord of mercy will spare you from ever knowing."

Boys and girls, can you bear to think that you might bring such sorrow on your dear father or mother? If you would not, be on your guard against intemperance. Let wine and liquors alone. Never touch them.—Selected.

* * * * *

"Ah, none but a mother can tell you, sir, how a mother's heart

will ache
   With the sorrow that comes of a sinning child,
     with grief for a lost one's sake,
   When she knows the feet she trained to walk have gone so far astray,
   And the lips grown bold with curses that she taught to sing and pray!
   A child may fear, a wife may weep, but of all sad things none other
   Seems half so sorrowful to me as being a drunkard's mother."

THE REPRIMAND

At the sound of Mr. Troy's bell, Eleanor Graves vanished into his private office. Ten minutes later she came out, with a deep flush on her face and tears in her eyes.

"He lectured me on the spelling of a couple of words and a mistake in a date," she complained to Jim Forbes. "Anybody's liable to misspell a word or two in typing, and I know I took the date down exactly as he gave it to me."

Jim looked uncomfortable. "I would not mind," he said awkwardly. "We all have to take it sometime or other. Besides," he glanced hesitatingly at the pretty, indignant face, "I suppose the boss thinks we ought not to make mistakes."

"As if I wanted to!" Eleanor retorted, stiffly.

But she worked more carefully the next week; for her pride was touched. Then, with restored confidence, came renewed carelessness, and an error crept into one of the reports she was copying. The error was slight, but it brought her a sharp reprimand from Mr. Troy. It was the second time, he reminded her, that she had made that blunder. At the reproof the girl's face flushed painfully, and then paled.

"If my work is not satisfactory, you had better find some one who can do it better," she said.

Whirling round in his swivel-chair, Mr. Troy looked at her. He had really never noticed his latest stenographer before, but now his keen eyes saw many things that showed that she came from a home where she had been petted and cared for.

"How long have you been at work?" he asked.

"This is my first position," Eleanor answered.

Mr. Troy nodded. "I understand. Now, Miss Graves, let me tell you something. You have many of the qualities of a good business woman; you are punctual, you are not afraid of work, you are fairly accurate. I have an idea that you take pride in turning out a good piece of work. But you must learn to stand criticism and profit by it. We must all take it sometime, every one of us. A weakling goes under. A strong man or woman learns to value it, to make every bit of it count. That is what I hope you will do."

Eleanor braced herself to meet his eyes.

"If you will let me, I will try again," she said.—Youth's Companion.

* * * * *

The Kingfisher

A kingfisher sat on a flagpole slim,
And watched for a fish till his eye was dim.
"I wonder," said he, "if the fishes know
That I, their enemy, love them so!
I sit and watch and blink my eye
And watch for fish and passers-by;
I must occasionally take to wing
On account of the stones that past me sing.
*
"I nearly always work alone;
For past experience has shown
That I can't gather something to eat,
And visit my neighbor across the street.
So whether I'm fishing early or late,
I usually work without a mate,
Since I can't visit and watch my game;
For fishing's my business, and Fisher's my name.
Maybe by watching, from day to day,
My life and habits in every way,
You might be taught a lesson or two
That all through life might profit you;
Or if you only closely look,
This sketch may prove an open book,
And teach a lesson you should learn.
Look closely, and you will discern."

CHAS. E. E. SANBORN.

An EXAMPLE

Stealing away from the ones at home, who would be sad when they found out about it; stealing away from honor, purity, cleanliness, goodness, and manliness, the minister's boy and the boy next door were preparing to smoke their first cigarettes. They had skulked across the back pasture, and were nearing the stone wall that separated Mr. Meadow's corn-field from the road; and here, screened by the wall on one side and by corn on the other, they intended to roll the little "coffin nails," and smoke them unseen.

The minister's boy, whose name was Johnny Brighton, and who was an innocent, unsuspicious child, agreed that it would be a fine, manly thing to smoke. So the lads waited and planned, and now their opportunity had come. The boy next door, whose name was Albert Beecher, saw old Jerry Grimes, the worst character in Roseland, drop a small bag of tobacco and some cigarette-papers. The lad, being unobserved, transferred the stuff from the sidewalk to his pocket, then hid it in the wood-shed.

At last their plan seemed about to be carried out. Albert's mother was nursing a sick friend, and the minister, secure in his study, was preparing a sermon. Johnny's mother was dead. His aunt Priscilla was his father's housekeeper, and she was usually so busy that she had little time for small boys. Today, as she began her sewing, Johnny slipped quietly from the house and joined his chum.

The boys reached the stone wall and sat down, with the tobacco between them, to enjoy (?) what they considered a manly deed. After considerable talk and a few blunders, each succeeded in rolling a cigarette, and was about to pass it to his lips, when a strange voice, almost directly above their heads, said, pleasantly, "Trying to kill yourselves, boys?"

With a guilty start, Johnny and Albert turned instantly, and beheld the strangest specimen of humanity that either had ever seen. An unmistakable tramp, with a pale, sickly face, covered

partly with grime and partly with stubby black beard, stood leaning with his arms on top of the wall, looking down at them. Although it was summer, he wore a greasy winter cap, and his coat,
too, spoke of many rough journeys through dirt and bad weather.
His lips were screwed into something resembling a smile; but as
he spoke, his haunted, sunken eyes roved restlessly from one upturned face to the other.

As the only answer the boys gave him was an astonished,
frightened stare, the man continued: "I would not do it, boys. It is
an awful thing—awful! I was trying to get a little sleep over here,"
he continued, "when I heard your voices, and thought I would
see what was going on. Did not any one ever tell you about cigarettes? Why, each one contains enough poison to kill a cat; if it
was fixed right, I mean." He passed a thin, shaking hand over his
face, and went on: "Do you want to fool with such things?—Not
if you are wise. You see, the cigarette habit will kill you sometime,
by inches, if not right away, or else drive you crazy; and no sane
person wants to kill himself or spoil his health. That is what I am
doing, though," he admitted, with a bitter smile and a sad shake
of his head. "But I cannot stop it now. I have gone too far, and I
cannot help myself. I am a wreck, a blot on the face of the earth."

Both lads had thrown their cigarettes to the ground, scrambled
to their feet. Johnny, sober-faced and round-eyed, was gazing in-
tently up at the man; but Albert, feigning indifference, stood dig-
ging his toe into the earth. He was listening, however.

"It is this way with me," the stranger went on, seeing he had an
audience: "I have gone from bad to worse till I cannot stop, no
matter how hard I try. Why, I was once a clean little chap like you,
but I got to reading trash, and then I began to smoke, and pretty
soon I had drifted so far into evil ways that I had no control over
myself."

Here Johnny and Albert exchanged a painful glance.

"The worst thing about cigarettes," the man continued, "is that
they usually lead to something worse. I am a drunkard and a
thief, because of evil associations. Tramps never have any ready
money; so when I have to have cigarettes, which is all the time, I
either steal them or steal the money to buy them with. Besides,"
with another sad shake of the head, "I am what is known as a

drug fiend, and—yes, I guess I am everything bad. If your folks knew who was talking to you, their blood would run cold.

"And it is all principally due to cigarettes!" he broke forth, savagely, emphasizing his words with his fist and speaking more excitedly. "Just look at me and behold a splendid example of the cigarette curse. Why, I was naturally bright; I might have been a man to honor. But a bad habit, uncontrolled, soon ruins one. My nerves are gone. I am only a fit companion for jailbirds and criminals. I cannot even look an honest man in the face, yet I am not naturally bad at heart. The best way is never to begin; then you will never have to suffer. Cigarettes will surely hurt you some day, though you may not be able to see the effects at first."

The speaker's manner had changed greatly during the past few moments. At first he had spoken calmly, but he was now more than agitated. His eyes rolled and flashed in their dark caverns, and he spoke vehemently, with excited gestures. Johnny and Albert stood close together, regarding him with frightened eyes.

"I wish I could reform," he exclaimed, "but I cannot! The poison is in my veins. A thousand devils seem dragging me down. I wish I could make every boy stop smoking those things. I wish I could warn them of the horrible end."

With a sudden shriek, the man threw up his hands, fell backward, and disappeared. After a second's hesitation, both lads ran to the wall, climbed up, and looked over. In an unmistakable fit, the man was writhing on the ground. Johnny and Albert ran quickly across lots and into Rev. Paul Brighton's study. After learning that the boys had found a man in a fit, Johnny's father hailed two passing neighbors, and the little party of rescuers followed the lads to the scene of the strange experience.

It was a sorry spectacle that greeted them. The poor fellow's paroxysm had passed, and he lay still and apparently lifeless, covered with dust and grime. The minister bent over him, and, ascertaining that he was alive and conscious, lifted him up; then, with the help of the two men, took the outcast to the parsonage.

That evening, before the minister had asked his boy three questions, Johnny broke into convulsive sobs, and made a clean breast of the matter from the beginning. Blaming himself for not having won the child's heart securely long before this, the minister did not censure him severely. He knew that after such an example, the sensitive lad would never go wrong as far as cigarettes were concerned.

Aunt Priscilla took her nephew in her arms, and, kissing the lips that were yet sweet and pure, said, "If I have neglected you, Johnny, I am sorry; and after this I am going to spend considerable time being good to my precious laddie."

Johnny slipped an arm around Aunt Priscilla's neck. "That is just what I want," he said, happily.

"I hope this will teach you a lesson, Albert," said Mrs. Beecher to her son, when he, with the help and advice of the minister, had made a full confession of his share in the matter. "After such an example, I should think you would never want to see another cigarette."

"I do not," said Albert, soberly, "and if I can help it, I am not going to;
I will fight them. Cigarettes certainly did not make a man of that fellow.
They unmade him."

For several days, during which the minister thought of what could be done for him, the outcast stayed at the parsonage. He was invited to try the gospel cure. "If you will put yourself unreservedly in the hands of God, and remain steadfast," said Mr. Brighton, "there is hope for you. Besides, I know of some medical missionaries who can help doctor the poison out of your system, if you will let them."

At last the poor fellow yielded. And after a hard, bitter struggle, during which a higher power helped him, he won the victory. He joined a band of religious people whose work is to help rebuild wrecked lives; and although weak at first and never robust, he was still able to point the right way to many an erring mortal. He did much good; and Johnny and Albert, at least, never forgot the practical example he gave them of what the cigarette can accomplish for its slaves.

BENJAMIN KEECH.

64

ƒIGHTING THE GOOD FIGHT

A number of years ago, at an orphan asylum in a Northern State, there lived a boy whom we shall call Will Jones. He was just an ordinary boy. No, he was not so in one respect, which I must point out, to his discredit. Will Jones had a temper that distinguished him from the general run of boys. Will's temper might have been inherited from a Spanish pirate, and yet Will was a boy whom every one loved; but this hair-trigger temper at times terribly spoiled things. It would be tedious to recount his uprisings of anger, and the direful consequences that often followed.

Mr. Custer, the superintendent of the asylum, had hopefully striven to lead
Will to the paths of right; but it was a difficult task.

Sometimes it needs but one small breach to begin the overthrow of a giant wall. One small key, if it is the right one, will open the most resisting door. One small phrase may start a germ-thought growing in a human mind which in after-years may become a mighty oak of character. So Will Jones, the incorrigible fighter was to demonstrate this principle, as we shall see.

On a Sabbath evening, as the hundred or more orphans met at vespers and sang, "Onward, Christian Soldiers!" they saw a stranger seated at the speaker's desk in the home chapel. He was a venerable old Wan, straight and dignified, his hoary head a crown of honor; for he was all that he appeared—a father in Israel.

In a brief speech he told the boys that he had once been a Union soldier, and had fought in the battles of his country. He told of the courage it required to face death upon the battle-field. He described the charges his company had made and met, the sieges and the marches, the sufferings they endured, and, lastly, the joys that victory and the end of the conflict brought.

Then, when the boys were at the height of interested expectancy, he skilfully drew the lesson he wanted them to learn. He told of a greater warfare, requiring a higher courage, and bringing as a reward a larger and more enduring victory. "Boys," he said, "the real soldiers are the Christian soldiers; the real battle is the battle against sin; the real battle-ground is where that silent struggle is constantly waging within our minds." Then he told of Paul, who said, "I have fought a good fight." "Did any of you boys ever fight a bad fight?" Every head but one turned to a common point at this juncture, and the eyes of only one boy remained upon the speaker. Will Jones had the record for bad fights, and that is why about ninety-nine pairs of eyes had involuntarily sought him out when the speaker asked the question, which he hoped each would ask himself. And the reason Will Jones did not look around accusingly at any of the other boys was because he had taken to heart all that had been said; and, because of this, the turning-point had come; his conversion had begun. Henceforth he determined so to live that he could say with Paul, "I have fought a good fight."

No sooner does a boy determine to fight the good fight than Satan accepts the challenge, and gives him a combat such as will seem like a "fiery trial" to try him. These struggles develop the moral backbone; and if a boy does not give in, he will find his moral courage increasing with each moral fight. Just let that thought stay in your mind, underscored in bold-faced italics, and printed in indelible ink; and if you have a tendency to be a spiritual "jelly-back," it will be like a rod of steel to your spine.

The fear of Will Jones's knuckles had won a degree of peace for him. He had lived a sort of armed truce, so to speak. Now he was subjected to petty persecutions by mean boys who took advantage of his new stand. He did not put on the look of a martyr either, but kept good-natured even when the old volcano within was rumbling and threatening to bury the tormentors in hot lava and ashes. The old desire to fight the bad fight was turned into the new channel of determination to fight the good fight. Today Will Jones is still a good fighter, and I hope he always will be, and some day will be crowned with eternal victory; for he who fights the good fight is fighting for eternity.

Will you not try so to live each day, subduing every sinful thought, that at night when you kneel to pray you can say to the Lord, "I have fought a good fight today"?

S. W. VAN TRUMP.

* * * * *

Our Help Is Near

Temptations dark and trials fall
  On all who labor here;
But we have One on whom to call:
  Our Lord is ever near.
So let us when these trials come,
  Lean on his strength alone,
Till we have reached the promised home
  Where sorrows are unknown.

MAX HILL.

TIGHTENING THE SADDLE-GIRTH

A time of grave crisis; upon the events of the next few minutes would hang the issue of a hard-fought battle. Already at one end of the line the troops seemed to be wavering. Was it indeed defeat?

Just where the fight was most fierce, a young officer was seen to leap from his horse. His followers, sore pressed though they were, could not help turning toward him, wondering what had happened. The bullets flew like hail everywhere; and yet, with steady hand, the gallant soldier stood by the side of his horse and drew the girth of his saddle tight. He had felt it slip under him, and he knew that upon just such a little thing as a loose buckle might hinge his own life, and, perhaps, the turn of the battle. Having secured the girth, he bounded into the saddle, rallied his men, and swept on to victory.

Many a battle has been lost on account of no greater thing than a loose saddle-girth. A loose screw will disable the mightiest engine in the world. A bit of sand in the bearing of an axle has brought many a locomotive to a standstill, and thrown out of order every train on the division. Lives have been lost, business houses wrecked, private fortunes laid in the balance, just because some one did not tighten his saddle-girth!

Does it seem a small thing to you that you forgot some seemingly unimportant thing this morning? Stop right where you are and go back and do the thing you know you should have done in the first place.

One of the finest teachers in the leading school of one of our cities puts stress day after day on that one thing of cultivating the memory so that it will not fail in time of stress. "Do the thing when it should be done," she insists. "If you forget, go back and do it. You have no right to forget; no one has."

Tighten up the loose screw the moment you see it is loose. Pull the strap through the buckle as soon as you feel it give. Wipe the axle over which you have charge, clean of dust or grit. If your soul is in the balance, stop now, today, this very moment, and see that all is right between you and God.—Kind Words.

* * * * *

If You But Knew

 O lad, my lad, if you but knew
 The glowing dreams I dream of you,—
 The true, straight course of duty run,
 The noble deeds, the victories won,
  And you the hero of them all,—
 I know that you would strive to be
 The lad that in my dreams I see;
  No tempter's voice could make you fall.

 Ah, lad, my lad, your frank, free smile
 Has cheered me many a weary mile;
 And in your face, e'en in my dreams,
 Potent of future manhood beams,—
  Manhood that lives above the small;
 Manhood all pure and good and clean,
 That scorns the base, the vile, the mean,
  That hears and answers duty's call

 And lad, my lad, so strong and true,
 This is the prayer I pray for you:
 Lord, take my boy, and guide his life
 Through all the pitfalls of the strife;
  Lead him to follow out thy plan,
 To do the deeds he ought to do,
 To all thy precepts ever true;
  Make him a clean and noble man.

MAX HILL.

69

"ℋERRINGS FOR NOTHING"

I want you to think of a bitter, east windy day, fast-falling snow, and a short, muddy street in London. Put these thoughts together, and add to them the picture of a tall, stout man, in a rough greatcoat, and with a large comforter round his neck, buffeting through wind and storm. The darkness is coming rapidly, as a man with a basket on his head turns the corner of the street, and there are two of us on opposite sides. He cries loudly as he goes: "Herrings! three a penny! Red herrings, good and cheap, three a penny!" So crying, he passes along the street, crosses at its end, and comes to where I am standing at the corner. Here he pauses, evidently wishing to fraternize with somebody, as a relief from the dull time and disappointed hopes of trade. I presume I appear a suitable object, as he comes close to me and begins conversation:—

"Governor, what do you think of these yer herrings?"—three in his hand, while the remaining stock are deftly balanced in the basket on his head. "Don't you think they're good?" and he offered me the opportunity of testing them by scent, which I courteously but firmly declined, "and don't you think they're cheap as well?"

I asserted my decided opinion that they were good and cheap.

"Then, look you, governor, why can't I sell 'em? Yet have I walked a mile and a half along this dismal place, offering these good and cheap 'uns; and nobody don't buy none!"

"I do not wonder at all at that," I answered, to his astonishment.

"Tell us why not, governor."

"The people have no work, and are starving; there are plenty of houses round here that have not a single penny in them," was my reply.

"Ah! then, governor," he rejoined, "I've put my foot in it this time; I knew they was werry poor, but I thought three a penny 'ud tempt 'em. But if they haven't the ha-pence, they can't spend 'em, sure enough; so there's nothing for it but to carry 'em back, and try and sell 'em elsewhere. I thought by selling cheap, arter buying cheap, I could do them good, and earn a trifle for myself. But I'm done this time."

"How much will you take for the lot?" I inquired.

First a keen look at me, then down came the basket from his head, then a rapid calculation, then a grinning inquiry, "Do you mean profit an' all, governor?"

"Yes."

"Then I'll take four shillin', and be glad to get 'em."

I put my hand in my pocket, produced that amount, and handed it to him.

"Right, governor, thank'ee! Now what'll I do with 'em?" he said, as he quickly transferred the coins to his own pocket.

"Go round this corner into the middle of the road, and shout with all your might, 'Herrings for nothing!' and give three to every man, woman, or child that comes to you, till the basket is emptied."

On hearing these instructions, he immediately reproduced the money, and examined it. Being satisfied of its genuineness, he again replaced it, and then looked keenly and questioningly at me.

"Well," I said, "is it all right and good?"

"Yes," replied he.

"Then the herrings are my property, and I can do as I like with them; but if you do not like to do as I tell you, give me back my money."

"All right, governor, an' they are yours; so if you say it, here goes!" Accordingly, he proceeded into the middle of the adjoining street, and went along, shouting aloud: "Herrings for nothing! Good red herrings for nothing!"

Out of sight myself, I stood at the corner to watch his progress; and speedily he neared the house where a tall woman stood at the first-floor window, looking out upon him.

"Here you are, missus," he bawled, "herrings for nothing! A fine chance for yer! Come an' take 'em."

The woman shook her head unbelievingly, and left the window.

"Vot a fool!" said he. "But they won't be all so. Herrings for nothing!" A little child came out to look at him, and he called to her, "Yer, my dear, take these in to your mother. Tell her how cheap they are—herrings for nothing." But the child was afraid of him and them, and ran indoors.

So down the street, in the snowy slush and mud, went the cheap fish, the vender crying loudly as he went, "Herrings for nothing!" and then adding savagely, "O you fools!" Thus he reached the very end; and, turning to retrace his steps, he continued his double cry as he came, "Herrings for nothing!" and then in a lower key, "O you fools!"

"Well?" I said to him calmly, as he reached me at the corner.

"Well!" he replied, "if yer think so! When you gave me the money for herrings as yer didn't want, I thought you was training for a lunatic 'sylum. Now I thinks all the people round here are fit company for yer. But what'll I do with the herrings, if yer don't want 'em and they won't have 'em?"

"We will try again together," I replied. "I will come with you, and we will both shout."

Into the road we both went; and he shouted, "Herrings for nothing!" and then I called out also, "Will any one have some herrings for tea?"

They heard the voice, and they knew it well; and they came out at once, in twos and threes and sixes, men and women and children, all striving eagerly to reach the welcome food.

72

As fast as I could take them from the basket, I handed three to each eager applicant, until all were speedily disposed of. When the basket was empty, the hungry crowd who had none, was far greater than those that had been supplied; but they were too late; there were no more herrings.

Foremost among the disappointed was the tall woman, who, with a bitter tongue, began vehemently: "Why haven't I got any? Ain't I as good as they? Ain't my children as hungry as theirs?"

Before I had time to reply, the vender stretched out his arm toward her, saying, "Why, governor, that's the very woman as I offered 'em to first, and she turned up her nose at 'em."

"I didn't," she rejoined passionately; "I didn't believe you meant it!"

"Yer just goes without, then, for yer unbelief!" he replied. "Good night, and thank'ee, governor!"

You smile at the story, which is strictly true. Are you sure you are not ten thousand times worse? Their unbelief cost them only a hungry stomach; but what may your unbelief of God's offer cost you? God—not man—God has sent his messenger to you repeatedly for years, to offer pardon for nothing! Salvation for nothing! He has sent to your homes, your hearts, the most loving and tender offers that even an Almighty could frame; and what have you replied? Have you not turned away, in scornful unbelief, like the woman?

God says, "Because I have called, and ye refused; I have stretched out my hand, and no man regarded;... I also will laugh at your calamity; I will mock when your fear cometh." Prov. I:24-26. But he also says, "Ho, every one that thirsteth, come ye to the waters, and he that hath no money; come ye, buy, and eat; yea, come, buy wine and milk without money and without price." Isa. 55:1. "For God so loved the world, that he gave his only begotten Son, that whosoever believeth in him should not perish, but have everlasting life." John 3: 16.

Answer him. Will you have it?—C. J. Whitmore.

Come

Ho, every one that thirsteth,
   Come to the living stream,
And satisfy your longing soul
   Where silver fountains gleam.

Come, weary, faint, and hungry;
   Before you now is spread
A rich supply for all your needs;
   Receive the living Bread.

Why do you linger longer?
   Come while 'tis called today.
Here's milk and honey without price;
   O, do not turn away!

Why feed on husks that perish?
   Enter the open door.
Thy Saviour stands with outstretched hands;
   Eat, drink, and want no more.

MAY WAKEHAM.

THE POWER OF SONG

My Own Experience

Near the summit of a mountain in Pennsylvania is a small hamlet called Honeyville, consisting of two log houses, two shanties, a rickety old barn, and a small shed, surrounded by a few acres of cleared land. In one of these houses lived a family of seven,—father, mother, three boys, and two girls. They had recently moved from Michigan. The mother's health was poor, and she longed to be out on the beautiful old mountain where she had spent most of her childhood. Their household goods had arrived in Pennsylvania just in time to be swept away by the great Johnstown flood of 1889.

The mother and her two little girls, Nina and Dot, were Christians, and their voices were often lifted in praise to God as they sang from an old hymn-book, one of their most cherished possessions.

One morning the mother sent Nina and Dot on an errand to their sister's home three and one-half miles distant. The first two miles took them through dense woods, while the rest of the way led past houses and through small clearings. She charged them to start on their return home in time to arrive before dark, as many wild beasts—bears, catamounts, and occasionally a panther— were prowling around. These animals were hungry at this time of the year; for they were getting ready to "hole up," or lie down in some cozy cave or hole for their winter's nap.

The girls started off, merrily chasing each other along the way, and arrived at their sister's in good time, and had a jolly romp with the baby. After dinner the sister was so busy, and the children were so absorbed in their play, that the time passed unheeded until the clock struck four. Then the girls hurriedly started for home, in the hope that they might arrive there before it grew very dark. The older sister watched until they disappeared up the road, anxiously wishing some one was there to go with them.

Nina and Dot made good time until they entered the long stretch of woods, when Nina said:—

"O, I know where there is such a large patch of wintergreen berries, right by the road! Let's pick some for mama."

So they climbed over a few stones and logs, and, sure enough, the berries were plentiful. They picked and talked, sometimes playing hide-and-seek among the bushes. When they started on again, the sun was sinking low in the west, and the trees were casting heavy shadows over the road, which lengthened rapidly. When about half of the distance was covered, Dot began to feel tired and afraid. Nina tried to cheer her, saying, "Over one more long hill, and we shall be home." But now they could only see the sun shining on the top of the trees on the hill.

They had often played trying to scare each other by one saying, "O, I see a bear or a wolf up the road!" and pretending to be afraid. So Dot said: "Let's scare each other. You try to scare me." Nina said, "All right." Then, pointing up the road, she said, "O, look up the road by that black stump! I see a—" She did not finish; for suddenly, from almost the very spot where she had pointed, a large panther stepped out of the bushes, turning his head first one way and then another. Then, as if seeing the girls for the first time, he crouched down, and, crawling, sneaking along, like a cat after a mouse, he moved toward them. The girls stopped and looked at each other. Then Dot began to cry, and said, in a half-smothered whisper, "O Nina, let's run!" But Nina thought of the long, dark, lonely road behind, and knew that running was useless. Then, thinking of what she had heard her father say about showing fear, she seized her little sister's hand, and said: "No, let's pass it. God will help us." And she started up the road toward the animal.

When the children moved, the panther stopped, and straightened himself up. Then he crouched again, moving slowly, uneasily, toward them. When they had nearly reached him, and Nina, who was nearest, saw his body almost rising for the spring, there flashed through her mind the memory of hearing it said that a wild beast would not attack any one who was singing. What should she sing? In vain she tried to recall some song, but her mind seemed a blank. In despair she looked up, and breathed a little prayer for help; then, catching a glimpse of the last rays of the setting sun touching the tops of the trees on the hill, she began the beautiful hymn,—

"There is sunlight on the hilltop,
  There is sunlight on the sea."

Her sister joined in, and although their voices were faint and trembling at first, by the time the children were opposite the panther, the words of the song rang out sweet and clear on the evening air.

The panther stopped, and straightened himself to his height. His tail, which had been lashing and switching, became quiet as he seemed to listen. The girls passed on, hand in hand, never looking behind them. How sweet the words,—

"O the sunlight! beautiful sunlight!
  O the sunlight in the heart!"

sounded as they echoed and reechoed through the woods.

As the children neared the top of the hill, the rumbling of a wagon fell upon their ears, so they knew that help was near, but still they sang. When they gained the top, at the same time the wagon rattled up, for the first time they turned and looked back, just in time to catch a last glimpse of the panther as he disappeared into the woods.

The mother had looked often and anxiously down the road, and each time was disappointed in not seeing the children coming. Finally she could wait no longer, and started to meet them. When about half-way there, she heard the words,—

"O the sunlight! beautiful sunlight!
  O the sunlight in the heart!
Jesus' smile can banish sadness;
  It is sunlight in the heart."

At first a happy smile of relief passed over her face; but it faded as she listened. There was such an unearthly sweetness in the song, so strong and clear, that it seemed like angels' music instead of her own little girls'. The song ceased, and the children appeared over the hill. She saw their white faces, and hurried toward them. When they saw her, how their little feet flew! But it was some time before they could tell her what had happened.

What a joyful season of worship they had that night, and what a meaning that dear old hymn has had to them ever since!

A few days later, a party of organized hunters killed the panther that had given the children such a fright. But the memory of that thrilling experience will never fade from the mind of the writer, who was one of the actors in it.—Nina Case.

JACK'S FIDELITY

There was held, in Hartford, some years ago, a convention of the colored Baptist Association of New England. I was invited to address one of the sessions. To show what those converted in early life are sometimes enabled to endure by God's grace, I related the following story:—

"What's dat, Willie?"

"That's a spelling-book, Jack."

"What's de spellin'-book for?"

"To learn how to read."

"How's you do it?"

"We learn those things first."

And so Jack learned A, B, C, etc., mastered the spelling-book, and then learned to read a little, though the law forbade any colored person to do it.

One day Willie brought home a little black book, and Jack said:—

"What's dat, Willie?"

"That is the New Testament, that tells about Jesus."

And, erelong, Jack learned to read the New Testament, and when he read that "God so loved the world, that he gave his only begotten Son, that whosoever believeth in him should not perish, but have everlasting life," and that he really loved us and died for us, and that "if we confess our sins, he is faithful and just to forgive us our sins," his heart went out in love to Jesus. He believed in him, his sins were forgiven, his heart was changed, and he became a happy Christian.

Though a mere child, he at once began to tell others of Jesus' love. When he became a young man, he was still at work for the Lord. He used to go to the neighboring plantations, read his Bible, and explain it to the people.

One day the master said to him, "Jack, I am told that you go off preaching every Sunday."

"Yes, mas'r, I must tell sinners how Jesus died on de cross for dem."

"Jack, if you go off preaching on Sunday, I will tell you what I will do on
Monday."

"What will do you on Monday, mas'r?"

"I will tie you to that tree, take this whip, and flog all this religion out of you."

Jack knew that his master was a determined man, but when he thought of Christ's sufferings for us, and heard his Lord saying unto him, "Be thou faithful unto death, and I will give thee a crown of life," he resolved to continue his work for the Lord the next Sunday.

With his New Testament in hand, he went down to the plantation and told them that his master might whip him half to death the next day, but if he did, he would not suffer more than Christ had suffered for us.

The next morning his master said, "Jack, I hear you were preaching again yesterday."

"Yes, mas'r. I must go and tell sinners how Jesus was whipped that we might go free."

"But, Jack, I told you that if you went off preaching Sunday, I should whip you on Monday, and now I will do it."

Blow after blow fell upon Jack's back, while oaths fell from the master's lips. Then he said:—

"There, Jack, I don't believe you will preach next Sunday. Now go down to the cottonfield and go to work."

When next Sunday came, Jack could not stand straight, for his back was covered with sores and scars. But, with his Testament in his hand, he stood before the people of the plantation, and said, "Mas'r whip me mos' ter death last Monday, an' I don't know but he will kill me tomorrow, but if he does, I shall not suffer more than Jesus did when he died on the cross for us."

Monday morning the master called him and said,

"Jack, I hear you have been preaching again."

"Yes, mas'r. I must go an' tell sinners how Christ was wounded for our transgressions, how he sweat drops of blood for us in the garden, an' wore that cruel crown of thorns that we might wear a crown of joy when he comes."

"But I don't want to hear your preaching. Now bare your back, and take the flogging I told you I should give you if you went off preaching."

Fast flew the cruel lashes, until Jack's back was covered with wounds and blood.

"Now, Jack, go down to the cotton-field and go to work. I reckon you'll never want to preach again."

When the next Sunday came, Jack's back was in a terrible condition. But, hobbling along, he found his friends in the neighboring plantation, and said:—

"Mas'r whipped me mos' ter death last Monday, but if I can only get you to come to Jesus and love him, I am willing to die for your sake tomorrow."

If there were scoffers there, do you not think they were led to believe there was a reality in religion? If any were there who were inclined to think that ministers preach only when they get money for it, do you not think they changed their minds when they saw

81

what wages Jack got? Many were in tears, and some gave themselves to that Saviour for whose sake Jack was willing to die the death of a martyr.

Next morning the master called Jack, and said,

"Make bare your back again; for I told you that just as sure as you went off preaching, I would whip you till you gave it up."

The master raised the ugly whip, and as he looked at Jack's back, all lacerated, he could find no new place to strike, and said:—

"Why do you do it, Jack? You know that as surely as you go off preaching Sunday, I will whip you most to death the next day. No one pays you anything for it. All you get is a terrible flogging, which is taking your life from you."

"Yer ax me, mas'r, what I'se doin' it fer. I'll tell you, mas'r. I'se goin' ter tak all dos stripes an' all dos scars, mas'r, up to Jesus, by an' by, to show him how faithful I'se been, 'cause he loved you an' me, mas'r, an' bled an' died on the cross for you an' me, mas'r."

The whip dropped, and that master could not strike another blow. In a subdued tone he said:—

"Go down in the cotton-field."

Do you think Jack went away cursing his master, saying, "O Lord, punish him for all his cruelty to me"?

No, no! His prayer was, "Lord, forgive him, for Jesus Christ's sake."

About three o'clock, a messenger came down to the cotton-field, crying:
"Mas'r dyin'! Mas'r's dyin'! Come quick, Jack. Mas'r's dyin'!"

In his private room, Jack found his master on the floor in agony, crying:
"O Jack, I'm sinking down to hell! Pray for me! Pray for me!"

"I'se been prayin' for you all de time, mas'r. You mus' pray for yourse'f."

"I don't know how to pray, Jack. I know how to swear, but I don't know how to pray."

"You mus' pray, mas'r."

And finally they both prayed, and God revealed Christ on the cross to him, and then and there he became a changed man.

A few days after, he called Jack to him and said:—

"Jack, here are your freedom papers. They give you your liberty. Go and preach the gospel wherever you will, and may the Lord's blessing go with you."

While telling this story at the convention, I noticed a man, perhaps sixty years of age, with quite gray hair, who was deeply moved. When I had finished, he sprang to his feet, and, with a clear but tremulous voice, said:—

"I stand for Jack. Mr. Hammond has been speaking of me. He has been trying to tell my sufferings, but he cannot describe the terrible agony I endured at the hands of my master, who, because I was determined to preach the gospel on the plantations around us, every Monday morning for three weeks called me up and laid the cruel lash upon my back with his own hands until my back was like raw beef. But God helped me to pray for him, until he was forgiven and saved through Christ. And, thank God, Jack still lives."

I have given you only a few of his burning words, but I can tell you there were many eyes filled with tears during this touching scene, which will not soon be forgotten by those who witnessed it.—E. Hammond, in "Early Conversion."

*H*ONOR THY FATHER AND THY MOTHER

Here is a touching story told of the famous Dr. Samuel Johnson which has had an influence on many a boy who has heard
it. Samuel's father Michael Johnson, was a poor bookseller in Li-
chfield, England. On market-days he used to carry a package of
books to the village of Ottoxeter, and sell them from a stall in the
market-place. One day the bookseller was sick, and asked his son
to go and sell the books in his place. Samuel, from a silly pride,
refused to obey.

Fifty years afterward Johnson became the celebrated author,
the compiler of the English Dictionary, and one of the most distinguished scholars in England; but he never forgot his act of
unkindness to his poor, hard-toiling father. So when he visited
Ottoxeter, he determined to show his sorrow and repentance. He
went into the market-place at the time of business, uncovered his
head, and stood there for an hour in the pouring rain, on the very
spot where the bookstall used to stand. "This," he says, "was an
act of contrition for my disobedience to my kind father."

The spectacle of the great Dr. Johnson standing bareheaded in
the storm to atone for the wrong done by him fifty years before, is
a grand and touching one. There is a representation of it in marble
on the doctor's monument.

Many a man in after-life has felt something harder and heavi-
er than a storm of rain beating upon his heart when he remembered his acts of unkindness to a good father or mother now in
the grave.

Dr. John Todd, of Pittsfield, the eminent writer, never forgot
how, when his old father was very sick, and sent him away for
medicine, he, a little lad, been unwilling to go, and made up a lie,
saying that the druggist had no such medicine.

The old man was dying when little Johnny came in, but he said to Johnny,

"My boy, your father suffers great pain for want of that medicine."

Johnny started, in great distress, for the medicine, but it was too late. On his return the father was almost gone. He could only say to the weeping boy, "Love God, and always speak the truth; for the eye of God is always upon you. Now kiss me once more, and farewell."

Through all his after-life, Dr. Todd often had a heartache over that act of falsehood and disobedience to his dying father. It takes more than a shower to wash away the memory of such sins.

The words, "Honor thy father and thy mother," mean three things,—always do what they bid you, always treat them lovingly, and take care of them when they are sick and grown old. I never yet knew a boy who trampled on the wishes of his parents who turned out well. God never blesses a wilful boy.

When Washington was sixteen years old, he determined to leave home and become a midshipman in the colonial navy. After he had sent off his trunk, he went to bid his mother good-by. She wept so bitterly because he was going away that he said to his Negro servant: "Bring back my trunk. I am not going to wake my mother suffer so, by leaving her."

He remained at home to please his mother. This decision led to his becoming a surveyor, and afterward a soldier. His whole glorious career in life turned on simple act of trying to make his mother happy, happy, too, will be the child who never has occasion to shed bitter tears for any act of unkindness to his parents. Let us not forget that God has said,

"Honor thy father and thy mother."—Theodore L. Cuyler, in Pittsburgh
Christian Advocate.

THE SLEIGH-RIDE

In one of the larger cities of New England, fifty years ago, a party of lads, all members of the same school, got up a grand sleigh-ride. There were about twenty-five or thirty boys engaged in the frolic. The sleigh was a large and splendid conveyance drawn by six gray horses. The afternoon was as beautiful as anybody could desire, and the merry group enjoyed themselves in the highest degree. It was a common custom of the school to which they belonged, and on previous occasions their teacher had accompanied them. Some engagement upon important business, however, occupying him, he was not at this time with them. It is quite likely, had it been otherwise, that the restraining influence of his presence would have prevented the scene which occurred.

On the day following the ride, as he entered the schoolroom, he found his pupils grouped about the stove, in high merriment, as they chatted about the fun and frolic of their excursion. He stopped awhile and listened; and, in answer to some inquiries which he made about the matter, one of the lads, a fine, frank, manly boy, whose heart was in the right place, though his love of sport sometimes led him astray, volunteered to give a narrative of their trip and its various incidents. As he drew near the end of his story, he exclaimed:—

"O, sir, there was one little circumstance which I almost forgot to tell you! Toward the latter part of the afternoon, as we were coming home, we saw, at some distance ahead of us, a queer-looking affair in the road. We could not exactly make out what it was. It seemed to be a sort of half-and-half monstrosity. As we approached it, it proved to be a rusty old sleigh fastened behind a covered wagon, proceeding at a very slow rate, and taking up the whole road. Finding that the owner was disposed not to turn out, we determined upon a volley of snowballs and a good hurrah. These we gave with a relish, and they produced the right effect, and a little more; for the crazy machine turned out into the deep snow by the side of the road, and the skinny old pony started on a full trot. As we passed, some one who had the whip gave the jilt of a horse a good crack, which made him run faster than he ever did before, I'll warrant. And so, with another volley of snow-balls pitched into the front of the wagon, and three times three cheers, we rushed by. With that, an old fellow in the wagon, who was buried up under an old hat and beneath a rusty cloak, and who had dropped the reins, bawled out, 'Why do you frighten my horse?'

"'Why don't you turn out, then?' said the driver.

"So we gave him three rousing cheers more. His horse was frightened again, and ran up against a loaded team, and, I be-lieve, almost capsized the old man; and so we left him."

"Well, boys," replied the instructor, "that is quite an incident. But take your seats; and after our morning service is ended, I will take my turn and tell you a story, and all about a sleigh-ride, too."

Having finished the reading of a chapter in the Bible, and all having joined in the Lord's Prayer, he began as follows:—

"Yesterday afternoon a very venerable and respectable old man, a clergyman by profession, was on his way from Boston to Salem to pass the residue of the winter at the house of his son. That he might be prepared for journeying, as he proposed to do in the spring, he took with him his light wagon, and for the winter his sleigh, which he fastened behind the wagon. He was, as I have just told you, very old and infirm. His temples were covered with thinned locks which the frosts of eighty years had whitened. His sight, and hearing, too, were somewhat blunted by age, as yours will be should you live to be as old.

"He was proceeding very slowly and quietly, for his horse was old and feeble, like his owner. His thoughts reverted to the scenes of his youth, when he had periled his life in fighting for the lib-erties of his country; to the scenes of his manhood, when he had preached the gospel of his divine Master to the heathen of the re-mote wilderness; and to the scenes of riper years, when the hard hand of penury had lain heavily upon him. While thus occupied, almost forgetting himself in the multitude of his thoughts, he was suddenly disturbed, and even terrified, by loud hurrahs from be-hind, and by a furious pelting and clattering of balls of snow and ice upon the top of his wagon. In his trepidation he dropped his reins; and as his aged and feeble hands were quite benumbed with cold, he found it impossible to gather them up, and his horse began to run away.

"In the midst of the old man's troubles, there rushed by him, with loud shouts, a large party of boys in a sleigh drawn by six horses.

"'Turn out, turn out, old fellow!' 'Give us the road, old boy!' 'What'll you take for your pony, old daddy?' 'Go it, frozen nose!' 'What's the price of oats?' were the various cries that met his ear.

"'Pray, do not frighten my horse,' exclaimed the infirm driver.

"'Turn out, then! Turn out!' was the answer, which was followed by repeated cracks and blows from the long whip of the grand sleigh, with showers of snowballs, and tremendous hurrahs from the boys.

"The terror of the old man and his horse was increased; and the latter ran away, to the imminent danger of the man's life. He contrived, however, after some exertion, to secure the reins, which had been out of his hands during the whole of the affray, and to stop his horse just in season to prevent his being dashed against a loaded team.

"As he approached Salem, he overtook a young man who was walking toward the same place, whom he invited to ride. The young man alluded to the grand sleigh which had just passed, which induced the old gentleman to inquire if he knew who the boys were. He replied that he did; that they all belonged to one school, and were a set of wild fellows.

"'Aha!' exclaimed the former, with a hearty laugh, for his constant good nature had not been disturbed, 'do they, indeed? Why, their master is very well known to me. I am now going to his house, and I think I shall give him the benefit of the affair.'

"A short distance brought him to his journey's end, the home of his son.

His old horse was comfortably housed and fed, and he himself provided for.

"That son, boys, is your instructor; and that aged and infirm old man, that 'old fellow,' that 'old boy,' who did not turn out for you, but who would gladly have given you the whole road had he heard your approach, that 'old boy,' that 'old daddy,' and 'frozen nose,' is Rev. Daniel Oliver, your master's father, now at my home, where he and I will gladly welcome any and all of you."

As the master, with an undisturbed and serene countenance, gave this version of the ride, it was very manifest from the expression of the boys' faces, and the glances they exchanged, that they recognized the history of their doings of the previous day; and it is not easy to describe nor to imagine the effect produced by this new translation of their own narrative. Some buried their heads behind their desks; some cried; some looked askance at one another; and many hastened down to the desk of the teacher, with apologies, regrets, and acknowledgments without end.

"We did not know it was your father," they said.

"Ah, my lads," replied the teacher, "what odds does it make whose father it was? It was probably somebody's father,—an inoffensive traveler, an aged and venerable man, entitled to kind treatment from you and everybody else. But never mind; he forgives it all, and so do I."

Freely pardoned, they were cautioned that they should be more civil for the future to inoffensive travelers, and more respectful to the aged and infirm.

Years have passed by. The lads are men, though some have found an early grave. The boy who related the incident to his master is "in the deep bosom of the ocean buried." They who survive, should this story meet their eye, will easily recall its scenes and throw their memories back to the schoolhouse in Federal Street, Salem, and to their friend and teacher.

—Henry K. Oliver.

* * * * *

The Tongue Can No Man Tame

Lord, tame my tongue, and make it pure,

And teach it only to repeat
Thy promises, all safe, all sure;
To tell thy love, so strong and sweet.

Lord, tame my tongue, and make it kind
The faults of others to conceal
And all their virtues call to mind;
Teach it to soothe, to bless, to heal.

ELIZABETH ROSSER

SAMUEL SMILES, THE AUTHOR OF "SELF-HELP"

When Samuel Smiles was a schoolboy in Scotland, he was fonder of frolic than of learning. He was not a prize-winner, and so was not one of his teacher's favorites. One day his master, vexed by his dulness, cried out, "Smiles, you will never be fit for anything but sweeping the streets of your native borough!" From that day the boy's mates called him by the name of the street sweeper in the little town. But he was not discouraged.

"If I have done anything worthy of being remembered," he wrote, more than sixty years later, when his name was known over the whole world, "it has not been through any superiority of gifts, but only through a moderate portion of them, accompanied, it is true, with energy and the habit of industry and application. As in the case of every one else, I had for the most part to teach myself.... Then I enjoyed good health, and health is more excellent than prizes. Exercise, the joy of interest and of activity, the play of the faculties, is the true life of a boy, as of a man. I had also the benefit of living in the country, with its many pleasures and wonders."

When he was fourteen, he was apprenticed to a physician. In the intervals of his work, he sought to continue his education by reading. Books were expensive then, but several libraries were open to him.

The death of his father near the end of his medical course, and consequent financial reverses, made him hesitate as to the wisdom of finishing his studies. In speaking of this, he made mention for the first time of his indebtedness to his mother. "You must go back to Edinburgh," she said, "and do as your father desired. God will provide." She had the most perfect faith in Providence, and believed that if she did her duty, she would be supported to the end. She had wonderful pluck and abundant common sense. Her character seemed to develop with the calls made upon her. Difficulties only brought out the essence of her nature. "I could not fail to be influenced by so good a mother."

But he was not to find his life-work as a doctor. For some years he practised medicine. Then he became editor of a political paper. Later, he was a railroad manager. Experience in writing gained in the newspaper office prepared him for literary work, by which he is best known.

These being the chief events and influences of his boyhood, the story of his most famous book, "Self-Help," is just what might be expected. It is a story full of inspiration.

In 1845, at the request of a committee of working men, he made an address to the society which they represented, on "The Education of the Working Classes." This excited such favorable comment that he determined to enlarge the lecture into a book. Thus "Self-Help" was written. But it was not to be published for many years. In 1854 the manuscript was submitted anonymously to a London publisher, and was politely declined. Undaunted, he laid it aside and began an account of the life of George Stephenson, with whom he had been associated in railway work. This biography was a great success.

Thus encouraged, he took from the drawer, where it had lain for four years, the rejected manuscript of "Self-Help," rewrote it, and offered it to his publishers. It was not his intention, even then, to use his name as author, so little did he think of himself. But, listening to the advice of friends, he permitted his name to appear. Very soon he was famous, for thirty-five thousand copies were sold during the first two years. In less than forty years two hundred and fifty-eight thousand copies have been disposed of in England alone. American publishers reprinted the book almost at once, and it soon became a favorite in school libraries in many States. It was translated into Dutch, German, Swedish, French, Portuguese, Czech, Croatian, Russian, Italian, Spanish, Turkish, Danish, Polish, Chinese, Siamese, Arabic, and several dialects of India.

But the author did not look on the fame and fortune brought to him by his book as his chief reward. It had been his desire to be helpful to the plodding, discouraged men and boys. As he expressed it himself: "It seemed to me that the most important results in daily life are to be obtained, not through the exercise of extraordinary powers, but through the energetic use of simple means, and ordinary qualities, with which all have been more or less endowed."

As his greatest reward he looked upon the grateful testimony of men of many countries who had been inspired by the book to greater effort, and so spurred on to success. An emigrant in New England wrote that he thanked God for the volume, which had been the cause of an entire alteration in his life. A working man wrote: "Since perusing the book I have experienced an entire revolution in my habits. Instead of regarding life as a weary course, which has to be gotten over as a task, I now view it in the light of a trust, of which I must make the most." A country schoolboy received a copy as a prize, and his life was transformed by the reading. By perseverance he secured an education, and became a surgeon. After a few years he lost his life in an attempt to help others. Such testimonies as these made Mr. Smiles happy, and are a fitting memorial to him. He died in 1904, at the age of ninety-two.

How much more satisfying to look back on a life of such usefulness than to say, as Jules Verne, author of many books, was compelled to say, "I amount to nothing ... in literature."—John T. Faris, D. D., in "Self-Help" published by Frederick A. Stokes Company, New York.

* * * * *

Life's Battles

Life's battles thou must fight all single-handed;
　No friend, however dear, can bear thy pain.
No other soul can ever bear thy burdens,
　No other hand for thee the prize may gain

Lonely we journey through this vale of sorrow;
　No heart in full respondeth to our own:
Each one alone must meet his own tomorrow,
　Each one must tread the weary way alone

Ah, weary heart! why art thou sad and lonely?
　Why this vain longing for an answering sigh?
Thy griefs, thy longings, trials, and temptations
　Are known and felt by Him who reigns on high.

ARTHUR V. FOX

DAVID LIVINGSTONE

On March 19, 1813, a hero was born in Blantyre, central Scotland. It was an age of great missionary activity, and the literal fulfilment of the spirit of the great commission had led Carey, Judson, Moffat, and scores of others to give their lives to the promulgation of the gospel of the kingdom of God in heathen lands. A dozen missionary societies were then in their youth. Interest in travel and exploration was at its height, and the attention of adventurers centered in the Dark Continent, the last of the great unknown regions of the world to be explored. Into the kingdom for such a time, and to do a divinely appointed work, came David Livingstone.

His home was a humble cottage. A rugged constitution came to him as a birthright, for his parents were of sturdy peasant stock. They served God devoutly, and though poor in this world's goods, were honest and industrious, being able to teach their children lessons in economy and thrift which proved of lifelong help to them.

David was a merry, brown-eyed lad, and a general favorite. Perseverance seemed bred in his very bone. When only nine years old, he received from his Sunday-school teacher a copy of the New Testament as a reward for repeating the one hundred nineteenth psalm on two successive evenings with only five errors. The following year, at the age of ten, he went to work in the cotton factory near his home, as a "piecer." Out of his first week's wages he saved enough to purchase a Latin grammar, and set himself resolutely to the task of thoroughly mastering its contents, studying for the most part alone after leaving his work at eight o'clock in the evening. His biographer tells us that he often continued his studies until after midnight, returning to work in the factory at six in the morning. Livingstone was not brighter than other boys, nor precocious in anything save determination. He was very fond of reading, and devised the plan of fastening a book on his spinning-jenny in the factory so that he could catch a sentence now and then while tending the machines. In this way he familiarized himself with many of the classics.

His aptitude for scientific pursuits early revealed itself, and he had a perfect passion for exploration. When only a boy, he usually chose to spend his holidays scouring the country for botanical, geological, and zoological specimens.

In his twentieth year the embryo missionary and explorer was led to accept Jesus Christ as his personal Saviour. Out of the fulness of peace, joy, and satisfaction which filled his heart, he wrote, "It is my desire to show my attachment to the cause of him who died for me by devoting my life to his service." The reading of an appeal by Mr. Gutzlaff to the churches of Britain and America in behalf of China brought to the young student's attention the need of qualified missionaries, and led him to dedicate his own life as well as all that he possessed to foreign service.

As a surgeon carefully selects the instruments with which he works, so it is ever with the divine Physician; and though Livingstone was anxious to enter his chosen field, providence led him to tarry for a little while in preparation. During this time of waiting he put into practise the motto which in later life he gave to the pupils in a Sunday-school, "Trust God and work hard." Having set his face toward China, he had no notion of turning back in the face of difficulties, and finally, after four years of untiring effort, he earned in 1840 a medical diploma, thus equipping himself with a training indispensable for one whose life was to be hidden for years in the fever jungles of Africa. He wrote, "With unfeigned delight I became a member of a profession which with unwearied energy pursues from age to age its endeavors to lessen human woe."

Livingstone also secured the necessary theological training, and was duly accepted by the London Missionary Society as a candidate for China. But the breaking out of the Opium war effectually closed the doors of that field. Just at this time came his providential acquaintance with Robert Moffat. The missionary was home on a furlough, and at a meeting which the young physician attended, stated that sometimes he had seen in the morning sunlight the smoke of a thousand villages in the Dark Continent where no missionary had ever been to tell the sweet old story of redeeming love. This message came to Livingstone as a Macedonian cry, and he willingly answered, "Here am I; send me." The purpose once formed, he never swerved from it.

The change of fields caused some alteration in his plans, and he remained for a time in England, further preparing for his mission with scrupulous care. On Nov. 17, 1840, Dr. Livingstone spent the last evening with his loved ones in the humble Blantyre home, going at once to London, where he was ordained as a missionary. He sailed for the Cape of Good Hope on the eighth of December.

Arrived in Africa, the new recruit immediately turned his steps toward the interior, where there were real things to do. After a brief stop at Kuruman, the home of the Moffats, he spent six months alone among the Bakwains, acquainting himself with their language, laws, and customs. In that time he gained not only these points, but the good will and affection of the natives as well. His door of opportunity had opened, and from the Bakwains he pressed farther north, until, within the first three years of his service in the Dark Continent, he was giving the gospel to heathen far beyond any point before visited by white men.

Both Livingstone and his wife learned early the secret of power that comes from living with the heathen, rather than merely living among them. He possessed a certain indefinable power of discipline over the native mind, which made for orderly, thorough, and effective service. The natives knew him for their friend as well as their teacher. Under his loving care, heathen chiefs became Christian leaders of their own people; Christian customs replaced heathen practises; and peace settled down where trouble had been rife.

Leaving his well-established work among the Namangwato, the Bakaa, the Makalaka, and the Bechuana tribes to be carried on by trained native helpers, this fearless man pressed on—always toward the dark interior. When his course was criticized, he wrote, "I will go anywhere, provided it be forward," and "forward" he went.

Livingstone's mind was one of that broad character which at the outset grasps the whole of a problem, and to those who have followed his later course it is clear why he saw no duty in settling down on one fixed spot to teach and preach in a slavery-harrowed land. He knew that, first, there must be a mighty clearing out of this evil. As for his own intent, he said, "Cannot the love of

Christ carry the missionary where the slave-trade carries the trader?" And so, right through to the west coast he marched, carrying and diffusing everywhere a knowledge of the redeeming Christ, and illustrating by his own kindly life and words and deeds the loving mercies of the Lord.

The physician and the scientist, the minister and the reformer, were all combined in this one purposeful man. The people believed him to be a wizard, and even credited him with power to raise the dead. Heathen, sick and curious, crowded about his wagon, but not an article was stolen. One day the chief of a savage tribe said: "I wish you would change my heart. Give me medicine to change it; for it is proud, proud and angry, angry always."

Livingstone left on record in his journals invaluable data of rivers, lakes, and streams, treacherous bogs, and boiling fountains, plants, animals, seasons, products, and tribes, together with the most accurate maps.

Near the mighty but then unknown Zambesi, Livingstone found the Makololo people, a tribe from which came his most devoted native helpers. When he left them to journey toward the west coast, as many men as he needed willingly agreed to accompany him. After a terrible journey of seven months, involving imminent starvation and endless exposure, the party at last reached their destination, St. Paul de Loanda, a Portuguese settlement.

Full as this journey was of incident, one of the most impressive things about it all was the horrors of the slave-trade, which came home to the missionary with heart-rending directness. "Every day he saw families torn asunder, dead bodies along the way, gangs chained and yoked, skeletons grinning against the trees by the roadside. As he rowed along on the beautiful river Shire, the paddles of his boat were clogged in the morning with the bodies of women and children who had died during the night, and were thus disposed of by their masters." And when he was sure that the wretched system was entrenched from the center of the continent to the coast, is it any wonder that he determined to make the exposure of this gigantic iniquity his principal work until "the open sore of the world" should be healed?

The slave-raiders were Livingstone's bitter enemies, and did everything possible to hinder his work. Just a story:—

Into a quiet little village on the shores of Lake Nyassa came some strangers one beautiful afternoon. The king sent to inquire as to their business. "We are Livingstone's children," they said. "Our master has found a road to the coast, and sent us back for his supplies. The day is late; we wish to spend the night in your village." "The white master is our friend," said the king, and he commanded his men to prepare the best huts for Livingstone's children. Some of the servants left at once to carry out the king's command, and soon the visitors were comfortably settled. The people flocked to their huts, bringing many gifts, and lingered about until the day was ended.

Late that night, when all the village was asleep, suddenly there was a piercing scream, then another, and another. The people rushed from their huts; for many of their homes were on fire. The white men, who called themselves Livingstone's children, were seizing women and children, and binding them with strong cords of leather. Around the necks of the men they fastened great Y-shaped sticks, riveting the forked ends together with iron. "We have been deceived," cried the natives. "The visitors were not Livingstone's children. They were slave-raiders. O! why did we ever trust them? If the white master were here, he would save us. He never takes slaves."

In the gray light of the morning, leaving their village a heap of smoldering ruins, the sad procession was marched off, heavily guarded. For two days their merciless captors drove them under the hot tropical sun without food or water. Late the second afternoon, they suddenly came upon a camp, at a sharp bend of the road, and there, in plain view, stood Dr. Livingstone. Every slave-driver took to his heels and disappeared in the thickets. They had all respect for that one white man. They knew he was in Africa to stop the slave-trade. The whole procession of slaves fell on their knees in thanksgiving, rejoicing in this unexpected deliverance, and were soon returning to their own country.

Do you wonder that the poor heathen loved the missionary? He never once betrayed their confidence. Almost immediately after reaching the Portuguese settlement on the coast, he was prostrated with a very severe illness. An English ship in the harbor was about to sail. In his great weakness, Livingstone longed for the bracing air of the Scottish highlands, and a sight of his beloved wife and children in the home land. But he prepared his reports, charts, and observations, put them aboard the ship, and, after watching it set sail, made ready to march back into the interior. Why did he not go home?—There was just one reason. He had promised his native helpers that if they would journey with him to the coast, he would see them back safely to their homes, and "his word to the black men of Africa was just as sacred as it would have been if pledged to the queen. He kept it as faithfully as an oath made to Almighty God. It involved a journey of nearly two years in length, a line of march two thousand miles long, through jungles, swamps, and desert, through scenes of surpassing beauty." But the result was worth the cost; for two years later, when he came out on the east coast at Quilimane, "he was the best known, best loved, and most perfectly trusted man in Africa."

Many times through all these wanderings he was in danger. Once, during his early explorations, he had an adventure with a lion, which nearly cost his life. He says of it in a letter: "The beast rushed from the bushes and bit me on the arm, breaking the bone. I hope I shall never forget God's mercy. It will be well before this reaches you. Do not mention it to any one. I do not like to be talked about." He never voluntarily referred to it; but "for thirty years thereafter, all adventures and exposures and hardships were undertaken with an arm so maimed that it was painful to raise a fowling-piece to his shoulder." After his death, the body was identified by that scar and the compound fracture made by the lion's teeth.

Livingstone's visits to the home land were brief, and each day was filled to the brim with interviews, lectures, and literary work. He returned to Africa for the third and last time in 1866, ascended the Rovuma, and for three years was lost to the outside world. During this time he visited lakes Meroe and Tanganyika, preaching the gospel to thousands and tens of thousands waiting in heathen darkness.

In 1871 his strength utterly gave way, and on October 23, reduced to a living skeleton, he reached Ujiji, after a perilous journey of six hundred miles taken expressly to secure supplies. He was bitterly disappointed to find that the rascal to whom the delivery of the goods had been charged had disposed of the whole lot. For eighty days he was obliged to keep his bed, and during this time he read his Bible through four times. On the fly-leaf he wrote: "No letters for three years. I have a sore longing to finish and go home, if God wills." Relief, letters, and supplies had all been sent him, but he never received them. Many of the letters which he wrote never even reached the coast, as the Portuguese destroyed them whenever possible.

During all this time England—and, in fact, the world—waited with intense anxiety for news of the hero. A report came that he was dead. Then a relief expedition brought back the word that Livingstone was alive, and in Africa, but that they had not been able to find him.

Just at this crucial moment Henry M. Stanley was sent out by James Gordon Bennett, of the New York Herald, with the order: "Take what money you want, but find Livingstone. You can act according to your own plans in your search, but whatever you do, find Livingstone—dead or alive." Stanley went. For eleven months he endured incredible hardships, but his expedition pressed forward into the interior. One day a caravan passed and reported that a white man had just reached Ujiji. "Was he young or old?" questioned Stanley anxiously. "He is old; he has white hair on his face; he is sick," replied the natives. As the searching party neared the village, flags were unfurled, and a salute fired from the guns. They were answered by shouts from hundreds of Africans. Stanley was greeted by Susi, Livingstone's servant, and soon stood face to face with the great missionary-explorer. He had found Livingstone.

The brief visit which they enjoyed meant much to both men. In vain did Stanley plead with the doctor to go home with him. The old explorer's heart was resolute, and he set his face as a flint. He did not feel that his work was done. At length the newspaper man and his company started eastward. Livingstone went some distance with them, and then, a broken old man, "clad in faded gray clothes," with bowed head and slow step, returned to his chosen solitude. Five months later the relief party reached Zanzibar, and news of Livingstone's safety and whereabouts was flashed to all parts of the world.

As the explorer again took up his weary way, physically weak and in constant pain, the buoyant spirit rose above hardship, and Scotch pluck smiled at impossibilities. He wrote in his diary: "Nothing earthly will make me give up my work in despair. I encourage myself in the Lord my God, and go forward." Weary months followed, filled with travel, toil, and physical suffering. The last of April, 1873, a year after Stanley left him, he reached the village of Ilala, at the southern end of Lake Bangweolo. He was so ill that his attendants were obliged to carry him as they journeyed, but the heroic spirit was still struggling to finish a work which would make possible the evangelization of the Dark Continent.

While the spirit was willing, the flesh was weak indeed, and on the morning of the first of May, his faithful servants found him kneeling at the bedside, with his head buried in his hands upon the pillow. "He had passed away without a single attendant, on the farthest of all his journeys. But he had died in the act of prayer—prayer offered in that reverential attitude about which he was always so particular; commending his own spirit, with all his dear ones, as was his wont, into the hands of his Saviour; and commending Africa, his own dear Africa, with all her woes and sins and wrongs, to the Avenger of the oppressed and the Redeemer of the lost."

LORA CLEMENT.

A TRUE INCIDENT OF THE SAN FRANCISCO EARTHQUAKE

He was by no means handsome; he had a turned-up nose, and a little squint in one eye; and Jennie Mills said you could not stick a pin anywhere on his face where there was not a freckle. And his hair, she said, was carrot color, which pleased the children so much that they called him "Carroty" for short. O, nobody ever thought of calling Tommy Carter handsome! For that matter, no one thought him a hero; yet even then he had some of the qualities which help to make heroes.

For instance, he was brave enough to go to school day after day with patched knees and elbows, the patches of quite a different color from the trousers and shirt-waist, and to say not a word at home of the boys who shouted, "Hello, Patchey!" or of Jennie Mills's asking whether she should not bring him a piece of her yellow cashmere for patches, to match his hair and freckles.

He had shed a few tears in private that day. The boys yelled and shouted so over what Jennie said that he could not help it. The scholars were used to laughing at Jennie Mills's sayings, and she was spoiling her character by always trying to think of something to say that would make people laugh. But on his way home Tommy stopped at the fountain on the square, and gave his eyes a good wash, so his mother would not suspect tears. Tommy knew that he had his mother to think about; she had been left in his care.

Tommy was only seven when his father, Tom Carter, was crushed between two engines. Nobody seemed to know just how it happened, only the man who had charge of the other engine had been drinking; anyway, it happened. They took Tom Carter home on a stretcher. Just before he died, he said; "Good-by, Tommy. Father trusts you to take care of mother and Sissy." After that would Tommy say anything to his mother about patches or teasing, or let her see tears?

There was another thing that Tommy had courage to do; that was to take constant care of Sissy. All day Saturday and all day Sunday, and just as much time as he could spare on school-days, Tommy gave to Sissy. It was he who fed her, and washed her face a great many times a day, and coaxed her to sleep, and took her to ride in her little cart, or walked very slowly when she chose to toddle along by his side, and changed her dress when she tumbled into the coal-box or sat down in a mud puddle. And he had been known to wash out a dress and a nightgown for Sissy when his mother was ill. There was really nothing too hard or too "girlish" for Tommy to do for his little sister. Once, somebody who saw him trying to mend a hole in the baby's petticoat called him "Sissy," and the name clung; for a time the school yard rang with shouts of "Sissy Carter." But not one word of this did Mother Carter hear.

"Did you have a good time today?" his mother would ask, and Tommy, with Sissy in his arms, crowing with delight that she had got him again, would answer, cheerfully: "A first-rate time. I got a big A for spelling, and teacher said I had improved in my writing." And not a word would be hinted about the nicknames or the jeers.

But better school-days came to Tommy before the last thing happened by which the people found out that he was a hero.

A new little girl came into the fourth grade. She was a pretty girl, and wore pretty dresses, and had a fluff of brown curls about her face. She was "smart," too, the boys said; they said she could say "lots funnier things than Jennie Mills." Then her name pleased them very much; it was Angela.

Whether or not she was smarter than Jennie Mills, it is true that Angela said some things that Jennie had never thought of.

"Tommy Carter is real good-natured," she said one day. "And he is not one
bit selfish. Don't you know how he gave the best seat to little Eddie
Cooper this morning, and stood off in a corner where he could not see much?
I like Tommy."

The scholars stared. Somehow it had never occurred to them to "like Tommy;" but, when once it had been mentioned, they seemed to wonder that they had not thought of it. Tommy was good-natured and very obliging. Not a day passed in which he did not in some small way prove this. As for his patches, Angela did not seem to notice them at all; and, if she did not, why should anybody? So in a few days a queer thing happened. The boys stopped teasing Tommy, and began in little ways to be kind to him. Some of the older ones, when they happened to have an extra apple or pear, fell into the habit of saying, "Here, want this?" and would toss it to Tommy. And when they discovered that he saved a piece of everything for Sissy, they did not laugh at all, for Angela said, "How nice for him to do that!"

Soon they began to save up bright little things themselves for Sissy—bits of paper, half-worn toys, once a new red ball. None of them realized it, but this really the influence of the new little girl with brown curls.

In that way it came to pass that Tommy lost many of his chances for being a hero; but a new chance was coming.

Tommy lived in a large tenement-house on one of the back streets of San Francisco. Seven other families lived in the same house. One Tuesday evening, Mrs. Carter told the woman who lived across the hall that she had done the hardest day's work of her life, and was so dead tired that she felt as if she would like to go to bed and never get up.

At five o'clock the next morning, she, Sissy, close beside her, and Tommy, in a little cot at the farther end of the room, were all sound asleep. Suddenly the walls of the big tenement-house began to sway from side to side in the strangest manner, and there was at the same second a terrible crashing noise. The kitchen table in the corner tipped over, and the dishes in the corner cupboard slid to the floor and went to pieces. The big wardrobe, which was a bureau and a clothes-closet all in one, moved out into the middle of the room, and the stove fell down. All these things happened so fast, and the earth was full of such strange, wild noises, that for a second nobody knew what was the matter.

Tommy Carter got to his mother's side before the noise was over, but he found that she could not stir; her bed was covered with bricks, and there was a great hole in the wall. Tommy did not know it then, but he understood afterward that the chimney had fallen on his mother's bed.

"Tommy," she gasped, "it is an earthquake! Take Sissy and run."

"But, mother," he cried, "O mother, I cannot leave you!"

"Never mind me, Tommy; take her quick! She is not hurt. Maybe there will be another. Tommy? you take care of Sissy! Run!"

And Tommy ran, with just the little shirt on in which he had been sleeping, and with an old quilt that his mother's hands had wrapped around the sleeping baby.

What an awful street was that into which he ran! What an awful road he had to go to get to it! Part of the side wall of the house was gone, and the stairs swayed from side to side as he stepped on them; but he reached the street, and it looked as if everything on it had tumbled down, and all the people in the world were running about, wringing their hands, and crying. Then suddenly an awful cry arose, "Fire! Fire! Fire!"

"Mother! O mother!" Tommy screamed, and he hurried to scramble back over the fallen walls by which he had come. He must take care of his mother. But a strong hand held him.

"Keep away, youngster. Don't you see that the wall is falling! Run!"

But where should he run? The whole city seemed to be burning, and everywhere was horror and terror. In trying to cross a street, Tommy was knocked down, and was for a second under the feet of a plunging horse. But he got out, and reached the sidewalk, with Sissy still safe, and he did not know that his arm was broken.

"Wasn't it lucky that Sissy was on the other arm?" he said, speaking to no one.

That awful day! Nobody who lived through it will ever forget it. Tommy Carter spent it struggling, pushing, panting, tugging, trying to get somewhere with Sissy. And Sissy cried for food and then for water, and there was none of either to give her; and then she lay back still, and he thought she was dying. The crowds swarmed and surged about him, crying, groaning, praying, cursing, yelling orders; and above all that fearful din arose the terrifying roar of the fire. The city was burning up! O, where was mother? And where was a safe place for Sissy? And why did his arm hurt so? What was the matter with him? His head was whirling round and round. Was he going to die and leave Sissy?—He never would!

Suddenly he roused with fresh energy. Somebody was trying to take Sissy.

"Don't you touch her!" he cried, fiercely. "Don't you dare! Let her alone,
I say!" and he fought like a wild animal.

"But, my poor boy," said the doctor, who was bending over him. But Tommy was insane with pain and fear.

"Let her be, I say!" he screamed. "Mother said I was not to let anybody take her, and I won't! I will kill you if you touch her! I'll, I'll—" and then Tommy fell back in a dead faint.

When he wakened, he was in a large, quiet room, in a clean bed. "Where is Sissy?" he called out in terror. A woman in white bent over him and spoke low: "Hush, dear; do not try to move. Sissy is safe and well and happy."

"Where is she, ma'am?" said Tommy. "I must have her right here by me. I can take care of her as well as not; I always do; and—I promised mother, you see; and she's awfully afraid of strangers."

"She is not afraid of us; she is very happy here. I have sent for her to come and see you. Ah, here she comes this minute!"

And there was Sissy, smiling, in the arms of a woman in a white gown and cap, and herself in the prettiest of white dresses. She laughed for joy at sight of Tommy, but was quite willing to stay in the young woman's arms.

"Little darling!" said the nurse. "She was not hurt a bit; and she is so sweet!"

"And where is mother, ma'am?" asked Tommy. "Was she hurt so that she cannot take care of Sissy? I am afraid that she was. When can I go to her? I have to take care of mother. Does she know that I kept Sissy safe?"

The two nurses looked at each other, and seemed not to know just how to answer so many questions; but the doctor, who had come up a moment before, stepped forward and spoke cheerily.

Tommy smiled gratefully.

"And when can I go and take care of her, sir? Was mother hurt? I remember all about it now. Is mother safe?"

"You have been very ill, and did not know what was happening. You did not even know Sissy when we brought her to see you."

"O!" said Tommy, with a faint smile. "How queer! Did not know Sissy! It is so nice that she takes to the pretty lady, and that mother is safe. I am very sleepy, sir. Would it be right to go to sleep if the pretty lady can take care of Sissy for a little while?"

"Quite right, my boy. We will take the best possible care of Sissy."

The doctor's voice was husky, and he turned away soon, with his own eyes dim, as Tommy's heavy eyes had closed.

"O doctor!" said both nurses.

"He is going, the brave little hero!" he said. "And we, you and I, will take care of Sissy for him."

"Yes, indeed!" said the pretty nurse, with a sob; she kissed Sissy.—Mrs.
G.R. Alden, in Junior Endeavor World, by permission of Lothrop, Lee &
Shepard Co.

LITTLE CORNERS

Georgia Willis, who helped in the kitchen, was rubbing the knives. Somebody had been careless and let one get rusty, but Georgia rubbed with all her might, rubbed, and sang softly a little song:—

"In the world is darkness,
  So we must shine,
You in your small corner,
  And I in mine."

"Why do you rub at the knives forever?" asked Mary. Mary was the cook.

"Because they are in my corner," Georgia said, brightly. "'You in your small corner,' you know, 'and I in mine.' I will do the best I can; that is all I can do."

"I would not waste my strength," said Mary. "I know that no one will notice."

"Jesus will," said Georgia; and then she sang again,—

"You in your small corner,
  And I in mine."

"Cooking the dinner is in my corner, I suppose," said Mary to herself. "If that child must do what she can, I suppose I must. If Jesus knows about knives, it is likely that he does about dinners." And she took particular pains.

"Mary, the dinner was very nicely cooked today," Miss Emma said.

"That is all due to Georgia," said Mary, with a pleased face. Then she told about the knives.

Miss Emma was ironing ruffles; she was tired and warm. "Helen will not care whether they are fluted or not," she said. "I will hurry them over." But after she heard about the knives, she did her best.

"How beautifully my dress is done!" Helen said. Emma, laughing, answered,
"That is owing to Georgia." Then she told about the knives.

"No," said Helen to her friend who urged, "I really cannot go this evening.
I am going to prayer-meeting; my 'corner' is there."

"Your 'corner'! What do you mean?"

Then Helen told about the knives.

"Well," the friend said, "if you will not go with me, perhaps I will with you," and they went to the prayer-meeting.

"You helped us ever so much with the singing this evening," their pastor said to them as they were going home. "I was afraid you would not be here."

"It was owing to our Georgia," said Helen. "She seemed to think she must do what she could, if it were only to clean the knives." Then she told him the story.

"I believe I will go in here again," said the minister, stopping before a poor little house. "I said yesterday there was no use; but I must do what I can."

In the house a sick man was lying. Again and again the minister had called, but the invalid would not listen to him. Tonight the minister said, "I have come to tell you a little story." Then he told him about Georgia Willis, about her knives and her little corner, and her "doing what she could." The sick man wiped the tears from his eyes, and said, "I will find my corner, too. I will try to shine for Jesus." And the sick man was Georgia's father.

Jesus, looking down at her that day, said, "She hath done what she could," and gave the blessing.

"I believe I will not go for a walk," said Helen, hesitatingly. "I will finish that dress of mother's; I suppose I can if I think so."

"Why, child, are you here sewing?" her mother said. "I thought you had gone for a walk."

"No, mother; this dress seemed to be in my 'corner,' so I thought I would finish it."

"In your 'corner'!" her mother repeated in surprise, and then Helen told about the knives. The doorbell rang, and the mother went thoughtfully to receive her pastor. "I suppose I could give more," she said to herself, as she slowly took out the ten dollars that she had laid aside for missions. "If that poor child in the kitchen is trying to do what she can, I wonder if I am. I will make it twenty-five dollars."

And I seemed to hear Georgia's guardian angel say to another angel, "Georgia Willis gave twenty-five dollars to our dear people in India today."

"Twenty-five dollars!" said the other angel. "Why, I thought she was poor?"

"O, well, she thinks she is, but her Father in heaven is not, you know! She did what she could, and he did the rest."

But Georgia knew nothing about all this, and the next morning she brightened her knives and sang cheerily:—

"In the world is darkness,
  So we must shine,
You in your small corner,
  And I in mine."

—The Pansy.

IN THE HOME

When John Howard Payne wrote the immortal words of "Home, Sweet Home," adapting them to the beautiful Sicilian melody, now so familiar to us all, he gave to the world a precious legacy, which has brought sunshine into millions of hearts. "Be it ever so humble, there's no place like home." And there is no other place in all the world where the little courtesies of life should be so tenderly given; where loving ministrations should be so cheerfully bestowed; in short, where good manners, in all the varied details of life, should be so diligently practised. "Home, sweet home!" the place where childhood days are spent, where habits are formed which are to continue through the future, and where the foundation is laid upon which the superstructure of after-years is to be built. What a halo lingers about the blessed spot! and how the soul of the exile cherishes the pictures which adorn the halls of memory,—pictures which the rude hand of time can never efface!

This earth has many lingering traces of Eden yet remaining, which enrapture the eye of the beholder. But there is no sight in all the world so beautiful as that of a well-ordered, harmonious Christian home,—a home where love reigns; where each esteems the other better than himself; where the parents are careful to practise what they preach; where the daily lessons instilled into the minds of the children from babyhood to maturity always and forever include the indispensable drills in good manners.

There is no school so important as the home school, no teacher so responsible as the parent, no pupil under such weighty obligations to deport himself creditably as is the son or daughter of the household. And may it not be asserted truthfully that there is no more thrilling commencement scene than that which sees the noble young man or young woman, having passed successfully through all the grades of the parental school, bid a regretful adieu to the dear childhood home, to enter upon a career of usefulness elsewhere, to spend and be spent in saving humanity? But how few such commencement scenes do we witness! How few pupils ever pass the test satisfactorily in the important branch of ethics!

When parents practice good manners toward their children; when they find as much pleasure in the unaffected "please" and "thank you" of the home kindergarten as they do in the same marks of politeness elsewhere; when the deportment in the grades of the home school is considered of greater importance than that in the schools away from home, our preparatory schools and colleges will have less trouble in securing good behavior on the part of those in attendance, and the problem of how to maintain proper decorum will have lost its perplexity.

Every time a child says "please" it is a reminder that he is not independent, that he is in need of assistance. Every time he says "thank you," he has yet another reminder that he is not independent, that he is under obligations to another for assistance received. Pure and undefiled religion and good manners cannot be separated. The child who is taught to say "please" because he is in need of human aid, may be made easily to comprehend the beautiful significance of prayer, because he is in need of divine aid. The child who is taught to say "thank you" for favors received from earthly friends, may be led easily to see the appropriateness of offering praise and thanksgiving for divine blessings.

Children who are made to realize that to appear well always in the society of home is infinitely more important than to try to appear well occasionally when away from home, cause little parental anxiety as to how they will deport themselves when absent. And children who practise good behavior in the home when no company is present, do not need to be called aside for a hasty lesson in this line when some one is about to call. Such lessons are very unsatisfactory, and are seldom remembered, being much like music lessons taken without the intervening practise.

Good manners cannot be put on and off with the best clothing, or donned momentarily to suit the occasion. But, unlike our ordinary apparel, the more they are worn, the more beautiful they appear. Good manners in the home means good manners everywhere; and each individual simply stands before the world an epitome of all his former training. If the child has learned to be honest and truthful in all the details of the home life, he may face the world in later years a worthy example of uprightness to all with whom he comes in contact. If he has learned to be habitually kind and courteous in the home, he is the same wherever he may be. If he always appears neat and tidy in the home, these pleasing characteristics will remain with him throughout life.

If the loved members of his own family circle never discover that he has a "temper of his own," there is little danger that any one else will ever find it out. If his habits and practises at home are such as to ennoble and beautify his own life, his influence will rest as a benign benediction upon the beloved of his household, and the great world outside will be better because of his having lived in it. O, that every boy and girl might rightly appreciate the vast difference between manners of the soul and manners of the head,—manners of the heart and manners of the outward appearance! One is Christian religion, the other is cold formality. One means the salvation of souls; the other is but vanity and outward show.

But we are instructed that "true refinement and gentleness of manners can never be found in a home where selfishness reigns." "We should be self-forgetful, ever looking out for opportunities, even in little things, to show gratitude for the favors we have received from others, and watching for opportunities to cheer others, and to lighten and relieve their sorrows and burdens, by acts of tender kindness and little deeds of love. These thoughtful courtesies that begin in our families, extend outside the family circle, and help to make up the sum of life's happiness; and the neglect of these little things makes up the sum of life's bitterness and sorrow."

Boys and girls who rightly appreciate good manners will be polite and courteous in the home, and will share cheerfully in all the little duties of the household. Some one has said that idleness is "the chief author of all mischief." And surely any individual who chooses to be idle rather than to be usefully employed, is exceedingly ill-bred. Children should be taught the nobility of labor, and to respect those who faithfully perform the humblest duties of life, just as much as those who accomplish the more difficult tasks.

There is pointed truth in the assertion that there is gospel in a loaf of good bread; but it is a sad comment on the home training of the present day that so few of our young people recognize this fact. It is to be deplored that the children nowadays receive so little training in the ins and outs of good housekeeping. No young lady should consider herself accomplished until she has acquired the art of making good bread, and of knowing how to prepare healthful and palatable meals. Even if it never should be her privilege to become the queen of a kitchen, there are always ample opportunities to impart such valuable knowledge to others.

The world is in direful need of practical boys and girls, practical young men and young women, who are not afraid to perform faithfully even the smallest duties that lie in the pathway of life, and who are willing to tax their thinking powers in order that their work may be done in the best possible manner. How much more in keeping with Christian manners that the son of the household should share in the burden of keeping the domestic machinery running smoothly, rather than misemploy his time, and grow up unacquainted with the practical duties of life! How much more appropriate that the daughter should assist the mother in performing the various household duties, rather than occupy a hammock or an easy chair, and spend her time in reading cheap books! Many a weary mother would appreciate such kindness on the part of her children more than words can express, and the children themselves would be the happier because of such thoughtful service.

The boy or girl who grows up in the belief that honorable labor in any direction is a God-given privilege, will realize that housework is not without its fascinations, and that manual training in the school is an important part of the daily curriculum. Such a child will realize that even an empty water-pail or a vacant wood-box presents a golden opportunity for usefulness which should not be slighted. He will not appropriate for himself the last pint of cold water from the pail, or the last cup of hot water from the tea-kettle, and complacently leave them for some one else to fill. That child, even though he be grown up who sees nothing in these little opportunities for usefulness, will let greater ones pass by with the same lack of appreciation.

Laziness is a deadly enemy to success; and the child who is indolent in the home, is likely to bring up the rear in the race of life. Laziness is no kin to true happiness. The lazy child is not the truly happy child. He lies in bed until late in the morning, is often careless about his personal appearance, is late to breakfast, late to school, and his name is entirely wanting when the highest credits are awarded. Such a child may be sometimes recognized by the neglected appearance of his teeth and finger-nails, the "high-water marks" about his neck and wrists, the dust on his clothing and shoes, his untidy hair, etc. In fact, he seems to have adopted as his life motto the paraphrase, "There is no excellence about great labor."

A trite story is told of a man who was to be executed because of his persistent laziness. While being driven to the scaffold, he was given one more chance for his life by a kind-hearted individual who offered him a quantity of corn with which to make a new start. Upon hearing the suggestion, the condemned man slowly raised himself up, and rather dubiously inquired, "I-s i-t s-h-e-l-l-e-d?" Being informed to the contrary, he slowly settled down again, with the remark, "W-e-l-l, then, drive on."

Now, boys and girls, you will find many occasions in life when it will be necessary for you to put forth an extra effort in order to succeed. But when some golden opportunity presents the corn to you, do not stop to inquire, "Is it shelled?" Learn to shell your own corn. Use your muscle as well as your brain, ever bearing in mind that increased strength, both physical and mental, comes as the result of the proper use of that which you now possess. Be workers, be thinkers, in the great world about you. The old saying that it is better to wear out than to rust out is not without forceful meaning.

In accordance with heaven-born manners, "let all things be done decently and in order." All things include even the little chores which may be done by the members of the home kindergarten; it also includes the greatest task of which man is capable. If we would learn how particular Heaven is in regard to neatness and order, we should become familiar with God's instructions to ancient Israel. The arrangement of the camp of Israel, and the whole round of tabernacle service, present a systematic demonstration of order and neatness such as Heaven approves. And the sad fate of Uzzah, Korah, Dathan, and Abiram, attests to how particular God is in regard to perfect order.

If systematic order and neatness are to be maintained in the home, the members of the household must be united in putting forth the necessary efforts. And blessed is that family who make of home "a little heaven to go to heaven in."

But let me repeat that "true refinement and gentleness of manners can never be found in a home where selfishness reigns." And how many temptations to selfishness there are in the home life! Every day brings the choice between selfishness and self-sacrifice. Shall I take for myself the choicest apple? or shall I share in that which is not so agreeable? These may appear to be very insignificant questions. But, boys and girls, do you know that the habitual decisions at which you arrive in childhood, determine largely whether or not you will live by principle later on? "As the twig is bent, so the tree inclines."

But the lesson of always giving cheerfully to others that which the natural heart would selfishly appropriate as its own, can be learned only in the school of Christ. And blessed is that parent or teacher who rightly appreciates the privilege of becoming an assistant in that school. Blessed is that pupil who realizes what it means to become such a devoted learner that he can find joy in denying self that he may minister to the comfort of others whenever an opportunity is afforded, recognizing that every heaven-appointed task is a part of the great cause of truth—the giving of the "gospel to all the world in this generation." Every kindness shown to others, if done in the right spirit, is counted in the records of heaven as done to Christ himself. Even the cup of cold water given in his name, is never forgotten.

Kind words and loving deeds are as pebbles cast upon the great sea of humanity, the ever-widening circle of whose influence extends beyond the limited vision of him who projects them; and the eternal ages alone will reveal how many souls have been saved, and saved forever, as the grand result. How many girls and boys are watching every opportunity to share in this blessed work?

MRS. M. A. LOPER.

SOMETIME, SOMEWHERE

You lent a hand to a fallen one,
  A lift in kindness given;
It saved a soul when help was none,
  And won a heart for heaven.
And so for the help you proffered there,
You'll reap a crown, sometime, somewhere.

D. G. BICKERS

GIANTS AND GRASSHOPPERS

"What is the matter?" asked Mrs. Hamlin. "What is hindering the work?"

Mr. Hamlin glanced up from his paper. "The work?" he said. "O, the old story; there are 'giants' in the land, and the committee feel like 'grasshoppers'!"

It was Earle's turn to look up. Earle was reading, but he generally had one ear for any conversation that was going on about him. His eyes went back to his book, but he kept wondering just what his father meant. Of course there were no giants in these days! He waited until his father was turning the paper to another page, then put in his question:—

"Father, what do you mean about 'giants' and 'grasshoppers'?"

Mr. Hamlin laughed. "Your ears heard that, did they? Why, I meant what the ten spies did when they whined about giants, and called themselves 'grasshoppers,' instead of seizing their chance, as the other two wanted them to do. Don't you remember the story? I fear you are not so well posted on Old Testament history as you are in your school history. The report of the spies makes very interesting reading; you would better look it up."

"I remember about it now," said Earle, "and I guess what you mean about the committee. There lots of giants around nowadays, aren't there?"

"Plenty of them!" said his father. "Look out that none of them scare you away from an opportunity."

Earle laughed, and went back to his book. He knew he was the sort of boy of whom the other boys said that he did not "scare worth a cent."

It was nearly twenty-four hours afterward that he was in the dining-room, which was his evening study, bent over his slate, his pencil moving rapidly. His friend and classmate, Howard East-man, sat on the arm of the large rocker, tearing bits from a news-paper wrapper and chewing them, while he waited for Earle.

"I do wish you would come on!" he said, between the bites of paper. "The boys will be waiting for us; I told them I would bring you right along, and the fun will all be over before we get there."

"Bother!" said Earle, consulting his book. "That is not anywhere near right."

"Of course it is not. I knew it would not be. There is not a fellow in the class, nor a girl, either, for that matter, who has got that example. Why, I know, because I heard them talking about that very one; and haven't I done that seventy-five times myself? My brother Dick tried to do it for me, and he did not get it either; he said there was some catch about it."

"I would like to find the catch," said Earle, wistfully.

"Well, you can't. I tell you there is not one of them who can. You need not think you are smarter than anybody else. We won't get marked on that example; they do not expect us to have it. I heard Professor Bowen tell Miss Andrews that there would not be a pu-pil in the room who could conquer it."

"Is that so?" said Earle, running his fingers through his hair, and looking wearily at the long rows of figures on his slate.

"I have not got it, that is certain; and I have tried it in every way I can think of. I do not know as there is any use of my going over it again."

"Of course there is not! It is just one of those mean old catch problems that nobody is expected to get So just put up your tools, and come on. I know the boys are out of all patience with us for being so late."

It happened that Cousin Carrol was in the library, which opened from the dining-room. Cousin Carrol was seventeen, and her thir-teen-year-old cousin admired her extremely. He had known her but three weeks, and already they were the best of friends; he valued her good opinion next to his father's and mother's. At that moment her face appeared in the doorway, and she said in the sweetest and gentlest of tones:—

"And there we saw the giants."

Howard Eastman made haste to take the wads of paper out of his mouth, and to get off the arm of the chair; but Miss Carrol's face vanished, and they heard her open the hall door and pass out. Earle's face, meantime, had reddened to his hair.

"What did she say?" inquired Howard, his eyes big with wonder.

"O, never mind what she said! She was talking to me. Look here, Howard Eastman, you may as well cut down to Timmy's, and tell them I cannot come; they need not wait for me any longer. There is no use in talking; I am going to conquer that example if I have to sit up all night to do it. I am no grasshopper, and it has got to be done!"

"O, say now! I think that is mean!" growled Howard. "There won't be half so much fun without you; and, besides—why, you almost got started. You began to put up your books."

"I know I did; but I am not starting now, and there is no hope of me. Skip along, and tell the boys I am sorry, but it is not my fault; it is this old giant of a problem that is trying to beat me; and he can't. I do not feel a bit like a grasshopper."

"Say," said Howard, "what have giants to do with that example? She said something about them."

"They have not a thing to do with it," said Earle with energy, "and I will prove that they have not. Now you skip, Howard, that's a good fellow, and let me alone. I have a battle to fight."

Howard groaned, and growled, and "skipped." Next morning, just as the hour for recitation arrived, and the arithmetic class were filing in, company was announced.

"Just our luck!" muttered Howard Eastman. "Any other morning this term I should have been ready for them. Did you know

119

they were coming, Earle?"

No, Earle did not. He looked up in surprise. There were not only his father and Cousin Carrol, but a stranger, a fine-looking man, who, it was presently telegraphed through the class, was Judge Dennison, of Buffalo, who used to attend this school when he was a boy. And then, behold, came Principal Bowen, who stood talking with his guests a moment, after which they all took seats and stayed through the entire hour.

Work went on well until that fatal thirty-ninth example was reached, and
Howard Eastman was called upon to go to the board and perform it.

"I cannot do it, Miss Andrews," he said, "I tried it as many as fifty times, I think, in fifty different ways, and I could not get near the answer."

"That is very sad!" said Miss Andrews, trying not to laugh. "If you had not tried so many ways, but worked faithfully at one, you might have done better."

Then she called on the boy next to him, with no better success. A long row of downcast eyes and blushing faces. Some of the pupils confessed that they had not even attempted the problem, but had been discouraged by the reports of others.

"Is there no one who is willing to go to the board," said Miss Andrews, "and attempt the work, carrying it as far as he can?"

At just that moment she caught sight of Earle Hamlin's face, and spoke to him.

"Will you try it, Earle?"

And Earle went. Silence in the class-room. All eyes on the blackboard, and the quick fingers of one boy handling the crayon. How fast he worked! Had be multiplied right?—No. Yes, that was right. O, but he had blundered in subtraction! No, he had not; every figure was right. Ah! now he had reached the place where none of them knew what to do next. But he knew! Without pause or confusion, he moved on, through to the very last figure, which he made with a flourish. Moreover, he knew how to explain his work, just what he did, and why he did it. As he turned to take his seat, the admiring class, whose honor he had saved, broke into applause, which the smiling teacher did not attempt to check.

"I think we owe Earle a vote of thanks," she said. "I confess my surprise as well as pleasure in his work; I did not expect any of you to succeed. In truth, I gave you the example rather as a trial of patience than in the hope that you could conquer it. You remember, however, that I gave you permission to secure help if you utterly failed. Will you tell us, Earle, if you had any help?"

"Yes'm," said Earle. "My Cousin Carrol helped me."

And then Cousin Carrol's astonishment suddenly broke into laughter.

"I have not the least idea what he means," she said, in her clear, silvery voice. "I was so far from helping him that I tried all by myself to do the example, and failed."

The class began to cheer again, but hushed suddenly to hear what Earle was saying.

"All the same, she helped me," he said, sturdily. Then, seeing that he must explain, he added, hurriedly "We had been talking about the giants, you know, and the grasshoppers, just the night before, and I thought to myself then that I was not a grasshopper, anyhow; but I never thought about the example being a giant, and I was just going to quit it when Cousin Carrol came to the door and spoke about the giants, and then I went at it again."

Some of the pupils looked hopelessly puzzled. Mr. Hamlin's face was one broad smile. "Students of Old Testament history have the advantage here today, I fancy," he said.

"Earle," said Miss Andrews, "are you willing to tell us how long you worked on the example?"

"I began it at six o'clock," said Earle, "and I got it just as the clock struck eleven."

There was no use in trying to keep that class from cheering.

They felt that their defeat had been forgotten in Earle's victory.

Mr. Hamlin and Judge Dennison stood talking together after the class was dismissed.

"Do you know, I like best of all that word of his about his cousin's helping him?" said Judge Dennison. "It was plucky in the boy to keep working, and it took brains to study out that puzzle; but that little touch which showed that he was not going to accept the least scrap of honor that did not belong to him was what caught me. You have reason to be proud of your son, Mr. Hamlin."—Pansy, by permission of Lothrop, Lee & Shepard Co.

As GOOD AS HIS BOND

I remember that a good many years ago, when I was a boy, my father, who was a stone-mason, did some work for a man named John Haws. When the work was completed, John Haws said he would pay for it on a certain day. It was late in the fall when the work was done, and when the day came on which Mr. Haws had said he would pay for it, a fearful storm of sleet and snow and wind raged from morning until night. We lived nine miles from the Haws home, and the road was a very bad one even in good weather. I remember that father said at the breakfast-table:—

"Well, I guess that we shall not see anything of John Haws to-day. It will not make any difference if he does not come, as I am not in urgent need of the money he owes me. It will make no difference if it is not paid for a month."

But about noon Mr. Haws appeared at our door, almost frozen, and covered with sleet and snow.

"Why, John Haws!" exclaimed my father, when he opened the door, and saw who it was that had knocked. "I had not the least idea that you would try to ride away out here in this fearful storm."

"Did I not say that I would come?" asked John Haws, abruptly.

"O, yes; but I did not regard it as a promise so binding that you must fulfil it on a day like this!"

"Any promise that I make is binding, regardless of wind and weather. I said that I would pay the money today, and I am here to keep my word."

"But, then, it is only a small sum, and I do not really need it."

"I need to keep my word. If the sum had been but ten cents, and you were a millionaire, and I had said that I could pay it today, I would be here to pay it if I had been compelled to ride fifty miles."

Do you wonder that it was often said of John Haws that his word was as good as his bond? He was as truthful as he was honest. I remember that a neighbor of ours stopped at our house one day on his way home from the town. He had an almost incredible story to tell about a certain matter, and father said:—

"Why, it hardly seems possible that such a thing can be true."

"John Haws told me about it."

"O, then it is true!"

"Yes, or John Haws never would have told it."

It is a fine thing to have a reputation like that. It is worth more than much worldly glory and honor when they are combined with the distrust of the people. There are men in high positions, with all that wealth can buy at their command, who are much poorer than humble John Haws, because their word is of no value, and they have none of that high sense of honor that glorifies the humblest life.—Selected,

$\mathcal{P}$LAIN BERNICE

The last stroke of the bell was dying away ere Bernice Dahl walked timidly across the schoolroom floor, and sat down in the nearest empty seat.

"O, my, my!" whispered Myrtle Fling across the aisle to her chum. "She is the plainest-looking girl I ever saw."

Elizabeth nodded her head very positively, and two or three others exchanged knowing glances. A moment later a little piece of paper fluttered down at Myrtle's feet from a desk top. On it was written: "She's so plain. She's Rocky Mountainy—all ridges and hubbles."

Meanwhile Bernice sat very still, her great black eyes fixed on the teacher's face.

Have you ever held a frightened bird in your hand, and felt its heart beat? That is the way Bernice's heart was going. She was a stranger. Her father had moved to this place from a distant town, and she had walked to school that morning with a pupil who lived on the same street, but who had fluttered away into a little bevy of children almost as soon as she had shown the new girl the cloak-room; and Bernice, naturally a bit diffident and sensitive, felt very much alone.

This feeling was heightened when the bell struck, and one by one the pupils filed past into the schoolroom, with only a rude stare or indifferent glance, quite as if she were some specter on exhibition. When the last one had passed her, she clasped and unclasped her hands nervously.

"It is because I am so homely!" she thought.

A month or more went by. Somehow Bernice and her school-mates had not made so much progress in getting acquainted as one would have thought. The new girl was unobtrusive, attended strictly to her studies, and made few demands on those about her; yet it was true that there was among them at least an unacknowledged conspiracy to taboo her, or an understanding that she was to be ignored almost completely. This Bernice attributed to her looks. Ever since she could remember, she had been called "homely," "ugly," "plain," and similar epithets. Now, though she preserved a calm exterior, she could not help being unhappy because she was thus slighted.

One Monday morning a little flurry of excitement was visible among the pupils of the up-town grammar-school. Elizabeth Weston had announced a party to come off later in the week, and several of them had been invited.

"Will you invite Bernice Dahl?" asked Myrtle, bending over her friend.

"I have been thinking about it," Elizabeth answered, slowly. "Miss Somers says she has the best lessons of any one in her class, and then she was so nice to Jimmy Flanders that day he sprained his arm. I have half a mind to." And she really did.

That night when Bernice was telling her mother of the invitation she had received, she said, doubtfully, "I think I shall not go."

"Why not?" was the reply. "It can do no good to stay away, and something may be gained by going."

So it chanced that Bernice found herself at Elizabeth's home on the evening of the party. Her hostess met her smilingly. "She is really glad that I came," thought Bernice. And she felt her soul suddenly warm to life, just as the thirsty earth brightens and glows and sends up little shoots of new green at a patter of summer rain.

The long parlor was decorated in green and white. The bright lights, the gay figures stirring beneath, and the shining faces, half of which were strange to Bernice, formed a pretty picture, and the girl moved here and there in the constantly shifting kaleidoscope with a freedom and happiness she had not known since coming to the town.

At last she found herself, with the others, sitting very quiet and listening to two girls playing a duet on the piano. Then one of them sang a Scotch song. There was warmth and richness, the warbling of birds, the melody of brooks, in the rendering, and Bernice heard a half-sigh close beside her.

"I wish I could sing! O, always I wanted to sing!"

Then for the first time she saw who sat there—a tall, handsome, beautifully gowned girl whom she had noticed several times during the evening, and to whom everybody seemed to defer. She had heard vaguely that this was Elizabeth's cousin, and wondered if it was for her that Elizabeth had given the party.

"And can't you?" she asked, evincing instant interest.

The girl turned toward her with a smile. "Not at all. Sometimes I used to try when no one heard, and once when I was in the hammock with my brother's little girl, I joined her in the song she was singing. She looked at me in a minute with a rueful countenance, and said, 'Aunt Helen, I can't sing when you are making such a noise!'" Bernice laughed. "I haven't tried much since," the tall girl added.

"We have singing lessons at school twice a week," Bernice said, presently, "but I like the every-day lessons better."

"Do you? I like mathematics, and sloyd, and a hammer and nails and saw.
Mama tells me I ought to be a carpenter."

"But you don't look like one," Bernice smiled, critically; and then continued: "We began physical geography this term. It is so interesting. And Miss Somers makes language beautiful; I can't help liking grammar!"

"I never understood it—it was always so blind!"

But Bernice was laughing again. The tall girl turned toward her inquiringly.

"I was thinking of what Johnny Weeks said down in the primary room the other day," Bernice began in explanation. "The teacher asked him what 'cat' was. I guess he was not paying attention. He looked all around, and finally said he did not know. She told him it was a noun. 'Then,' he said, after some deliberation, 'kitten must be a pronoun.'"

An hour afterward, all the lights but one in the house were out. Elizabeth sat with her cousin talking over the events of the evening.

"And how do you like Bernice Dahl?" she asked, and lent an eager ear; for
Helen's word could make or mar things irretrievably.

"Like her? I have never liked any one better. Perhaps I would not have noticed, had you not spoken particularly about her."

"Well?" said Elizabeth, as her cousin paused.

"She is all life and vivacity. I thought you said she was 'dum-mified.'"

"But she was. I never saw her like this before."

"Then something woke her. If any seemed ill at ease or lonely, she went to them, and, behold, they chatted like magpies! I saw some of her schoolmates look at her wonderingly, and at least one sneered, but I watched. She had just one thought, and that was to make every one happy. You could have spared any one of the girls better; in fact, any three of them."

Long after Helen had gone to sleep, Elizabeth lay thinking. "Jimmy Flanders," she said, and counted off one finger; another followed, and then another. After all, it was wonderful how many good deeds she could reckon up, and all so quietly done. Strange she had never thought of them en masse before. How could Bernice be gay among so many frowns and slights?

The next forenoon session of the grammar-school was well under way. Bernice opened her history, and in it was a little slip of paper that she had used as a book-mark since that first morning. An odd spirit seized her, and almost before she knew it, she had gone up the aisle, and laid it on Elizabeth's desk. The next instant she would have given much to withdraw it. Elizabeth glanced down and flushed painfully. There it was: "She's so plain. She's Rocky Mountain—all ridges and hubbles." But Bernice was back at her work again, evidently unruffled.

When the bell tapped for intermission, Elizabeth went to her. "Bernice, I did write it. O, I am so ashamed!" and, bursting into tears, she hid her face on Bernice's shoulder.

One of those smiles that somehow have the power of transforming the harshest features, swept over the girl's face, and, picking up Elizabeth's hand, she kissed it softly again and again. "I won't kiss her face," she thought, "I am so homely!" but from that day she slipped into the queenly place she had a right to occupy, and it was not long before every one forgot her plainness.

And let me whisper you a secret, girls,—for even now Bernice does not seem to know,—as she grew older, the rough lines mellowed and softened, the short figure stretched upward, till she was beautiful as ever her dearest wish had pictured. Was it not lovely spirit within, for Bernice was a Christian, molding and modeling the clay into a fit dwelling-place for itself? That is a beauty that never quite withers away. Its roots are planted in the soul beautiful, and a beautiful soul can never die.

MRS. CORA WEBBER.

Say "Thank You"

I saw a needy one relieved,
And forth he went, and glad,
But not one word of gratitude
That lightened spirit had.
His benefactor, bent by cares,
Went wearily all day;
While him his kindnesses had served
Went careless on his way.

If you have given aught for me,
Ought not my voice return
One little word of graciousness?
O, breaking spirits yearn
Just for the human touch of love
To cheer the aching heart,
To brighten all the paths of toil,
And take away the smart!

Say "Thank you!" then. 'Tis small enough
Return for help bestowed
Say "Thank you!" You would spurn to slight
The smallest debt you owed;
But is not this a debt?—Ah, more!
And honor, if true blue
Your loyal heart of rectitude,
Impels to say "Thank you!"

B. F. W. SOURS.

*H*OW THE BOY WITHOUT A REFER-
ENCE FOUND ONE

John was fifteen, and anxious to get a desirable place in the office of a well-known lawyer, who had advertised for a boy. John doubted his success in obtaining this position, because, being a stranger in the city, he had no reference to present.

"I am afraid I will stand a poor chance," he thought, despondently; "however, I will try to appear as well as I can, and that may help me a little."

So he was careful to have his dress and person neat, and when he took his turn to be interviewed, went in with his hat in his hand and a smile on his face.

The keen-eyed lawyer glanced him over from head to foot. "Good face," he thought, "and pleasant ways." Then he noted the neat suit,—but other boys had appeared in new clothes,—saw the well-brushed hair, and clean skin. Very well; but there had been others quite as cleanly. Another glance, however, showed the finger-nails free from soil. "Ah, that looks like thoroughness," thought the lawyer.

Then he asked a few direct, rapid questions, which John answered as directly. "Prompt," was his mental comment; "can speak up when necessary."

"Let's see your writing," he added aloud.

John took a pen and wrote his name.

"Very well; easy to read, and no flourishes. Now, what references have you?"

The dreadful question at last! John's face fell. He pad begun to feel some hope of success, but this dashed it again.

"I haven't any," he said, slowly. "I am almost a stranger in the city."

"Cannot take a boy without references," was the brusque rejoinder.

As he spoke, a sudden thought sent a flush to John's cheek. "I haven't any reference," he said, with hesitation; "but here is a letter from mother I just received. I wish you would read it."

The lawyer took it. It was a short letter:—

"MY DEAR JOHN: I want to remind you that wherever you find work, you must consider that work your own. Do not go into it, as some boys do, with the feeling that you will do as little as you can and get something better soon, but make up your mind that you will do as much as possible, and make yourself so necessary to your employer that he will never let you go. You have been a good son to me, and I can truly say that I have never known you to shirk. Be as good in business, and I am sure God will bless your efforts."

"H'm!" said the lawyer, reading it over the second time. "That's pretty good advice, John, excellent advice. I rather think I will try you, even without the references."

John has been with him six years, and last spring was admitted to the bar.

"Do you intend taking that young man into partnership?" asked a friend lately.

"Yes, I do. I could not get along without John; he is my right-hand man!" exclaimed the lawyer, heartily.

And John always says the best reference he ever had was his mother's good advice and honest praise.

—Selected.

AN HOUR A DAY FOR A YEAR

"Only an hour a day!" that does not seem much; it hardly seems worth mentioning.

But let us consider a little. An hour a day may mean more than we think. In a year it represents three hundred and sixty-five hours, and, allowing sixteen hours for a waking day, three hundred and sixty-five hours gives nearly twenty-three days,—waking days, too, which is worth taking note of, not days one third of which is spent in necessary sleep.

Now, time is a possession to be parted with for something else; indeed, it forms a large part of the capital with which we trade. We give it and labor, and in exchange get education, money, dexterity, and almost all other things of value. To be watchful of time, then, is wise economy. A person who had astonished many by his achievements was once asked how he had contrived to do so much.

"The year," he replied, "has three hundred and sixty-five days, or eight thousand seven hundred and sixty hours. In so many hours great things may be done; the slow tortoise makes a long journey by losing no time."

Just think what an hour's reading daily would amount to in a year. You can read easily a page of an ordinary youth's paper in twenty minutes, and at that rate could get through, in three hundred and sixty-five hours, no fewer than one thousand and ninety-five pages. And suppose the matter were printed in small pages, of, say, three hundred words apiece, your daily reading for one hour would in a year cover something like twelve thousand pages.

As to the books in which the year's reading is to be found, let every one take his choice, remembering that people are known by the company they keep, and that to lead a noble life one should associate as much as possible with the noble.

Instead of reading, suppose one took to writing: an hour a day would then produce quite as remarkable results. Even the short rule of "no day without a line," has resulted in the production of volumes—we might say almost of libraries.

What results may, indeed, be arrived at by an hour's daily industry in anything! "An hour in every day," says a writer, "withdrawn from frivolous pursuits, would, if properly employed, enable a person of ordinary capacity to go far toward mastering a science. It would make an ignorant man a well-informed one in less than ten years."

Of course, the hour's work must not be done listlessly. "Whatsoever thy hand findeth to do, do it with thy might." It is an advantage, too, to work at intervals instead of a long period at a time. We come to the work fresher, and in better condition to do it justice. When working hours come together, the best work is usually done during the first hour; after that even the most energetic fall off.

In music, an hour's practising every day will carry one far in a year. But remember that practising must be gone through with strict attention. An hour with strict attention is worth more than three hours with carelessness; and if a girl who wants to get on has only one hour to spare each day, she must be to herself a very exacting music master.

It is wise to spend an hour a day in exercise. In an hour one can, without making too great haste, walk three miles. At this rate, a year's walking represents over a thousand miles. Relaxation is essential to keep up the spirit and prevent life from becoming monotonous, as if one were sentenced to perpetual treadmill. Recreation is necessary, and the pursuit of pleasure is sometimes a duty.

If we had but an hour a day to spare, what would be the best conceivable use to put it to?—The best use, perhaps, would be to sit down and think. Suppose we came every day to a full stop for an hour, and thought: "What am I doing? What is to be the end of all this busy life for me? How may I so act that when I go out of the world, it will be the better for my having been in it?" This thinking and planning would make us better characters altogether, would prepare us to face the future, ready for anything that might happen, and would fit us for coming duties. An hour a day spent thus would be a bright streak running through the year.

You say it is easy to talk about devoting an hour a day to anything, and easy to make a start, but very difficult to keep it up. True enough, but there is no end of wonders that can be wrought by the exercise of the human will.

"We all sorely complain," says Seneca, "of the shortness of time. And yet we have much more than we know what to do with. Our lives are either spent in doing nothing at all, or in doing nothing that we ought to do. We are always complaining that our days are few, and acting as if there would be no end to them."

An hour a day for a year squandered in idleness or in foolish pursuits means the sacrifice of all the advantages just mentioned. And any one who keeps up idleness or folly for a year, usually ends in having a lifetime of it.—Selected.

"PLEASE, SIR, I WOULD RATHER NOT"

An old sailor tells the following story of a boy who suffered much in resisting temptation:—

When offered a drink, the lad said, "Excuse me; I would rather not."

They laughed at him, but they never could get him to drink liquor. The captain said to the boy:—

"You must learn to drink grog if you are to be a sailor."

"Please excuse me, captain, but I would rather not."

"Take that rope," commanded the captain to a sailor, "and lay it on; that will teach him to obey orders."

The sailor took the rope, and beat the boy most cruelly.

"Now, drink that grog," said the captain.

"Please, sir, I would rather not."

"Then go into the foretop and stay all night."

The poor boy looked away up to the masthead, trembling at the thought of spending the night there, but he had to obey.

In the morning the captain, in walking the deck, looked up, and cried,
"Halloo, up there!"

No answer.

"Come down!"

Still no answer.

One of the sailors was sent up, and what do you think he found? The poor boy was nearly frozen. He had lashed himself to the mast, so that when the ship rolled, he might not fall into the sea. The sailor brought the boy down in his arms, and they worked upon him until he showed signs of life. Then, when he was able to sit up, the captain poured out some liquor and said:—

"Now, drink that grog."

"Please, sir, I would rather not. Let me tell you why, and do not be angry. In our home in the cottage we were so happy, but father took to drink. He had no money to get us bread, and at last we had to sell the little house we had lived in, and everything we had. It broke my poor mother's heart. In sorrow she pined away, till, at last, before she died, she called me to her bedside, and said: 'Jamie, you know what drink has made of your father. I want you to promise your dying mother that you will never taste drink. I want you to be free from that curse that has ruined your father,' O, sir," continued the little fellow, "would you have me break the promise I made to my dying mother? I cannot, and I will not do it."

These words touched the heart of the captain. Tears came into his eyes. He stooped down, and, folding the boy in his arms, said: "No, no, my little hero. Keep your promise, and if any one tries again to make you drink, come to me, and I will protect you."— Selected.

* * * * *

"There were plans of mischief brewing;
    I saw, but gave no sign,
  For I wanted to test the mettle
    Of this little knight of mine.
'Of course, you must come and help us,
    For we all depend on Joe,'
  The boys said; and I waited
    For his answer—yes or no.

"He stood and thought for a moment;
    I read his heart like a book,

137

For the battle that he was fighting
  Was told in his earnest look.
Then to his waiting playmates
  Outspoke my loyal knight:
'No, boys; I cannot go with you,
  For I know it wouldn't be right.'"

THE RIGHT WORD

An instance of the transforming power of the right word is furnished by the following incident:—

Many years ago a minister was passing through a prison crowded with convicts showing every phase of ignorance and brutality. One gigantic fellow crouched alone in a corner, his feet chained to a ball. There was an unhealed wound on his face, where he had been shot when trying to escape. The sight of the dumb, gaunt figure touched the visitor.

"How long has he to serve?" he asked of the guard.

"For life."

"Has he anybody outside to look after him—wife or child?"

"How should I know? Nobody has ever noticed him all the time he has been here."

"May I speak to him?"

"Yes, but only for a minute."

The minister hesitated. What could he say in one minute? He touched the man's torn cheek.

"I am sorry," he said. "I wish I could help you."

The convict looked keenly at him, and he nodded to indicate that he believed in the sympathy expressed.

"I am going away, and shall never see you again, perhaps; but you have a
Friend who will stay here with you."

The keen, small eyes were upon him. The prisoner dragged

himself up, waiting and eager.

"Have you heard of Jesus?"

"Yes."

"He is your friend. If you are good and true, and will pray to God to help you, I am sure he will care for you."

"Come, sir," called the keeper. "Time's up."

The clergyman turned sorrowfully away. The prisoner called after him, and, catching his hand, held it in his own while he could. Tears were in the preacher's eyes.

Fourteen years passed. The convict was sent into the mines. The minister went down one day into a mine, and among the workmen saw a gigantic figure bent with hardship and age.

"Who is that?" he asked the keeper.

"A lifer, and a steady fellow—the best of the gang."

Just then the "lifer" looked up. His figure straightened, for he had recognized the clergyman. His eyes shone.

"Do you know me?" he said. "Will He come soon? I've tried to be good."

At a single word of sympathy the life had been transformed, the convict redeemed.—Selected.

A Friend

A friend—how much it means
  To be so true
  In all we do
That others speak of us as such,
And call us by that noble name.

A friend—how much it means
  To have a friend
  Who'll gladly lend

A helping hand to help us on
When weary seems the path we tread.

A friend—may we be such to Christ,
  Who gladly gave,
  Our lives to save.
His life a willing sacrifice,
And showed himself a friend of men.

E. C. JAEGER

THE SADDEST OF INDIA'S PICTURES (1912)

I saw a sad little picture when I was at the hills; it haunts me even now. It was a sight that should be seen; for words convey very little idea of the pathos of the scene. We were walking through the thick jungle on the hillside when on the narrow path we saw a little procession wending its way toward us. In front walked a big, hardened-looking man, in the prime of life; behind him came a child, a slim, wonderfully fair girl of about ten years, lithe and graceful, with large, expressive dark eyes. After her came a woman prematurely old, her face lined and seamed in every direction.

Just after they passed us, the little girl and woman stopped; and the child bent low to the earth and caressed her mother's feet. Then she flung herself into her mother's arms and clung to her, while the big, beautiful eyes filled with tears. The mother embraced her lovingly; then she tried to thrust her away from her, her own tears running down her face all the time. The child clung piteously, with a yearning love in her eyes. Then she glanced toward that hardened figure still continuing its way, and, O, the awful look of terror on that sweet face! It is that look which continues to haunt me, the look of sweet, yearning love giving place to that awful terror. Then terror overcame, and the child sped swiftly and silently after that man, ever and anon turning back for one more gaze at her heartbroken mother. Then she was lost to sight in the thick jungle.

The wretched mother over and over again lifted up her voice and called her child by name, but there was no voice, and none that gave answer, and she turned her dreary steps homeward. We questioned her, and it was just as we feared. This sweet, innocent girl was leaving her mother's care for the first time, to go and live with that man to whom she now belonged. And only those who know something of the East know what that would mean to that frail, innocent little one.

For days that scene haunted me in all its freshness, and it haunts me still. My heart bleeds for the little girls of India, for I love them so. O, that something could be speedily done for these little sisters of ours!

VERA CHILSON.

A Plea for Missions

O, SOULS that know the love of God,
And know it deep and true,
The love that in your heart is shed abroad
Shall others share with you?

And do you count it joy to give
Of what to you is given,
That erring souls may hear the word, and live
In hope of rest and heaven?

If not, lift up your blinded eyes,
And let the light break in;
Behold a world that, bruised and groaning, lies
Beneath the curse of sin.

Then higher lift your eyes, to meet
Your Master's tender gaze,
And say, "Dear Lord, thy will in us complete,
And pardon our delays."

—Jessie H. Brown.

ONE LITTLE WIDOW

Seven years a widow, yet only eleven years old! The shadow—nay, the curse—of widowhood had hung over little Sita ever since she remembered anything. The little brown girl often wondered why other little girls living near her had such happy, merry times while she knew only drudgery and ill treatment from morning until night. One day when six of the weary years had passed, and she was ten years old, Sita found out what widow meant. Then, to the cruelties she had already endured, was added the terrors of the woe to come. She had gone, as usual, in her tattered garments, with three large brass water-pots on her head, to the great open well from which she drew the daily supply of water for a family of nine. She was so tired, and her frail little back ached so pitifully, that she sat down on a huge stone to rest a minute. Resting her weary head on one thin little hand, she was a picture of childish woe. Many deep sorrows had fallen on her young heart, but she was still a child in mind and years, yearning for companionship and love.

Many Brahman servants were drawing water near her, and looked bright and happy in their gay-colored cotton saris. A woman so poor that she must draw her own drinking-water, but still a Brahman, came near, and to her Sita appealed for help.

"Will you not draw a little water for me? I am ill and tired, and the well is very deep."

The woman turned angrily, and uttered, in a scathing tone, the one word, "Widow!" then she burst out: "Curse you! How dare you come between me and the glorious sun! Your shadow has fallen upon me, and I'll have to take the bath of purification before I can eat food! Curse you! Stand aside!"

Poor Sita stood bewildered. She made no answer, but the tears coursed down her cheeks. Something akin to pity made the woman pause. Halting at a safe distance from the shadow of the child, she talked to her in a milder tone. She was thinking, perhaps, of her two soft-eyed daughters, very dear to her proud heart, though she mourned bitterly when they were born, because the gods had denied her sons.

"Why should I help you," she said, "when the gods have cursed you? See, you are a widow!"

Then, in answer to the child's vacant gaze, she continued: "Don't you understand? Didn't you have a husband once?"

"Yes, I think so," Sita answered; "an old, bad man who used to shake me, and tell me to grow up quickly to work for him; perhaps he was my husband. When he died, they said I killed him, but I did not."

"So you call him bad?" the woman cried. "Ah, no wonder the gods hate you! No doubt you were very wicked ages and ages ago, and so now you are made a widow. By and by you will be born a snake or a toad." And, gathering up her water-pots, she went away.

The slender, ill-fed child hurriedly filled the brass vessels, knowing that abuse awaited her late return. Raising the huge jars to her head, she hastened to her house—a home she never knew. The sister-in-law met the little thing with violent abuse, and bade her prepare the morning meal. The child was ill, and nearly fell with fatigue.

"I'll show you how to wake up!" the woman cried, and, seizing a hot poker, she laid it on the arms and hands of the child.

Screaming with pain, the poor little creature worked on, trembling if the sister-in-law even looked her way. This was one day. Each of the seven long years contained three hundred and sixty-five such days, and now they were growing worse. The last year, in token of the deep disgrace of widowhood, the child's soft dark tresses had been shaved off, and her head left bare. When that has been done, but one meal a day is permitted a widow, no matter how she works.

Most of the little girls who saw Sita ran from her, fearing pollution. But there was one who shone on her like a gleam of sunshine whenever she saw her. One day after the woman had abused her at the well, Sita found a chance to tell Tungi about it.

"There is a better God than that," Tungi said. "Our people do not know him, and that is why I am not allowed to talk with you. I am married, and my husband lives in a distant city. If I speak to you, they believe that he will die. But in the school I attend, many do not believe these things."

"How can you go to school?" Sita asked. "My sister-in-law says that only bad people learn to read."

"So my mother used to think," said Tungi; "but my husband is in school, and he has sent word that I must go until he calls for me to come to his home. Then he can have a wife who can understand when he talks about his books. He says the English have happy families, and it is this that makes them so. The wives know books, and how to sing, and how to make home pleasant. My mother says it is all very bad, but he is my husband, and I must do as he says. I am very glad; for it is very pleasant there."

Thus the bright-eyed little Brahman wife chatted away, as gay as a bird.

The fount of knowledge was opened to her—the beaming eye, the elastic

figure, and the individuality of her Western sisters were becoming hers.

But none of these things seemed for Sita.

For nine weary months after Tungi went to school, the shaven-headed child, living on one meal a day, went about sad and lonely. When she again saw her bright-faced little friend, her condition had grown worse. Her neck and arms were full of scars where bits of flesh had been pinched out in vindictive rage by her husband's relatives, who believed her guilty of his death. Brutality, growing stronger with use, made them callous to the sufferings of the little being in their power. No one who cared knew of the pangs of hunger, the violent words, and the threats of future punishment. Once or twice she had looked down into the cool depths of the well, and wondered how quickly she could die. Only the terror of punishment after death kept this baby widow from suicide.

One day as she was weeping by the gateway of Tungi's house,

the little child wife told the little child widow of a safe refuge for such as she, where neither poverty nor ignorance could exclude her—a home under the loving care of one who knew the widow's curse. After many difficulties, Sita found this shelter. Here she forgot her widowhood, and found her childhood. Here, in the beautiful garden, or at her lessons, helping with cooking, or leaning lovingly on the arms of Ramabai's chair, she passed many sweet and useful years. By and by she found the greatest joy in love, higher and better than human love can ever be. Later, when a beautiful young womanhood had crowned her, she was sought by an earnest young Christian as his wife.

Many of the millions of the child widows in India never find release from the bonds of cruel custom and false religion. In Hinduism there is no hope for such accursed ones.—"Mosaics From India," published by Fleming H. Revell Company.

WHY THE MITE BOXES WERE FULL

Rosella had a blue mite box, and so had her brother Drew. The mite boxes had been given out in Sunday-school, and were to be kept two months. All the money saved in the mite boxes was to go toward sending the news about Jesus to the heathen girls and boys across the ocean. The Sunday-school superintendent said so, and so did the sweet old blind missionary woman, who had talked to the scholars.

Rosella and Drew carried their mite boxes across the fields toward their tent. They and their mother and aunt and cousins had come several miles from their farm to tent, with a number of other folks, near the Farmers' Cooperative Fruit Drying buildings, during the fruit season, to cut fruit for drying.

Another girl was going across the fields with a blue mite box. She was the Chinese girl, Louie Ming, whose father and mother had come from the city to cook for some of the owners here.

"Louie Ming's got a mite box!" said Rosella.

Drew laughed. "Do you suppose she'll save anything in it?"

"I don't believe she will," said Rosella.

Rosella and Drew carried their mite boxes into their mother's tent.

"We're going to cut apricots and peaches to help the heathen!" announced
Rosella.

Mother nodded.

"We'll have a whole lot of money in our mite boxes when we carry them back," said Rosella.

"We'll see," said mother.

For two or three mornings Rosella and Drew rose early, and after breakfast hurried to the cutting-sheds to work. But, after a while, Rosella and Drew grew tired. It was more fun to run over the fields, and mother never said Rosella and Drew must cut fruit, anyhow, though she looked sober.

"The heathen children won't know," said Rosella to herself. "Suppose the heathen children were me, I wonder if they'd cut apricots every day to send me Bibles and missionaries? I don't believe they would."

The first month melted away. When it was over, Rosella had two nickels in her mite box, and Drew had three in his.

"The heathen children won't know," said Rosella.

But one Saturday night Rosella and Drew were going by the tent where Louie
Ming lived. Inside the tent sat Louie Ming, with her week's pay in her lap.
In the Chinese girl's hand was her blue mite box. Louie Ming was putting
her money into her mite box, and did not notice Rosella and Drew.

"Why-ee!" whispered Rosella. "See there! Why, Drew! I do believe Louie Ming's putting every bit of her pay into her mite box! Do you suppose she knows what she's doing?"

Rosella and Drew stood watching.

"Do you suppose Louie Ming understands?" whispered Rosella again. "Why, she's giving it all! Drew, she's been working in the cutting-sheds every time I've been there. She didn't cut fruit till she got her mite box. There, she's given every cent!"

When Louie Ming looked up, and suddenly discovered Rosella and Drew, she looked half scared. Rosella stepped toward the tent, and said:—

"What made you give all your money? Why didn't you save

149

some? You've worked hard for it. The heathen children wouldn't know if you kept some for candy and things."

Louie Ming looked shy.

"You say wha' fo' I give money?" she asked softly.

"Yes," said Rosella. "Why do you give so much?"

Louie Ming looked down at the blue mite box. Somehow it seemed hard for her to answer, at first. Then she spoke softly: "One time I have baby brudder. He die. Mudder cry, cry, cry. I cry, cry all time. I say, 'Never see poor little baby brudder again, never again!' An' I love little brudder. Then I go mission school. Teacher say, 'Louie Ming, love Jesus, an' some day you see your baby brudder again.' O, teacher make me so happy! See little brudder again! I go home and tell my mudder. She not believe, but I get teacher to come and tell. She tell about Jesus to my fadder and mudder. They learn love him. Some day we all go heaven and see little brudder! Now I save money to put in mite box. Way over in China many little girls don't know about Jesus. Their little brudders die. They cry, cry, all the same me did. Maybe some my money send teacher tell those poor Chinese girls how go to heaven, see their baby brudders again. So I work very hard to put money in my box, because Jesus come into my heart."

Rosella did not answer, but stood looking at Louie Ming. Then she suddenly turned and caught Drew's hand, and pulled him along till they were running toward their own tent. Rosella rushed in. The baby was sitting on the straw floor, and Rosella caught him up, crying:—

"O baby, baby brother, don't you ever die! I couldn't spare you!"

"Goo!" said baby brother, holding out his arms to Drew.

Drew did not say anything, but he took baby brother.

"Drew," said Rosella, "I'm going straight to work. Aren't you? I'm ashamed of myself. To think that a Chinese girl who once did not know about Jesus, would work so hard now for her mite box, and you and I haven't! Why, Drew Hopkins, I haven't acted as though I cared whether the heathen boys and girls knew about

Jesus or not! I'm going to work to fill my mite box. Why, Drew, Louie Ming's box is most full, and she used to be a heathen!"

Drew nodded, and hugged baby brother tighter.

The next Monday Rosella and Drew began working hard cutting fruit. How they cut fruit the remaining month! How they saved! And how glad they were that their mite boxes were heavy when the day came to carry them back!

The blind missionary woman was at Sunday-school again. After the school closed, the superintendent, who knew Rosella and Drew, introduced them to the missionary. And the blind missionary said, "Bless the dear girl and boy who have cut peaches for two whole months to help send the gospel to heathen children!"

Then Rosella, being honest, could not bear to have the missionary think it had been two months instead of one, and she suddenly burst out, half-crying, and said, "O, I wasn't so good as that! I didn't work two months, and I—I'm afraid if Louie Ming hadn't loved Jesus better than I did, Drew and I wouldn't have had hardly any money in our mite boxes."

The blind missionary wanted to know about Louie Ming, and Rosella told the missionary all about her. Then the blind missionary kissed Louie Ming's cheek, and said, "Many that are last shall be first."

But Rosella was glad that she and Drew had worked to send the news about
Jesus to heathen children.—Mary E. Bamford, in "Over Sea and Land."

Ti-TO AND THE BOXERS

A True Story of a Young Christian

It was late in May when we last saw Ti-to's father. He was attending the annual meeting of the North China Mission at Tung-chou, near Peking when word came that the Boxers were tearing up the railway between Peking and Pao-ting-fu. For twelve years he had been the pastor of the Congregational Church in Pao-ting-fu, having been the first Chinese pastor ordained in north China. Without waiting for the end of the meeting, he hastened to the assistance of the little band of missionaries.

During the month of June dangers thickened about the devoted band of missionaries and Christian Chinese who lived in the mission compound not far from the wall of Pao-ting-fu. There was no mother in Pastor Meng's home to comfort the hearts of five children living face to face with death. But thirteen-year-old Ti-to, the hero of our story, was as brave a lad as ever cheered the hearts of little brothers and sisters. Straight as an arrow, his fine-cut, delicate face flushed with pink, with firm, manly mouth and eyes that showed both strength and gentleness, Ti-to was a boy to win all hearts at sight.

By the twenty-seventh of June it was plain that all who remained in that compound were doomed to fall victims to Boxer hate. Pastor Meng called his oldest boy to his side, and said: "Ti-to, I have asked my friend, Mr. Tien to take you with him and try to find some place of refuge from the Boxers. I cannot forsake my missionary friends and the Christians, who have no one else to depend upon, but I want you to try to escape."

"Father," said the boy, "I want to stay here with you. I am not afraid to die."

"No," the father replied. "If we are all killed, who will preach Jesus to these poor people?"

So, before the next day dawned, Ti-to said good-by, and started with Mr. Tien on his wanderings. That same afternoon Pastor Meng was in the chapel when a company of Boxers suddenly burst into the room and seized him. A Christian Chinese who was with him escaped over the back wall, and took the sad tidings to his friends. The Boxers dragged Pastor Meng to a temple, and there, having learned that his eldest son had fled, tortured him to make him tell Ti-to's hiding-place. But the secret was not revealed. In the early morning scores of Boxer knives slowly stabbed him to death. But the face of the Master smiled upon this brave soul, "faithful unto death."

Three days later, four of his children, his only sister and her two children, and the three missionary friends for whom he had laid down his life, were killed.

But what of the little one who had left home four days before? Determined that not one member of the family should be left, the Boxers searched for him in all directions. But Mr. Tien had taken Ti-to to the home of a relative only a few miles from Pao-ting-fu, and they escaped detection. This relative feared to harbor them more than two or three days, so they turned their faces northward, where a low range of sierra-like mountains was outlined against the blue sky. Seventeen miles from Pao-ting-fu, and not far from the home of an uncle of Mr. Tien's, they found a little cave in the mountainside, not high enough to allow them to stand upright. Here they crouched for twenty days. The uncle took them a little food, but to get water they were obliged to go three miles to a mountain village, stealing up to a well under cover of darkness. In that dark cave, hunger and thirst were their constant companions, and the howling of wolves at night made their mountain solitude fearsome.

Ti-to had lived for five days in this retreat when word was brought to him that father, brothers, sisters, aunt, cousins, and all the missionaries belonging to the three missions in Pao-ting-fu, had been cruelly massacred, and that churches, schools, homes, were all masses of charred ruins.

After twenty days of cave life, Mr. Tien's uncle sent them warning that Boxers were on their track, and that they must leave their mountain refuge immediately. Then began long, weary wanderings toward the southwest, over mountain roads, their plan being to go to Shansi. One day in their wanderings they had just passed the village of Chang-ma, about sixteen miles south of Pao-ting-fu, when a band of Boxers, some armed with rifles, some brandishing great swords, rushed after them, shouting, "Kill! kill! kill the secondary foreign devils!"

Escape was impossible. Before this howling horde had overtaken them, a man who was standing near them asked Ti-to, "Are you a Christian?"

"Yes," the boy replied. "My father and mother were Christians, and from a little child I have believed in Jesus."

"Do not be afraid," the stranger said; "I will protect you."

Then the Boxers closed about them. Mr. Tien was securely bound, hand and foot. Ti-to was led by his queue, and soon they were back by the Boxer altar in the village. When the knives were first waved in his face, and the bloodthirsty shouts first rang in his ears, a thrill of fear chilled Ti-to's heart; but it passed as quickly as it came, and as he was dragged toward the altar, it seemed as if some soft, low voice kept singing in his ear the hymn, "I'm not ashamed to own my Lord." All fear vanished.

When they began to bind Mr. Tien to the altar, he spoke no word for himself, but pleaded most earnestly for the little charge committed to his care, telling how all his relatives had been murdered, and begging them to spare his life. Perhaps it was those earnest, unselfish words, perhaps it was the boy's gracious mien and winsome face, that moved the crowd; for one of the village Boxers stepped forward, saying: "I adopt this boy as my son. Let no one touch him. I stand security for his good behavior."

Ti-to's deliverer was one of the three bachelor brothers, the terror of the region. But it was evident that Mr. Chang's heart was completely won by the boy. For three months he kept him in his home, tenderly providing for every want. Let Ti-to tell the story of those days in his own words:—

"Of course I could not pray openly. But sometimes when my adopted father was away with the Boxers on their raids, I would shut the door tight and kneel in prayer. Then every evening when the sun went down, I would turn my face to the west, and in my heart repeat the hymn:—

"'Abide with me: fast falls the eventide; The darkness deepens: Lord, with me abide.'

"Mr. Chang was in Pao-ting-fu when my father was killed, and told me how they stabbed and tortured him. I supposed that my uncle and his wife, who had gone to Tung-chow, had been killed, too, and all the missionaries in China. But I knew that the people in America would send out some more missionaries, and I thought how happy I would be sometime in the future when I could go into a chapel again and hear them preach."

But Ti-to had not long to wait for this day of joy In October expeditions of British, German, French, and Italian soldiers from Peking and Tientsin arrived at Pao-ting-fu, and the Boxer hordes scattered at their coming. Soon to the brave boy in the Boxer's home came the glad tidings that his uncle was still living, and had sent for him to come to Pao-ting-fu.

Mr. Chang loved the boy so deeply that he could not but rejoice with him, sad though he felt at the thought of parting with him. Fearful of some treachery or of harm coming to Ti-to, he went with him to Pao-ting-fu, then returned to the village home from which the sunshine had departed.

Later Ti-to studied in the Congregational Academy in Peking, and then in Japan. He is now an earnest teacher of Christianity, for which he so bravely faced death.—Selected.

What the Flowers Say to Me

Our Father made us beautiful,
And breathed on us his love,
And gave us of the spirit that
Prevails in heaven above.

We stand here meekly blooming for
The stranger passing by;
And if unnoticed we are left,
We never stop to sigh,

But shed our fragrance all abroad,

And smile in shine or rain
And thus we do the will of God
Till he restores again

A realm of peace on earth, to last
The countless ages through;
Where flowers bloom and never fade;
And there is room for you.

IDA REESE KURZ.

HOW NYANGANDI SWAM TO CHURCH

Nyangandi lived in west Africa, near the Ogowe River. She was going away from the missionary's house one afternoon, where she had been to sell bunches of plantains to the missionary, when his wife said:—

"Now, you must not forget that you have promised to come to-morrow to church."

"Yes," the girl replied, "I will surely come if I am alive."

The next morning she found that somebody had stolen her canoe, and no one would lend her one to go to church in. But she had promised to go, and she felt that she must. She swam all the way! The current was swift, the water deep, and the river fully a third of a mile wide, but by swimming diagonally she succeeded in crossing the river.

Remember this little heathen girl in west Africa when you feel tempted to stay away from the house of God for some trivial reason.—Selected.

To Those Who Fail

"All honor to him who shall win the prize!"
The world has cried for a thousand years;
But to him who tries, and who fails and dies,
I give honor and glory and tears.

O, great is the hero who wins a name!
But greater many and many a time
Some pale-faced fellow who dies in shame,
And lets God finish the thought sublime.

And great is the man with the sword undrawn,
And good is the man who refrains from wine,
But the man who fails and who still fights on,
Lo! he is the twin brother of mine.
—Selected.

THE LITTLE PRINTER MISSIONARY

A ragged printer's boy, who lived in Constantinople, was in the habit of carrying the proof-sheets to the English editor during the noon lunch-time. The editor was a busy man, and exchanged no words, except such as were necessary, with him. The boy was faithful, doing all that he was bidden, promptly and to the best of his ability, but he was ragged, and so dirty as to be positively repulsive. This annoyed the editor; but, as he was no worse in this respect than most of the boys of his class, the busy man did not urge him to improve his personal appearance, much as he would have enjoyed the change. But one morning the boy came in with clean face, hands, and garments. Not a trace of the old filth was to be seen about his person; and so great was the change that his master did not recognize him.

"Why, you are a new boy entirely!" he said when convinced of the lad's identity.

"I am going away, back to my own home." said the boy, quickly, "and I came to ask a favor of you. Will you pray for me after I am gone?"

"Pray for you!" exclaimed the editor.

"Yes," returned the boy. "You think I am a heathen, but I am not. I have been attending chapel and Sunday-school in the Bible house. I have learned to read and to write, and, best of all, I have learned to love Jesus, and am trying to be his boy. But I cannot stay here while my father, mother, brothers, and sisters do not know about him. So I go back to my own village to tell friends and neighbors about him. I don't know much yet, and I want you to pray that I may be helped when I try to tell my people what he is to me."

"And it is because you are going away that you have washed and fixed yourself up so well?" asked the editor, thinking what a fine boy clothes and cleanliness had made of him.

"It is because I am Christ's boy now," was the answer. "I want to be clean and to have my clothes whole in honor of the Master I am trying to serve."

"I hope your friends will receive as much from Christ's love as you have," said the man.

"And you will pray for them and for me?" urged the boy.

The man promised; and, full of hope, the lad started on his long walk homeward, to tell the story of the cross to the dear ones there, in his own wretched home first, and afterward to the neighbors among whom he had spent his childhood days.—Selected.

Consecration

Ready to go, ready to wait,
Ready a gap to fill;
Ready for service, small or great,
Ready to do His will.

—Phillips Brooks

THE MISSIONARY'S DEFENSE

The following occurrence was related by Missionary von As-
selt, a Rhenish missionary in Sumatra from 1856-76, when on a
visit to Lubeck:—

"When I first went to Sumatra, in the year 1856 I was the first
European missionary to go among the wild Battas, although
twenty years prior, two American missionaries had come to them
with the gospel; but they had been killed and eaten. Since then
no effort had been made to bring the gospel to these people, and
naturally they had remained the same cruel savages.

"What it means for one to stand alone among a savage people,
unable to make himself understood, not understanding a single
sound of their language, but whose suspicious, hostile looks and
gestures speak only a too-well-understood language,—yes, it is
hard for one to realize that. The first two years that I spent among
the Battas, at first all alone and afterward with my wife, were so
hard that it makes me shudder even now when I think of them.
Often it seemed as if we were not only encompassed by hostile
men, but also by hostile powers of darkness; for often an inexpli-
cable, unutterable fear would come over us, so that we had to get
up at night, and go on our knees to pray or read the Word of God,
in order to find relief.

"After we had lived in this place for two years, we moved several hours' journey inland, among a tribe somewhat civilized, who
received us more kindly. There we built a small house with three
rooms,—a living-room, a bedroom, and a small reception-room,—
and life for us became a little more easy and cheerful.

"When we had been in this new place for some months, a man
came to me from the district where we had been, and whom I had
known there. I was sitting on the bench in front of our house, and
he sat down beside me, and for a while talked of this, that, and
the other. Finally he began, 'Now tuan [teacher], I have yet one
request.'

"'And what is that?'

"'I should like to have a look at your watchmen close at hand.'

"'What watchmen do you mean? I do not have any.'

"'I mean the watchmen whom you station around your house at night, to protect you.'

"'But I have no watchmen,' I said again; 'I have only a little herdsboy and a little cook, and they would make poor watchmen.'

"Then the man looked at me incredulously, as if he wished to say, 'O, do not try to make me believe otherwise, for I know better!'

"Then he asked, 'May I look through your house, to see if they are hid there?'

"'Yes, certainly,' I said, laughing; 'look through it; you will not find anybody.' So he went in and searched in every corner, even through the beds, but came to me very much disappointed.

"Then I began a little probing myself, and requested him to tell me the circumstances about those watchmen of whom he spoke. And this is what he related to me: 'When you first came to us, tuan, we were very angry at you. We did not want you to live among us; we did not trust you, and believed you had some design against us. Therefore we came together, and resolved to kill you and your wife. Accordingly, we went to your house night after night; but when we came near, there stood always, close around the house, a double row of watchmen with glittering weapons, and we did not venture to attack them to get into your house. But we were not willing to abandon our plan, so we went to a professional assassin [there still was among the savage Battas at that time a special gild of assassins, who killed for hire any one whom it was desired to get out of the way], and asked him if he would undertake to kill you and your wife. He laughed at us because of our cowardice, and said: "I fear no God, and no devil. I will get through those watchmen easily." So we came all together in the evening, and the assassin, swinging his weapon about his head, went courageously on before us. As we neared your house, we remained behind, and let him go on alone. But in a short time he came running back hastily, and said. "No, I dare not risk it to go through alone; two rows of big, strong men stand there, very close together, shoulder to shoulder, and their weapons shine like fire."

"Then we gave it up to kill you. But now, tell me, tuan, who are these watchmen? Have you never seen them?"

"'No, I have never seen them.'

"'And your wife did not see them also?'

"'No, my wife did not see them.'

"'But yet we have all seen them; how is that?'

"Then I went in, and brought a Bible from our house, and holding it open before him, said: 'See here; this book is the Word of our great God, in which he promises to guard and defend us, and we firmly believe that Word; therefore we need not to see the watchmen; but you do not believe, therefore the great God has to show you the watchmen, in order that you may learn to believe.'"—Selected.

⟁IGHT AT LAST

Dr. Kirkpatrick, with the Baptist Mission in the Shan States of Burma, tells in the Missionary Review of an aged woman whom he met on a tour in a mountain district, where no missionary had ever before set foot:—

"This old woman listened attentively, and apparently believed. She had never seen a white man, although, according to her birth certificate, she was one hundred and twenty-three years old. As she sat huddled together by the fire, she said: 'Teacher, is it true that the Lord can and will save me, a woman? Do not deceive me; I am very old, and must soon fall into hell, unless this new religion is true. I have made many offerings, and made many long pilgrimages to the most sacred shrines, and still find no relief from the burden of sin. Please teach me to pray to this Jesus that can save.'

"I explained the plan of salvation, and God's love for her, and taught her a simple prayer of a few words. She seemed very grateful. As I was about to leave her, she said:—

"'Teacher, you come from the great American country, do you not?'

"'Yes,' I answered.

"'Is your country greater than the Shan country?'

"I assured her that it was.

"'Are the people there all Christians?'

"I had to confess that they were not, but that there were many Christians.

"'Were your parents Christians?'

"'Yes, and my grandparents, and ancestors for several generations.'

"'My parents,' she said, 'died when I was young My brothers and sisters all are dead. I have been married three times, and my husbands are all dead. I had nine children, and they are all dead. I had many grandchildren, and they are all dead except this one with whom I am living. I have seen three generations fall into hell. Now I believe in Jesus, and hope to go to the heavenly country when I die. If there are so many Christians in your country, and you have known about this Lord that can save for so long, why did you not come and tell us before, so that many of my people could have been saved?' With the tears running down her cheeks, she said: 'I am so glad to hear this good news before it it too late; but all of my loved ones have fallen into hell. Why did you not come before?'

"That question still haunts me. I wish every Christian in America could hear it as I did.

"A few weeks later I saw some of the men from this village, in the bazaar at Namkhamm, and asked them about the 'old grandmother of the village.' They told me that she died the day before, and that they had come to buy things for the funeral. After much questioning, they said they were ashamed to tell me that she was crazy. As she grew weaker, she told everybody that she was going to die in a few days, and she was very happy about it. She was going to the heavenly country, and other such foolish things. When she was too weak to speak aloud, she kept whispering, 'Yasu hock sung; Yasu hock sung' (Jesus loves me; Jesus loves me), with her last breath. The first and only time this woman ever heard the gospel, she accepted it. It is an exceptional case, but there are others like it."

THE BROWN TOWEL

"One who has nothing can give nothing," said Mrs. Sayers, the sexton's wife, as the ladies of the sewing society were busily engaged in packing the contents of a large box, destined for a Western missionary.

"A person who has nothing to give must be poor, indeed," said Mrs. Bell, as she deposited a pair of warm blankets in the already well-filled box.

Mrs. Sayers looked at the last-named speaker with a glance which seemed to say, "You who have never known self-denial cannot feel for me," and remarked, "You surely think one can be too poor to give?"

"I once thought so, but have learned from experience that no better investment can be made, even from the depths of poverty, than lending to the Lord."

Seeing the ladies listening attentively to the conversation, Mrs. Bell continued: "Perhaps, as our work is finished, I can do no better than to give you my experience on the subject. It may be the means of showing you that God will reward the cheerful giver.

"During the first twenty-eight years of my life, I was surrounded with wealth; and not until I had been married nine years did I know a want which money could satisfy, or feel the necessity of exertion. Reverses came with fearful suddenness, and before I had recovered from the blow, I found myself the wife of a poor man, with five little children dependent upon our exertions.

"From that hour I lost all thought of anything but care of my family. Late hours and hard work were my portion, and to my unskilled hands it seemed first a bitter lot. My husband strove anxiously to gain a subsistence, and barely succeeded. We changed our place of residence several times, hoping to do better, but without improvement.

"Everything seemed against us. Our well-stocked wardrobe had become so exhausted that I felt justified in absenting myself from the house of God, with my children, for want of suitable apparel. While in this low condition, I went to church one evening, when my poverty-stricken appearance would escape notice, and took my seat near the door. An agent from the West preached, and begged contributions to the home missionary cause. His appeal brought tears to my eyes, and painfully reminded me of my past days of prosperity, when I could give of my abundance to all who called upon me. It never entered my mind that the appeal for assistance in any way concerned me, with my poor children banished from the house of God by poverty, while I could only venture out under the friendly protection of darkness.

"I left the church more submissive to my lot, with a prayer in my heart that those whose consciences had been addressed might respond. I tried in vain to sleep that night. The words of the text, 'Give, and it shall be given unto you; good measure, pressed down, and shaken together, and running over, shall men give into your bosom,' seemed continually sounding in my ears. The eloquent entreaty of the speaker to all, however poor, to give a mite to the Lord, and receive the promised blessing, seemed addressed to me. I rose early the next morning, and looked over all my worldly goods in search of something worth bestowing, but in vain; the promised blessing seemed beyond my reach.

"Hearing that the ladies of the church had filled a box for the missionary's family, I made one more effort to spare something. All was poor and thread-bare. What should I do? At last I thought of my towels. I had six, of coarse brown linen, but little worn. They seemed a scanty supply for a family of seven; and yet I took one from the number, and, putting it into my pocket, hastened to the house where the box was kept, and quietly slipped it in. I returned home with a light heart, feeling that my Saviour's eye had seen my sacrifice, and would bless my effort.

"From that day success attended all my husband's efforts in business. In a few months our means increased so that we were able to attend church and send our children to Sabbath-school, and before ten years had passed, our former prosperity had returned fourfold. 'Good measure, pressed down, and shaken together, and running over,' had been given us.

"It may seem superstitious to you, my dear friends, but we date all our success in life to God's blessing, following that humble gift out of deep poverty. He may not always think best to reward so signally those who give to him, but he is never unmindful of the humblest gift or giver. Wonder not that from that day I deem few too poor to give, and that I am a firm believer in God's promise that he will repay with interest, even in this life, all we lend to him."

Glances of deep interest, unmixed with envy, were cast from the windows at Mrs. Bell, as, after bidding the ladies adieu, she stepped into her carriage. Her consistent benevolence had proved to all that in her prosperity she retained the same Christian spirit which, in her days of poverty, had led to the bestowal of the brown towel.

"Well," exclaimed Mrs. Sayers, "if we all had such a self-denying spirit, we might fill another box at once. I will never again think that I am too poor to give."—Our Young Folks.

ONLY A BOY

More than half a century ago a faithful minister coming early to the kirk, met one of his deacons, whose face wore a very resolute expression.

"I came early to meet you," he said. "I have something on my conscience to say to you. Pastor, there must be something radically wrong in your preaching and work; there has been only one person added to the church in a whole year, and he is only a boy."

The old minister listened. His eyes moistened, and his thin hand trembled on his broad-headed cane.

"I feel it all," he said; "I feel it, but God knows that I have tried to do my duty, and I can trust him for the results."

"Yes, yes," said the deacon, "but 'by their fruits ye shall know them,' and one new member, and he, too, only a boy, seems to me rather a slight evidence of true faith and zeal. I don't want to be hard, but I have this matter on my conscience, and I have done but my duty in speaking plainly."

"True," said the old man; "but 'charity suffereth long and is

167

kind; beareth all things, hopeth all things.' Ay, there you have it; 'hopeth all things'! I have great hopes of that one boy, Robert. Some seed that we sow bears fruit late, but that fruit is generally the most precious of all."

The old minister went to the pulpit that day with a grieved and heavy heart. He closed his discourse with dim and tearful eyes. He wished that his work was done forever, and that he was at rest among the graves under the blossoming trees in the old kirk-yard. He lingered in the dear old kirk after the rest were gone. He wished to be alone. The place was sacred and inexpressibly dear to him. It had been his spiritual home from his youth. Before this altar he had prayed over the dead forms of a bygone generation, and had welcomed the children of a new generation; and here, yes, here, he had been told at last that his work was no longer owned and blessed!

No one remained—no one?—"Only a boy."

The boy was Robert Moffat. He watched the trembling old man. His soul was filled with loving sympathy. He went to him, and laid his hand on his black gown.

"Well, Robert?" said the minister.

"Do you think if I were willing to work hard for an education, I could ever become a preacher?"

"A preacher?"

"Perhaps a missionary."

There was a long pause. Tears filled the eyes of the old minister. At length he said: "This heals the ache in my heart, Robert. I see the divine hand now. May God bless you, my boy. Yes, I think you will become a preacher."

Some few years ago there returned to London from Africa an aged missionary. His name was spoken with reverence. When he went into an assembly, the people rose. When he spoke in public, there was a deep silence. Priests stood uncovered before him; nobles invited him to their homes.

He had added a province to the church of Christ on earth; had brought under the gospel influence the most savage of African chiefs; had given the translated Bible to strange tribes; had enriched with valuable knowledge the Royal Geographical Society; and had honored the humble place of his birth, the Scottish kirk, the United Kingdom, and the universal missionary cause.

It is hard to trust when no evidence of fruit appears. But the harvests of right intentions are sure. The old minister sleeps beneath the trees in the humble place of his labors, but men remember his work because of what he was to one boy, and what that one boy was to the world.

"Do thou thy work: it shall succeed
    In thine or in another's day;
And if denied the victor's meed,
    Thou shalt not miss the toiler's pay."

—Youth's Companion.

When Some One's Late

Some one is late,
    And so I wait
A minute, two, or ten;
    To me the cost
    Is good time lost
That never comes again.

He does not care
How I shall fare,
Or what my loss shall be;
    His tardiness
    Is selfishness
And basely rude to me.

My boys, be spry,
    The moments fly;
Meet every date you make.
    Be weather fair
    Or foul, be there
In time your place to take.

169

And girls, take heed,
And work with speed;
Each task on time begin;
On time begun,
And work well done,
The highest praise will win.

MAX HILL.

THE LITTLE PROTECTOR

He was such a little fellow, but he was desperately in earnest when he marched into the store that snowy morning. Straight up to the first clerk he went. "I want to see the 'prietor," he said.

The clerk wanted to smile, but the little face before her was so grave that she answered solemnly, "He is sitting at his desk."

The little fellow walked up to the man at the desk. Mr. Martin, the proprietor, turned around. "Good morning, little man. Did you want to see me?" he asked.

"Yes, sir. I want a wrap for my mama. I can make fires and pay for it."

"What is your name, my boy?"

"Paul May."

"Is your father living?"

"No, sir; he died when we lived in Louisville."

"How long have you lived here?"

"We haven't been here long. Mama was sick in Louisville, and the doctor told her to go away, and she would get well."

"Is she better?"

"Yes, sir. Last Sunday she wanted to go to church, but she didn't have any wrap, and she cried. She didn't think I saw her, but I did. She says I'm her little p'tector since papa died. I can make fires and pay for a wrap."

"But, little man, the store is steam-heated. I wonder if you could clean the snow off the walk."

"Yes, sir," Paul answered, quickly.

"Very well. I'll write your mama a note and explain our bargain."

When the note was written, Mr. Martin arose.

"Come, Paul, I will get the wrap," he said. At the counter he paused. "How large is your mother Paul?" he asked.

Paul glanced about him. "'Bout as large as her." he said, pointing toward a lady clerk.

"Miss Smith, please see if this fits you," requested Mr. Martin. Paul's eyes were shining.

Miss Smith put on the wrap and turned about for Paul to see it. "Do you like it?" she asked him.

"Yes, I do," he answered very emphatically.

The wrap was marked twelve dollars, but kind-hearted Mr. Martin said: "You may have it for five dollars, Paul. Take it to Pauline and have her take the price tag off," he added to Miss Smith. When she brought the bundle back to him, he put it in Paul's arms. "Take it to your mama, Paul. When the snow stops falling, come and sweep off the walk. I will pay you a dollar each time you clean it. We shall soon have enough to pay for the wrap."

"Yes, sir," answered Paul, gravely. He took the bundle and trudged out into the snow.

When he reached home, his mother looked in surprise at his bundle. "Where have you been, dear?"

"I went to town, mama," Paul answered. He put the note into her hand. She opened it and read:—

"MRS. MAY: This little man has bought a wrap for you. He says he is your protector. For his sake keep the wrap and let him work to pay for it. It will be a great pleasure to him. He has the making of a fine man in him. WILLIAM MARTIN."

Paul was astonished to see tears in his mothers eyes; he had thought she would be so happy, and she was crying. She put her arm about him and kissed him. Then she put on the wrap and told how pretty she thought it.

When the snow stopped falling, Paul went down to the store and cleaned the snow from the front walk. He did not know that Mr. Martin's hired man swept it again, for the little arms were not strong enough to sweep it quite clean.

The days passed, and one morning Paul had a very sore throat.

"You mustn't get up today, dear," his mother said. When she brought his breakfast, she found him crying. "What is making you cry? Is your throat hurting much?"

"No, mama. Don't you see it is snowing, and I can't go and clean the walk?" cried Paul.

"Shall I write a note to Mr. Martin and explain why you are not there?"

"Yes, please, mama. Who will take it?"

"I'll ask Bennie to leave it as he goes to school."

The note was written, and Bennie, a neighbor boy, promised to deliver it.

While Paul was eating his dinner, there was a knock at the door. Mrs. May answered it, and ushered in Mr. Martin.

"How is the sick boy?" he asked. He crossed the room and sat by Paul. He patted the boy's cheek, and then turned to the mother. "Mrs. May," he said, "my wife's mother is very old, but will not give up her home and live with us. She says she wants a home for her children to visit. She has recently lost a good housekeeper, and needs another. Since I met Paul the other day, I have been wondering if you would take the housekeeper's place. Mother would be glad to have you and Paul with her, and would make things easy for you, and pay you liberally."

"I shall be very glad to accept your offer, Mr. Martin. I am sorely in need of work. I taught in the public school in Louisville until my health failed. Since then I have had a hard struggle to get along," answered Mrs. May.

"I will give you mother's address. You can go out and arrange matters. Make haste and get well little protector," said Mr. Martin, as he rose to go.

When he had gone, the mother put her arms about her boy. "You are my protector," she said. "You brought me a wrap, and now you have helped me to get work to do."—Mrs. P. Binford, in the Visitor.

If I Ought To

> There's a voice that's ever sounding.
> With an echo oft rebounding,
> In my heart a word propounding,
>   Loudly speaking, never still;
> Till at last, my duty viewing,
> Heart replies to charge renewing,
> Let my willing change to doing,—
>   If I ought to, then I will.
> MAX HILL

MOFFAT AND AFRICANER

Robert Moffat, the poor Scotch lad, who, by living on beggar's fare, managed to get an education in theology and medicine, must evermore stand as one of the great pioneers of Central African exploration. When on the last day of October, 1816, that memorable year in missions, he set sail for the Cape of Good Hope, he was only twenty years of age. But in all the qualities that assure both maturity and heroism, he was a full-grown man.

As not infrequently occurs, his greatest obstacles were found, not in the hopeless paganism of the degraded tribes of the Dark Continent, but in the apathy, if not antipathy, of the representatives of Christian governments. The British governor would have penned him up within the bounds of Cape Colony, lest he should complicate the relations of the settlers with the tribes of the interior. While fighting out this battle, he studied Dutch with a pious Hollander, that he might preach to the Boers and their servants.

Afterward, when permission was obtained, while traveling to the country of the Bechuanas, at the close of his first day's journey he stopped at a farmhouse and offered to preach to the people that evening. In the large kitchen, where the service was to be held, stood a long table, at the head of which sat the Boer, with his wife and six grown children. A large Bible lay on the table, and underneath the table half a dozen dogs. The Boer pointed to the Bible as the signal for Mr. Moffat to begin. But, after vainly waiting for others to come in, he asked how soon the working people were to be called.

"Working people?" impatiently cried the farmer.

"You don't mean the Hottentots,—the blacks! You are not waiting for them surely, or expecting to preach to them? You might as well preach to those dogs under that table!" A second time, and more angrily he spoke, repeating the offensive comparison.

Young as Mr. Moffat was, he was disconcerted only for a moment. Lifting his heart to God for guidance, the thought came into his mind to take a text suggested by the rude remarks of the Boer. So he opened the Bible to the fifteenth chapter of Matthew and read the twenty-seventh verse: "Truth, Lord: yet the dogs eat of the crumbs which fall from their masters' table." Pausing a moment, he slowly repeated these words, with his eyes steadily fixed on the face of the Boer. Again pausing, a third time he quoted these appropriate words. Angrily the Boer cried out, "Well, well, bring them in." A crowd of blacks then thronged the kitchen, and Moffat preached to them all.

Ten years passed, and the missionary was passing that way again. Those work-people, who held him in the most grateful remembrance, seeing him, ran after him to thank him for telling them the way to Christ in that sermon.

His whole life in Africa was a witness to miracles of transformation. He had no scorn nor contempt for the sable sons of Africa. He found the most degraded of them open to the impressions of the gospel, and even the worst and unimpressionable among them were compelled to confess the power of that gospel to renew. One savage, cruel chief, who hated the missionaries, had a dog that chewed and swallowed a copy of the book of Psalms for the sake of the soft sheepskin in which it was bound. The enraged chief declared his dog to be henceforth worthless: "He would no more bite or tear, now that he had swallowed a Christian book."

This godly, devoted missionary preached and taught the warlike Bechuanas till they put away their clubs and knives, and farming utensils took the place of bows and arrows and spears. This strange change in African savages came to be talked over among the people. It was so wonderful that the other tribes could account for it only as an instance of supernatural magic. There was nothing they knew of that would lead men like the Bechuanas to bring war to an end, and no longer rob and kill.

Mr. Moffat was especially warned against the notorious Africaner, a chief whose name was the terror of the whole country. Some prophesied that he would be eaten by this monster; others were sure that he would be killed, and his skull turned into a drinking-cup, and his skin into the head of a drum. Nevertheless, the heroic young missionary went straight for the kraal of the cruel marauder and murderer. He was accompanied by Ebner, the missionary, who was not in favor in Africaner's court, and who soon had to flee, leaving Mr. Moffat alone with a bloodthirsty monarch and a people as treacherous as their chief.

But God had armed his servant with the spirit, not of fear, but of power, and of love, and of a sound mind. He was a man of singular grace and tact. He quietly but firmly planted his foot in Africaner's realms, and began his work. He opened a school, began stated services of worship, and went about among the people, living simply, self-denyingly, and prayerfully.

Africaner himself was his first convert. The wild Namoqua warrior was turned into a gentle child. The change in this chief was a moral miracle. Wolfish rapacity, leonine ferocity, leopardish treachery, gave way before the meekness and mildness of the calf or kid. His sole aim and ambition had been to rob and to slay, to lead his people on expeditions for plunder and violence, but he now seemed absorbed by one passion, zeal for God and his missionary. He set his subjects to building a house for Mr. Moffat, made him a present of cows, became a regular and devout worshiper, mourned heartily over his past life, and habitually studied the Word of God. He could not do enough for the man who had led him to Jesus.

When the missionary's life hung in the balance with African fever, he nursed him through the crisis of delirium. When he had to visit Cape Town, Africaner went with him, knowing that a price had been set for years upon his own head as an outlaw and a public enemy. No marvel that when he made his appearance in Cape Colony, the people were astonished at the transformation! It was even more wonderful than when Saul, the arch-persecutor, was suddenly transformed into Paul, the apostle.

Mr. Moffat once said that during his entire residence among this people, he remembered no occasion on which he had been grieved with Africaner or found reason for complaint; and even his very faults leaned to the side of virtue. On his way to Cape Town with Mr. Moffat, a distance of six hundred miles, the whole road lay through a country which had been laid waste by this robber and his retainers. The Dutch farmers could not believe that this converted man was actually Africaner; and one of them, when he saw him, lifted his hands and exclaimed: "This is the eighth wonder of the world! Great God, what a miracle of thy power and grace!"

He who had long shed blood without cause would now with as little hesitation shed his own for Christ's sake. When he found his own death approaching, he gathered his people around him, and charged them, as Moses and Joshua did Israel: "We are not now what we once were, savages, but men professing to be taught according to the gospel. Let us, then, do accordingly." Then, with unspeakable tenderness and gentleness, he counseled them to live peaceably with all men, to engage in no undertaking without the advice of Christian guides, to remain together as one people, and to receive and welcome all missionaries as sent from God. Then he gave them his parting blessing.

His dying confession would have graced the lips of the apostle of the Gentiles: "I feel that I love God, and that he has done much for me, of which I am totally unworthy. My former life is stained with blood: but Jesus Christ has bought my pardon, and I shall live with him through an eternity. Beware of falling back into the same evils into which I have so often led you, but seek God, and he will be found of you, and direct you."

Having said this, Africaner fell asleep, himself having furnished one of the most unanswerable proofs that the gospel is the power of God unto salvation.—Arthur T. Pierson, in "The Miracles of Missions," second series, copyright by Funk and Wagnalls Company, New York.

TWO TRIFLES

"Isn't Aunt Sue the dearest person you ever saw!" exclaimed Helen Fairmont as she and her visitor sank into a garden seat in the beautiful grounds surrounding Mrs. Armour's lovely home. "Nothing ever seems to be too much trouble for her, if she can make others happy."

"Yes," answered Mary Sutton, "I just felt like giving her a good hug when she told you her plan. It is really just for me that she is going to let you give the picnic here."

"Just for that very reason. It will be simply fine. O, she is so sweet! You see, two weeks ago, when you wrote that finally you could arrange to visit me for the summer, I was so full of the good news that I couldn't get to Aunt Sue's quickly enough to tell her about it,—somehow one always wants to tell Aunt Sue about things,—and she said she used to go to school with your mother, and was very fond of her, and she was all ready to like you, too, and that just the very minute you reached here, we were both to come over—I mean you and I were."

"O, dear," laughed Mary, "I think you'd better stop and take a good long breath, and get the we's and you's straightened."

"I don't care," Helen went chattering on. "You know what I mean, just what we've done. We, you and I,—is that right?—were to come to her house and choose what kind of entertainment we wanted her to give, so you might meet my friends."

"Who thought of the garden picnic?" inquired Mary, her face all animation. Then, not waiting for Helen's answer, she said, enthusiastically, "Isn't this a beautiful spot in which to have a picnic?"

The girls stopped talking long enough to look about at the pride of Mrs. Armour's heart, the lovely grounds round her home. They surrounded a fine old house of colonial type, for which they made a pretty setting. A double row of dignified and ancient elms flanked a pathway leading from the gate. The lawn on each side of the walk made one think of the answer the English gardener gave to the inquiry as to the cause of the velvety beauty of England's lawns. "Why, sir," said he, "we sows 'em, and we mows 'em, and we mows 'em, and we sows 'em." Mrs. Armour's lawn had the appearance of having undergone a like experience. At the back and sides of the house was a variety of shrubs and bushes whose blossoms in the spring made the place indescribably sweet. Mrs. Armour boasted that there were forty kinds of bushes, but her husband laughingly said that he had never been able to count more than thirty-nine and a half; "for you certainly couldn't call that Japanese dwarf a whole one!"

June roses ran riot in season. Later, more cultivated varieties, blooming regularly through the summer, took their part in providing fragrance. Sweet, old-fashioned garden plants and more valuable products, procured at much trouble and expense, helped to make a bower that might have satisfied even more fastidious eyes than those which reveled in them now.

Mrs. Armour's great delight was in using her garden, and she had given Helen the privilege of inviting all her young friends to picnic there the following Thursday evening.

"And, O Mary, you just can't imagine how pretty it is here with the Chinese lanterns swung from tree to tree, and the dainty tables scattered round!" Helen scarcely contain herself.

Mary laughed merrily. She was equally delighted but naturally she took everything in a more quiet manner. Smiling at Helen's exuberance of spirit, she asked, "What was it your aunt said about the sandwiches?"

"She wants to help us make them, and she was telling me she'd like me to cut them a little more carefully than I did the last time I helped her. You'd never think Aunt Sue has a hobby, would you?"

"No, I don't think I should."

"Well, she has. She's the most particular old darling about little things that you ever saw. Now those sandwiches I made I will admit were not cut very evenly, but, dear me! they tasted good enough. Tom Canton ate six. I told her so, but she said they should have looked good, too."

"Well, what's her hobby?"

"I just told you. It's trifles. She says life is made of them, and trifles with the rough edges polished off make beautiful lives. And she loves to quote such things as, 'Trifles make perfection, but perfection is no trifle.' She says trifles decide almost everything for us, and shape our characters. She says it is interesting to study how most big things grow from little ones.

"Helen, I think she's right." Mary's dark, thoughtful eyes looked into her friend's.

"O, I don't! It isn't trifles, trifles, that decide things and make the real difference. It is the big things. For instance, it is brother Tom's education in the school of technology that placed him in the responsible position we are all so proud of him for obtaining."

"Yes, but I heard him say himself that he just happened, by mistake, to leave one of his scribbled figures on your uncle's desk, and your uncle, picking it up by mistake, too, said that a boy who could do that should have a chance at the right training."

"Why, that's a fact, Mary mine," said Helen, in surprise. "I never thought of it in that way. Well, I won't agree that it happens so often. For example,"—glancing about for an idea, she caught sight of a young man, a former schoolmate, passing just in front of the Armour home,—"for example, I don't suppose it was a trifle that made Alson Jarvis turn out the kind of individual he has become lately. He used to be a fine boy, but I am afraid he is getting dissipated. He doesn't go with our crowd much now. I guess he is not invited the way he used to be before he began going with those South Town boys."

"I wish I could prove to you my side of the argument. Let's try your Aunt Sue's idea of studying how the big things come from little ones. Wouldn't it be interesting to find the cause of this one case? I would not be one bit surprised if it were just some little thing which was the pivot that turned him."

"All right," agreed Helen. "I don't believe your theory, but it would be fun, as you say, to try it. Will"—Will was her brother—"insists Al's not so black as he has been painted lately. We will get Will to find out for us if he can."

Then the talk drifted to the more absorbing subject of sandwiches and cakes.

At dinner-time the two girls confided to the accommodating Will their desire to find what had changed Al.

"Trying to pry into private closets, regardless of the kind of welcome their enclosed skeletons may accord you, are you?" said Will, banteringly.

Mary, not accustomed to his teasing, blushed, wondering if she had really been guilty of an indelicate presumption, but Helen spoke up quickly in their defense:—

"Now, Will you know perfectly well it is not any such thing. As a pledge of our good faith—does that sound nice and lawyer-like?" Will was studying law, and Helen, too, liked to tease occasionally—"I do affirm that if you will do that for us, I will do something nice for him, on your account."

"Then I certainly will. It is what I have been trying to convince you for a month that you ought to do."

The girls told him why it was they were so anxious to know more of Alson's private affairs.

"I would like to prove that your Aunt Sue and I are right, you know," said
Mary.

"Well," said Will, turning to his sister's guest, "don't let them prejudice you against Al. He is off the track just now, I know. The girls are not having much to do with him, but I have seen worse than he is." Will went off whistling. The next day he was ready with his report.

"Girls," he began, "Mary wins in the argument about trifles, and as a result I am feeling pretty mean about the business. I guess I am the trifle in the case."

Both girls laughed as they glanced at his six feet of length, and his great, broad shoulders.

"O, it is no laughing matter," he said, good-naturedly. "This is the way it happened: Washington's birthday, you know, everything in town was closed, and I thought, as Al was living in a boarding-house, I would better ask mother if I might bring him home the night before, and have him spend the day here with us; we were going to have a kind of celebration anyway, you know. So about seven o'clock that evening, just before I started for the travel lecture, I ran up to mother's room. It was on the tip of my tongue to ask her if she would not include Al in the number of her guests, when I noticed that she looked pretty blue. I know she whisked away a tear so I should not get sight of it. I pretended I didn't see it but I said, 'Got some troubles, little mother?'"

Helen knew in just what a hearty, cheerful way he said it.

"'Not very many, dear,' she said; but I didn't feel like bothering her about anything then, and decided it would do just as well to bring Al home the following Saturday night and keep him over Sunday."

Will looked dubious.

"But it didn't do," he continued. "Having nothing to keep him busy that holiday, Al went off with a crowd he had always before refused to join—a pretty gay set, I am afraid. The man who had half promised him the position he had been slaving for during the past year happened to see him with those people, and the very next day he informed Al very curtly that, after due consideration, he found he had no place for him. Alson guessed why, and now he feels reckless, and says he might as well have the game as the name, might as well be really bad since he has to suffer anyway. He talked in a desperate sort of way this morning when he told me about it. Somehow I feel responsible for the whole thing, because I hesitated about asking mother."

Will looked thoughtfully across at the girls, whose faces expressed real sympathy. Suddenly Helen exclaimed:—

"The night before Washington's birthday, you say?"

"Yes."

"Mother was nearly crying alone in her room?"

"Yes."

"About seven o'clock?"

"Yes. Is this a cross-examination?"

"Then," said Helen, sitting upright and paying no attention to her brother's question, "it's all my fault."

"How?"

"Bridget was out that evening, and I had to stay home from the lecture to put away the dinner things and I said I did not see why I always had to do such disagreeable things. I did not see why all our relations were rich, and why we had to be always scrimping and missing everything. Of course I repented in a little while and apologized. It made mother feel pretty bad, I knew, but I did not think she minded it as much as that, though."

"It was a pretty serious mix-up all around, wasn't it, sister?" Will spoke consolingly, but he looked worried.

"Well," came Mary's soothing tones, "you must not take all the blame, for probably there were a great many more 'little nothings' that had something to do with it. Al must take his share, too."

"Yes, perhaps," said Will; "but we have to take the blame that belongs to us."

Helen was aghast at the enormous result of her few minutes' irritability. Such outbursts were not common with her. There was a catch in her voice as she said, "Poor Al!"

Mary went directly to the heart of the matter. "It is done," she said. "It is somebody's fault, of course, but what is to be done first to rectify it?"

"I don't know, I am sure," Helen answered, musingly. "I have not had a thought of anything but the garden picnic for the last two days, and I don't seem to have any idea but picnic in my head."

"O, good!" ejaculated Mary. The joy of the discoverer shone in her eyes.

"The picnic! That is just the thing. Ask him, of course."

Alson Jarvis had hidden the hurts of his schoolmates' recent slights under a nonchalant manner. Each one, while it cut deeply, seemed to aggravate him to greater wilfulness. Well bred as he was, took no real pleasure in the sports of the company of which he had made a part since the loss of the position he so desired, and for which he had worked so faithfully. He felt himself disgraced and barred from the old associates; so, from pure discouragement, he continued with the new.

Helen Fairmont's note of invitation came as a surprise. It ran:—

"DEAR ALSON: I am inviting, for Aunt Sue, a number of my friends to meet Miss Mary Sutton, my guest from Amosville. We are to have a garden picnic Thursday evening. I think you will enjoy meeting Miss Sutton, as she has the same love for golf you have, and I have already told her of the scores you made last summer. Yours sincerely,

"HELEN FAIRMONT."

He read it with pleasure. Then the accumulated unkindnesses of his old friends came before him. A spirit of resentment took hold of him. No, they had shown how little they cared for him. Why should he go among them again? There was plenty of other company he could enter. But why had she asked him if she did not want him? O, well, they were all alike anyway! Even if she had not already done so, Helen would pass him by sooner or later, like so many of the others. But Will Fairmont had stuck to him. Maybe he had got his sister to pity him. Al winced at the thought. "I am getting contemptible. Will Fairmont would not do that. O, well, I might as well be done with them all right now!" His eyes flashed defiantly. Then he caught sight of the little note.

"Friendly enough," he said. "Sounds as honest and sincere as her brother."

Then he added: "I might give her the benefit of the doubt, I suppose. Yes,

I will go, if for no other reason than that she is Will's sister."

He went. And he enjoyed himself thoroughly thanks partially to Mrs. Armour's knowledge of human nature. Where others saw only weakness, she found smarting hurts. She felt that he was on dangerous ground, that he was ashamed of himself, and that his self-pride and self-respect needed propping, and she immediately proceeded to prop them.

Helen's grief over her own unsuspected part in his career resulted in an especial effort to make the picnic a pleasure and success for him. With that kindly compliance which is more common in those about us than we sometimes think, the other young people accepted the idea of Alson's being one of them again, and he found himself, before the termination of the evening, on almost his old footing with them.

"Wasn't it a success all round?" said Mary that night. "I congratulate you,
Helen, on your ability to extend real hospitality. It was just lovely."

"They did seem to have a good time, didn't they? Al Jarvis was on my conscience all the evening. Do you think he enjoyed himself?"

"Yes, I do, Helen."

"After what I did it was such a little return to make."

Simultaneously the girls laughed.

"Trifles again! They keep bobbing up, don't they? I suppose this is one of those of little consequence."

"'Time will tell,'" sententiously quoted Mary.

Time did tell. Years afterward two successful lawyers sat in an office, one congratulating the other on his brilliant speech of the day.

"It might never have been, Will," said Alson Jarvis, "if your aunt hadn't somehow, without a single definite word on the subject, shown me the broken road down which I had about decided to

185

travel through It was at a party she had in her grounds one night long ago for your sister and Mary Sutton. Do you remember it?"

Did he? Will's heart glowed with pleasure and gratitude as he thought of the great result of Mary's little suggestion about inviting Al. How unlike this was the outcome of that miserable trifle which had played so important a part in the lawyer's experience.—Elisabeth Golden, in the Wellspring.

Finish Thy Work

No other hand thy special task can do,
Though trivial it may seem to thee.
Thou canst not shirk
God-given work
And still be blest of Heaven, from sin be free.
O idler in life's ripened harvest-field,
Perform thy task, that rich thy work may yield!

Ah, sweet the thought that comes at set of sun,
If finished is the work of that one day.
But O the joy
Without alloy,
Awaiting him who at life's close can say,
"I'm ready, Father, to go home to thee;
The work is finished which thou gavest me."

MRS. M A LOPER.

THE SIN OF EXTRAVAGANCE A SECOND TRIAL

A College Scene

It was commencement day at college. The people were pouring into the church as I entered. Finding the choice seats already taken, I pressed onward, looking to the right and the left for a vacancy, and on the very front row I found one. Here a little girl moved along to make room for me, looking into my face with large gray eyes, whose brightness was softened by very long lashes. Her face was open and fresh as a newly blown rose. Again and again I found my eyes turning to the rose-like face, and each time the gray eyes moved, half-smiling, to meet mine. Evidently the child was ready to make friends with me. And when, with a bright smile, she returned my dropped handkerchief, we seemed fairly introduced.

"There is going to be a great crowd," she said to me.

"Yes," I replied; "people always like to see how schoolboys are made into men."

Her face beamed with pleasure and pride as she said: "My brother is going to graduate; he's going to speak. I have brought these flowers to throw at him."

They were not greenhouse favorites, but just old-fashioned domestic flowers, such as we associate with the dear grandmothers. "But," I thought, "they will seem sweet and beautiful to him, for his little sister's sake."

"That is my brother," she went on, pointing with her nosegay.

"The one with the light hair?" I asked.

"O, no;" she said, smiling and shaking her head in innocent reproof; "not that homely one with red hair; that handsome one with brown, wavy hair. His eyes look brown, too; but they are not, they are dark blue. There! he's got his hand up to his head now. You see him, don't you?"

In an eager way she looked from him to me, as if some important fate depended on my identifying her brother.

"I see him," I said. "He is a very good-looking brother."

"Yes, he is beautiful," she said, with artless delight, "and he's good, and he studies so hard. He has taken care of me ever since mama died. Here is his name on the program. He is not the valedictorian, but he has an honor for all that."

I saw in the little creature's familiarity with these technical college terms that she had closely identified herself with her brother's studies, hopes, and successes.

"He thought at first," she continued, "that he would write on 'The Romance of Monastic Life.'"

What a strange sound these long words had, whispered from her childish lips! Her interest in her brother's work had stamped them on the child's memory, and to her they were ordinary things.

"But then," she went on, "he decided that he would write on 'Historical Parallels,' and he has a real good oration, and says it beautifully. He has said it to me a great many times. I almost know it by heart. O, it begins so pretty and so grand! This is the way it begins," she added, encouraged by the interest she must have seen in my face: "'Amid the combinations of actors and forces that make up the great kaleidoscope of history, we often find a turn of Destiny's hand.'"

"Why, bless the baby!" I thought, looking down into her proud face. I cannot describe how very odd and elfish it did seem to have those sonorous words rolling out of the smiling mouth. The band striking up put an end to the quotation and to the confidences. As the exercises progressed and approached nearer and nearer the effort on which all her interest was concentrated, my little friend became excited and restless. Her eyes grew larger and brighter; two deep red spots glowed on her cheek. She touched up the flowers, manifestly making the offering ready for the shrine.

"Now it's his turn," she said, turning to me a face in which pride and delight and anxiety seemed equally mingled. But when the overture was played through, and his name was called, the child seemed, in her eagerness, to forget me and all the earth except him. She rose to her feet and leaned forward for a better view of her beloved as he mounted to the speaker's stand. I knew by her deep breathing that her heart was throbbing in her throat. I knew, too, by the way her brother came to the front, that he was trembling. The hands hung limp: his face was pallid, and the lips blue, as with cold. I felt anxious. The child, too, seemed to discern that things were not well with him. Something like fear showed in her face.

He made an automatic bow. Then a bewildered, struggling look came into his face, then a helpless look, and he stood staring vacantly, like a somnambulist, at the waiting audience. The moments of painful suspense went by, and he still stood as if struck down. I saw how it was; he had been seized with stage fright.

Alas, little sister! She turned her large, dismayed eyes on me. "He's forgotten it," she said. Then a swift change came over her face, a strong, determined look; and on the funeral-like silence of the room broke the sweet child voice:—

"'Amid the combinations of actors and forces that make up the great kaleidoscope of history, we often find that a turn of Destiny's hand—'"

Everybody about us turned and looked. The breathless silence, the sweet, childish voice, the childish face, the long, unchildlike words, produced a weird effect.

But the help had come too late; the unhappy brother was already staggering in humiliation from the stage. The band quickly struck up, and waves of lively music were rolled out to cover the defeat.

I gave the sister a glance in which I meant to show the intense sympathy which I felt, but she did not see. Her eyes, swimming with tears, were on her brother's face. I put my arm around her. She was too absorbed to feel the caress, and before I could appreciate her purpose she was on her way to the shame-stricken young man, sitting with a face like a statue's. When he saw her by his side, the set face relaxed, and a quick mist came into his eyes. The young men got closer together to make room for her. She sat down beside him, laid her flowers upon his knee, and slipped her hand into his. I could not keep my eyes from her sweet, pitying face. I saw her whisper to him, he bending a little to catch her word. Later, I found out that she was asking him if he knew his "piece" now, and that he answered yes.

When the young man next on the list had spoken, and the band was playing, the child, to the brother's great surprise, made her way up the platform steps, and pressed through the throng of professors, trustees, and distinguished visitors, to the president.

"If you please, sir," she said, with a little courtesy, "will you and the trustees let my brother try again? He knows his 'piece' now."

For a moment, the president stared at her through his gold-bowed spectacles, and then, appreciating the child's petition, he smiled on her, and went down and spoke to the young man who had failed.

So it happened that when the band had again ceased playing, it was briefly announced that Mr. Duane would now deliver his oration, "Historic Parallels."

"'Amid the combinations of actors and forces that——'" This the little sister whispered to him as he arose to answer the summons.

A ripple of heightened and expectant interest passed over the audience, and then all sat stone-still as if fearing to breathe lest the speaker might again take fright. No danger. The hero in the youth was aroused. He went at his "piece" with a set purpose to conquer, to redeem himself, and to bring back the smile into the child's tear-stained face. I watched the face during the speaking. The wide eyes, the parted lips, the whole rapt being, said the breathless audience was forgotten, that her spirit was moving with his.

And when the address was ended, with the ardent abandon of one who catches enthusiasm, in the realization that he is fighting down a wrong judgment and conquering a sympathy, the effect was really thrilling. That dignified audience broke into rapturous applause; bouquets intended for the valedictorian rained like a tempest. And the child who had helped save the day, that one beaming little face, in its pride and gladness, is something to be forever remembered.—Our Dumb Animals.

THE SIN OF EXTRAVAGANCE

"It may be a folly, but you would not think of calling extravagance a sin?" asked a young man of his minister.

"I do not care to offend you by harsh terms, but if we agree that it is a folly, that is reason enough for wishing to be wiser."

"But it is very easy to spend money when one is with others, and one does not like to be called 'tight.'"

"John," said the minister, "I do not propose to argue with you, but I want to tell you two stories, both of them true, recent, and out of my own experience. They will illustrate the reason why, knowing you as well as I do, having baptized you and received you into the church, I cannot view without concern your growing extravagance, and the company into which it leads you, and the interests from which it tends to separate you.

"A few months ago a young man came to this city, and spent his first days here under my own roof. I have known his father for many years, an earnest, faithful man, who has denied himself for that boy, and prayed for him, and done everything that a father ought.

"I chance to remember a word which his father spoke to me a number of years ago, when the boy was a young lad, and was recovering from a sickness that made it seem possible he would need a change of climate. I happen to remember meeting his father, who told me of this, and how he was arranging in his own mind to change his business, to make any sacrifice, to move to the ends of the earth, if necessary, for that boy's sake.

"The boy is not a bad boy. But he had not been in my home an hour before he asked me for the address of a tailor, and when his new suit came,—a suit which I thought he might very well have waited to earn,—it was silk-lined throughout. I do not believe the suit which his father wears as he passes the plate in church every

Sunday is silk-lined.

"I knew what the boy was to earn, and could estimate what he could afford, and I knew that he could not buy that suit out of his own earnings.

"I had a letter from his father a few days ago. Shall I read it to you? It is very short. It reads as follows:—

"'MY DEAR FRIEND: I hope you will never know how hard it is for me to write to you to say that you must not under any circumstances lend money to my dear boy.'

"And those last three words make it the more pathetic.

"The second story, too, is recent. Another boy, from another State, came to this city, and for the first few Sundays attended our church. We tried to interest him in good things; we liked him, and did our best for him. I saw little in him to disturb me, except that he was spending more money than I could think he earned. Recently I received a letter from his father. It is longer, and I will not read it, but will tell you the substance of it. He wrote saying that his son was employed in a business where, with economy, he ought to be able to make a living from the start, and with hope for advancement, but that from the first week he had written home for money. Not only so, but the father had all too good reason to believe that the boy was still leaving bills unpaid. The father wrote to ask me whether he could not arrange with some one connected with the church to receive the boy's money from home week by week, and see that it was applied to the uses for which it was sent. He added that he would be glad to consider himself a contributor to the church during the period of this arrangement.

"I had little hope that any arrangement of this kind would help matters, but I took it as indicating that the boy needed looking after, and I sent at once to look him up. Where do you think we found him?—In jail.

"These are not imaginary stories, nor are they of a remote past. And I see other young men for whom I am anxious. Wear the coat a little longer, but pay for it out of your own money. Be considered 'tight' if necessary, but live within your means. It is good sense; more than that, it is good religion.

"And now I will answer your question, or rather, you may answer it: Is extravagance merely a folly, or is it also a sin? What do you think?"—Youth's Companion.

𝒜 LITTLE CHILD'S WORK

Near one of the tiny schoolhouses of the West is a carefully tended mound, the object of the tenderest interest on the part of a man known far and wide as "Preacher Jim," a rough, unministerial-looking person, who yet has reached the hearts and lives of many of the men and women in that region, and has led them to know the Master whom he serves in his humble fashion.

Twenty years ago Preacher Jim was a different man. Rough and untaught, his only skill was shown by the dexterity with which he manipulated the cards that secured to him his livelihood. Then, as now, he was widely known, but in those days his title was "Gambler Jim."

It was during a long, tiresome trip across the Rockies that a clergyman and his wife, having undressed their little boy and tucked him snugly into his berth, repaired to the observation-car in order to watch the November heavens.

An hour passed swiftly; then suddenly a rough-looking fellow made his way toward the group of which the clergyman was one.

"Anybody here got a kid what's dressed in a red nightgown and sings like a bird?" he demanded, awkwardly.

The father and mother sprang excitedly to their feet, gasping in fear. The man nodded reassuringly.

"The' ain't nothing the matter of him," he said, with yet deeper embarrassment. "The matter's with—us. You're a parson, ain't you? The kid, he's been singin' to us—an' talkin'. If you don't mind, we'd take it mighty good of you to come with me. Not you, ma'am. The kid's all safe, an' the parson'll bring him back in a little while."

With a word to his wife, the minister followed his guide toward the front of the train, and on through car after car until thirteen of them had been traversed. As the two men opened the door of the smoking compartment, they stopped to look and listen.

Up on one of the tables stood the tiny boy, his face flushed, his voice shrill and sweet.

"Is you ready?" he cried, insistently. "My papa says the Bridegroom is Jesus, an' he wants everybody to be ready when he comes, just 'cause he loves you." Then, with a childish sweetness, came the song which had evidently made the deepest impression upon the child's mind: "Are you ready for the Bridegroom when he comes?"

"He's sung it over 'n' over," whispered the clergyman's companion, "'nd I couldn't stan' no more. He said you'd pray, parson."

As the two approached, the boy lifted his sweet, serious eyes to his father's.

"They want to get ready," he said, simply. And, his boy snuggled childishly in his arms, the minister prayed, as he never had prayed before, for the men gathered about the child.

It was only a few moments before the clergyman bore the child back to the sleeping-car, where the mother anxiously awaited his coming. Then he returned to talk with the men, four of whom that night decided to "get ready," and among them was, of course, the man who sought out the father of the child, Gambler Jim.

To this day it remains a mystery how the child succeeded in reaching the smoking-car unnoticed and unhindered.

As for the little fellow himself, his work was early done, for a few weeks later, upon the return trip through the mountains, he was suddenly stricken with a swift and terrible disease, and the parents tenderly laid the little form under the sod near the schoolhouse where Preacher Jim now tells so often the story, which never grows old.—Youth's Companion.

Christ Is Coming

Little children, Christ is coming,
Coming through the flaming sky,

To convey his trusting children
  To their glorious home on high

Do you love the Lord's appearing?
  Are you waiting for the day
When with all his shining angels
  He will come in grand array?

All who keep the ten commandments
  Will rejoice his face to see;
But the wicked, filled with anguish,
  From his presence then will flee

Now while yet probation lingers,
  Now while mercy's voice is heard,
Haste to give your heart to Jesus,
  Seek to understand his Word

Quickly help to spread the message,
  You to Christ some soul may turn.
Though the multitudes his goodness
  And his tender love may spurn.

Little children, Christ is coming,
  Even God's beloved Son;
When in glory he descendeth,
  Will he say to you, "Well done"?
DORA BRORSEN.

THE HANDY BOX

"Grandmother, do you know where I can find a little bit of wire?" asked Marjorie, running from the shed, where an amateur circus was in preparation.

Grandmother went to a little closet in the room and disappeared a moment, coming out presently with the wire.

"O, yes! and Fred wanted me to ask if you had a large safety-pin." Marjorie looked a little wistful, as if she did not quite like to bother grandmother.

There was another trip made to the closet, and the safety-pin was in

Marjorie's hand.

"You are a pretty nice grandma," she said, over her shoulder, as she ran out.

Not very long after, Marjorie came into the kitchen again. This time she stood beside the sink, where grandmother was washing dishes, and twisted her little toes in her sandals, but seemed afraid to speak.

"Fred wants to know"—began grandmother, laughing.

"Yes'm," said Marjorie, blushing.

"If I can't find him a piece of strong string?" finished grandmother.

"O, no—it's a little brass tack!" declared Marjorie, soberly.

She was a patient, loving grandmother, and she went to the little closet again. Marjorie could hardly believe her eyes when she saw the tacks, for there were three!

"He—said—" she began slowly, and stopped.

"You ought to tell him to come and say it himself," and grandmother laughed; "but we will forgive him this time. Was it 'Thank you,' he said?"

"He feels 'Thank you' awfully, I'm sure," said Marjorie, politely, "but what he said was that if wasn't too much bother—well, he could use a kind of hook thing."

Her grandmother produced a long iron hook, and Marjorie looked at her wonderingly. "Are you a fairy?" she asked, timidly. "You must have a wand and just make things."

Grandmother laughed. "Come here," she said. And she opened the little dark closet, and from the shelf took a long wooden box. This she brought to the table, and when she opened it, Marjorie gave a little cry of delight. It seemed to her that there was a little of everything in it. There were bits of string, pins, colored paper, bobbins, balls, pieces of felt, and every sort of useful thing generally thrown away.

"When I knew my grandchildren were coming here to spend the summer," she said, "I began on this box, and whenever I find anything astray that would naturally be thrown out I just put it in."

"Do you want me to help save, too?" asked Marjorie, who thought the story should have a moral.

"You must start a handy box of your own when you go back, and keep it in the nursery. You don't know how many times a day you will be able to help the others out. A little darning yarn, an odd thimble, a bit of soft linen, and all the things that clutter and would be thrown away, go to fill up a handy box. You can be the good fairy of the nursery."

"It is just wonderful!" said Marjorie. "If I had a little—just a little wooden box, I would begin today, and when I go home I can have a larger one."

Grandmother smiled, and brought out a smaller wooden box, just the right size. From that moment Marjorie was a collector, and her usefulness began.—Mira Jenks Stafford, in Youth's Companion.

THE RESULT OF DISOBEDIENCE

My parents and their six children, including myself, lived in Flintville, Wisconsin, near the Suamico River and Pond, where a great number of logs had been floated in for lumber. On the opposite side from us were woods, where wintergreen berries were plentiful. One pleasant Sunday morning in October, 1857, one of our playmates came to ask mother if we, my older sister, a younger brother, and I, might go with her to pick some of these berries.

Mother said we might go if we would go down the river and cross the bridge. She knew that we had crossed the pond several times on the logs, but the water was unusually high for that time of the year, and there was danger in crossing that way. We promised to cross by the bridge, really intending when we left home to do so. Mother let my two younger sisters, one four and the other six years old, go with us.

We left the house as happy as could be. My mother smiled as she stood in the door and watched us go. She had always trusted us, and we seldom disobeyed her. But this time we had our playmate with us, and the had been in the habit of having her own way. As she was a little older than we were, we thought that what she said or did was all right.

We had gone but a short distance when this girl, whose name was Louise, suggested that we run across the logs, and get to the berries so much the sooner. We reminded her of what our mother had told us; but she said, "Your mother does not know how snug the logs are piled in, and that it would be such fun, and no danger, to cross on them."

We began to look at the matter in the same way, and after playing a few minutes, we started across. I took one of my little sisters, and Louise was going to take the younger one; but, as she was about to start, her brother, whom she had not seen for some time, drove up and took her home with him. My brother, thinking he could take our little sister across, started with her, but I called to him to go back and wait for me to do it; for I was then about half-way over. The stream was not wide, and he thought he could take her over as well as I.

Just as I started back, O, what a sight met my eyes! I saw my little sister slip off the log into the water. I ran to catch her, but was not quick enough. As I reached for her, my brother and I both rolled from the log into the water with her. Then my sister, who had been standing on the bank to see if we got over safely, came to our rescue; but we were so frightened that we caught hold of her, and, instead of her pulling us out, we pulled her in with us.

By that time our screams had reached our mother's ears, and she came running to see what the trouble was. She saw only one of us, as the others were under water, or nearly so, and, supposing there was only one in the water, she came on the logs to help. By the time she got to us, the logs were under motion, so that she could not stand on them; and she, too, fell into the water.

The six-year-old sister, whom I had taken across, saw it all and made an attempt to come to us. Mother called to her to go back. She turned back, and reached the shore all right. Just as mother spoke, she felt something come against her feet. She raised her foot with the weight, and caught the dress of little Emeline, who was sinking for the last time. Mother managed to hold her till help came.

It being Sunday, nearly every man that lived near was away from home. Fortunately, a Mr. Flint, who had company visiting him, was at home. The men were eating their dinner when a woman who had seen us in the water rushed into the dining-room and told them that Mr. Tripp's family were in the mill-pond drowning. They rushed from the table, tipping it over and breaking some dishes.

When they reached us, the logs and water were so disturbed that nothing could be done for us until boards were brought to lay on the logs. During this time I had caught hold of a log that was crowded between others, so I could pull myself up without rolling, but could get no farther. My sister Sarah and brother Willard were helped ashore. Emeline, whom mother had been trying hard to hold up, was taken out, but showed no signs of life. She was laid on a log while they helped mother out.

As soon as mother saw Emeline, she told the men to turn her on her stomach. They then saw that there was life. She was quickly taken to the house, and cared for by an old lady we called Aunt Betsey, who had come to help.

While taking mother to shore, the nine men who had come to our rescue fell into the water. They all had to walk on the same long board to get to shore. The boards having been placed so very quickly, it was not noticed, until too late, that one was unsafe. The men were near enough to shore where they fell in, so that they could touch bottom, and were not long in getting out.

Mother had to be taken home, where she was cared for by the best help we could procure. It was impossible to get a doctor where we lived in those days. Little Emeline and mother were watched over all night, and at sunrise the next morning they were pronounced out of danger.

The men who fell in got off with only an unpleasant wetting. The water was quite cold; the pond froze over the following night. They did not start for home that day, as they were intending to do, but spent the rest of the day drying their clothing.

About noon our father, who had been away for three days, came home. When he heard the story of our disaster, he wept, and thanked God for sparing our lives.

All this happened because we did not obey our mother; and we children never forgot the lesson.
MRS. M. J. LAWRENCE.

Likes and Dislikes

I had a little talk today—
  An argument with Dan and Ike:
First Dan, he said 'twas not his way
  To do the things he didn't like.

And Ike, he said that Dan was wrong;
  That only cowards dodged and hid.
Because it made him brave and strong,
  The things he didn't like, he did!

But then I showed to Ike and Dan
 An easy way between the two:
I always try, as best I can,
 To like the things I have to do.

—Arthur Guiterman, in Youth's Companion.

ᴌIVINGSTONE'S BODY-GUARD

The work of David Livingstone in Africa was so far that of a missionary-explorer and general that the field of his labor is too broad to permit us to trace individual harvests. No one man can quickly scatter seed over so wide an area. But there is one marvelous story connected with his death, the like of which has never been written on the scroll of human history. All the ages may safely be challenged to furnish its parallel.

On the night of his death he called for Susi, his faithful servant, and, after some tender ministries had been rendered to the dying man, Livingstone said: "All right; you may go out now," and Susi reluctantly left him alone. At four o'clock the next morning, May 1, Susi and Chuma, with four other devoted attendants, anxiously entered that grass hut at Ilala. The candle was still burning, but the greater light of life had gone out. Their great master, as they called him, was on his knees, his body stretched forward, his head buried in his hands upon the pillow. With silent awe, they stood apart and watched him, lest they should invade the privacy of prayer. But he did not stir; there was not even the motion of breathing, but a suspicious rigidity of inaction. Then one of them, Matthew, softly came near and gently laid his hands upon Livingstone's cheeks. It was enough; the chill of death was there. The great father of Africa's dark children was dead, and they were orphans. The most refined and cultured Englishmen would have been perplexed as to what course to take. They were surrounded by superstitious and unsympathetic savages, to whom the unburied remains of the dead man would be an object of dread. His native land was six thousand miles away, and even the coast was fifteen hundred. A grave responsibility rested upon these simple-minded sons of the Dark Continent, to which few of the wisest would have been equal. Those remains, with his valuable journals, instruments, and personal effects, must be carried to Zanzibar. But the body must first be preserved from decay, and they had no skill nor facilities for embalming; and if preserved, there were no means of transportation—no roads nor carts. No beasts of burden being available, the body must be borne on the shoulders of human beings; and, as no strangers could be trusted, they must themselves undertake the journey and the sacred charge.

These humble children of the forest were grandly equal to the occasion, and they resolved among themselves to carry the body to the seashore, and not give it into other hands until they could surrender it to his countrymen. Moreover, to insure safety to the remains and security to the bearers, it must be done with secrecy. They would gladly have kept secret even their master's death, but the fact could not be concealed. God, however, disposed Chitambo and his subjects to permit these servants of the great missionary to prepare his emaciated body for its last journey, in a hut built for the purpose, on the outskirts of the village.

Now watch these black men as they rudely embalm the body of him who had been to them a savior. They tenderly open the chest and take out the heart and viscera. These they, with a poetic and pathetic sense of fitness, reserve for his beloved Africa. The heart that for thirty-three years had beat for her welfare must be buried in her bosom. And so one of the Nassik boys, Jacob Wainright, read the simple service of burial, and under the moula-tree at Ilala that heart was deposited, and that tree, carved with a simple inscription, became his monument. Then the body was prepared for its long journey; the cavity was filled with salt, brandy poured into the mouth, and the corpse laid out in the sun for fourteen days, and so was reduced to the condition of a mummy, Afterward it was thrust into a hollow cylinder of bark. Over this was sewed a covering of canvas. The whole package was securely lashed to a pole, and so at last was ready to be borne between two men upon their shoulders.

As yet the enterprise was scarcely begun, and the most difficult part of their task was before them. The sea was far away, and the path lay through a territory where nearly every fifty miles would bring them to a new tribe, to face new difficulties.

Nevertheless, Susi and Chuma took up their precious burden, and, looking to Livingstone's God for help, began the most remarkable funeral march on record. They followed the track their master had marked with his footsteps when he penetrated to Lake Bangweolo, passing to the south of Lake Lumbi, which is a continuation of Tanganyika, then crossing to Unyanyembe, where it was found out that they were carrying a dead body. Shelter was hard to get, or even food; and at Kasekera they could get nothing for which they asked, except on condition that they would bury the remains they were carrying.

Now indeed their love and generalship were put to a new test. But again they were equal to the emergency. They made up another package like the precious burden, only it contained branches instead of human bones; and this, with mock solemnity, they bore on their shoulders to a safe distance, scattered the contents far and wide in the brushwood, and came back without the bundle. Meanwhile others of their party had repacked the remains, doubling them up into the semblance of a bale of cotton cloth, and so they once more managed to procure what they needed and go on with their charge.

The true story of that nine months' march has never been written, and it never will be, for the full data cannot be supplied. But here is material waiting for some coming English Homer or Milton to crystallize into one of the world's noblest epics; and it deserves the master hand of a great poet artist to do it justice.

See these black men, whom some scientific philosophers would place at one remove from the gorilla, run all manner of risks, by day and night, for forty weeks; now going around by circuitous route to resort to strategem to get their precious burden through the country; sometimes forced to fight their foes in order to carry out their holy mission. Follow them as they ford the rivers and travel trackless deserts; facing torrid heat and drenching tropical storms; daring perils from wild beasts and relentless wild men; exposing themselves to the fatal fever, and burying several of their little band on the way. Yet on they went, patient and persevering, never fainting nor halting, until love and gratitude had done all that could be done, and they laid down at the feet of the British consul, on the twelfth of March, 1874, all that was left of Scotland's great hero.

When, a little more than a month later, the coffin of Livingstone was landed in England, April 15, it was felt that no less a shrine than Britain's greatest burial-place could fitly hold such precious dust. But so improbable and incredible did it seem that a few rude Africans could actually have done this splendid deed, at such a cost of time and such risk, that not until the fractured bones of the arm, which the lion crushed at Jabotsa thirty years before, identified the body, was certain that this was Livingstone's corpse. And then, on the eighteenth of April, 1874, such a funeral cortege entered the great abbey of Britain's illustrious dead as few warriors or heroes or princes ever drew to that mausoleum.

The faithful body-servants who had religiously brought home every relic of the person or property of the great missionary explorer were accorded places of honor. And well they might be. No triumphal procession of earth's mightiest conqueror ever equaled for sublimity that lonely journey through Africa's forests. An example of tenderness, gratitude, devotion, heroism, equal to this, the world had never seen. The exquisite inventiveness of a love that lavished tears as water on the feet of Jesus, and made tresses of hair a towel, and broke the alabaster flask for his anointing; the feminine tenderness that lifted his mangled body from the cross and wrapped it in new linen, with costly spices, and laid it in a virgin tomb, have at length been surpassed by the ingenious devotion of the cursed sons of Canaan.

The grandeur and pathos of that burial scene, amid the stately columns and arches of England's famous Abbey, pale in luster when contrasted with that simpler scene near Ilala, when, in God's greater cathedral of nature, whose columns and arches are the trees, whose surpliced choir are the singing birds, whose organ is the moaning wind, the grassy carpet was lifted, and dark hands laid Livingstone's heart to rest, In that great cortege that moved up the nave no truer nobleman was found than that black man, Susi, who in illness had nursed the Blantyre hero, had laid his heart in Africa's bosom, and whose hand was now upon his pall.

Let those who doubt and deride Christian missions to the degraded children of Africa, who tell us that it is not worth while to sacrifice precious lives for the sake of these doubly lost millions of the Dark Continent,—let such tell us whether it is not worth while, at any cost, to seek out and save men with whom such Christian heroism is possible.

Burn on, thou humble candle, burn within thy hut of grass,
Though few may be the pilgrim feet that through Ilala pass;
God's hand hath lit thee, long to shine, and shed thy holy light
Till the new day-dawn pour its beams o'er Afric's long midnight.

—Arthur T. Pierson, in "The Miracles of Missions," second series.

❮PARE MOMENTS

A lean, awkward boy came to the door of the principal of a celebrated school one morning, and asked to see him. The servant eyed his mean clothes, and thinking he looked more like a beggar than anything else, told him to go around to the kitchen. The boy did as he was bidden, and soon appeared at the back door.

"I should like to see Mr. Slade," said he.

"You want a breakfast, more like," said the servant girl, "and I can give you that without troubling him."

"Thank you," said the boy; "I should like to see Mr. Slade, if he can see me."

"Some old clothes maybe you want," remarked the servant again, eying the boy's patched clothes. "I guess he has none to spare; he gives away a sight." And, without minding the boy's request, she went about her work.

"May I see Mr. Slade?" again asked the boy, after finishing his bread and butter.

"Well, he is in the library; if he must be disturbed, he must. He does like to be alone sometimes," said the girl in a peevish tone.

She seemed to think it very foolish to admit such a fellow into her master's presence. However, she wiped her hands, and bade him follow. Opening the library door, she said:—

"Here's somebody, sir, who is dreadful anxious to see you, and so I let him in."

I do not know how the boy introduced himself, or now he opened the business, but I know that, after talking awhile, the principal put aside the volume that he was studying, and took up some Greek books, and began to examine the boy. The examination lasted for some time. Every question the principal asked was answered promptly.

"Upon my word," exclaimed the principal, "you do well!" looking at the boy from head to foot over his spectacles. "Why, my boy, where did you pick up so much?"

"In my spare moments," answered the boy.

Here was a poor, hard-working boy, with few opportunities for schooling, yet almost fitted for college by simply improving his spare moments.

Truly are spare moments the "gold-dust of time"! How precious they should be regarded! What account can you give for your spare moments? What can you show for them? Look and see. This boy can tell you how very much can be laid up by improving them; and there are many, very many other boys, I am afraid, in jail and in the house of correction, in the forecastle of a whaleship, in the gambling-house, in the tippling-shop, who, if you should ask them when they began their sinful course, might answer, "In my spare moments." "In my spare moments I gambled for marbles." "In my spare moments I began to swear and drink." "It was in my spare moments that I began to steal chestnuts from the old woman's stand." "It was in my spare moments that I gathered with wicked associates."

Then be very careful how you spend your spare moments. The tempter always hunts you out in small seasons like these; when you are not busy, he gets into your hearts, if he possibly can, in just such gaps. There he hides himself, planning all sorts of mischief Take care of your spare moments.—Selected.

$\mathcal{A}$ GOLD MEDAL

[Right and generous deeds are not always rewarded nor always recognized; but the doing of them is our duty, even diough they pass unnoticed. Sometimes, however, a noble, unselfish, manly act is met by a reward that betrays, on the part of the giver, the same praiseworthy spirit as that which prompted the act. Do right, be courteous, be noble, though man may never express his appreciation. The God of right will, in his own good time, give the reward.]

I shall never forget a lesson I once received. We saw a boy named Watson driving a cow to pasture. In the evening he drove her back again, we did not know where. This was continued several weeks.

The boys attending the school were nearly all sons of wealthy parents, and some of them were dunces enough to look with disdain on a student who had to drive a cow. With admirable good nature Watson bore all their attempts to annoy him.

"I suppose, Watson," said Jackson, another boy, one day, "I suppose your father intends to make a milkman of you?"

"Why not?" asked Watson.

"O, nothing! Only don't leave much water in the cans after you rinse them, that's all."

The boys laughed, and Watson, not in the least mortified, replied:—

"Never fear. If ever I am a milkman, I'll give good measure and good milk."

The day after this conversation, there was a public examination, at which ladies and gentlemen from the neighboring towns were present, and prizes were awarded by the principal of our school.

Both Watson and Jackson received a creditable number; for, in respect to scholarship, they were about equal. After the ceremony of distribution, the principal remarked that there was one prize, consisting of a gold medal, which was rarely awarded, not so much on account of its great cost, as because the instances were rare which rendered its bestowal proper. It was the prize of heroism. The last medal was awarded about three years ago to a boy in the first class, who rescued a poor girl from drowning.

The principal then said that, with the permission of the company, he would relate a short anecdote:—

"Not long ago some boys were flying a kite in the street, just as a poor lad on horseback rode by on his way to the mill. The horse took fright and threw the boy, injuring him so badly that he was carried home, and confined some weeks to his bed. Of the boys who had unintentionally caused the disaster, none followed to learn the fate of the wounded lad. There was one boy, however, who witnessed the accident from a distance, who not only went to make inquiries, but stayed to render service.

"This boy soon learned that the wounded boy was the grandson of a poor widow, whose sole support consisted in selling the milk of a cow, of which she was the owner. She was old and lame, and her grandson, on whom she depended to drive her cow to the pasture, was now helpless with his bruises. 'Never mind,' said the friendly boy, 'I will drive the cow.'

"But his kindness did not stop there. Money was wanted to get articles from the apothecary. 'I have money that my mother sent me to buy boots with,' said he, 'but I can do without them for a while.' 'O, no,' said the old woman, 'I can't consent to that; but here is a pair of heavy boots that I bought for Thomas, who can't wear them. If you would only buy these, we should get on nicely.' The boy bought the boots, clumsy as they were, and has worn them up to this time.

"Well, when it was discovered by the other boys at the school that our student was in the habit of driving a cow, he was assailed every day with laughter and ridicule. His cowhide boots in particular were made matter of mirth. But he kept on cheerfully and bravely, day after day, never shunning observation, driving the widow's cow and wearing his thick boots. He never explained why he drove the cow; for he was not inclined to make a boast of his charitable motives. It was by mere accident that his kindness and self-denial were discovered by his teacher.

"And now, ladies and gentlemen, I ask you, Was there not true heroism in this boy's conduct? Nay, Master Watson, do not get out of sight behind the blackboard. You were not afraid of ridicule; you must not be afraid of praise."

As Watson, with blushing cheeks, came forward, a round of applause spoke the general approbation, and the medal was presented to him amid the cheers of the audience.—The Children's Own.

$\mathcal{A}$ GIRL'S RAILWAY ACQUAINTANCE

Most young people do not adequately realize what consummate address and fair seeming can be assumed by a deceiving stranger until experience enlightens them, and they suffer for their credulity. The danger, especially to young girls traveling alone, is understood by their parents; and no daughter is safe who disregards their injunction to permit no advances by a new and self-introduced acquaintance, either man or woman.

A lady gave, some years ago, in one of the religious papers, an experience of her own when she was a girl, which shows one of the artful ways by which designing men win the confidence of the innocent.

Traveling from Boston to New York, she had the company of a girl friend as far as Springfield. For the rest of the way she was to ride alone, and, as she supposed, unnoticed, save by the watchful conductor, to whose care her father had entrusted her.

She was beginning to feel lonely when a gentlemanly looking man of about forty-five approached her seat with an apology, and, by way of question, spoke her name. Surprised, but on her guard, for she remembered her home warnings, she made no reply; but the pleasant stranger went on to say that he was a schoolmate of her mother, whom he called by her girl name. This had its effect; and when he mentioned the names of other persons whom she knew, and begged to hear something of these old friends with whom he once went to school, she made no objection to his seating himself by her side.

The man made himself very agreeable; and the young girl of sixteen thought how delighted her mother would be to know she had met one of her old playmates, who said so many complimentary things about her. He talked very tenderly about the loss of his wife, and once went back to his own seat to get a picture of his motherless little girl, and a box of bonbons.

The conductor passed just then, and asked the young lady if she ever saw that gentleman before. She told him No; but, though the question was put very kindly and quietly, it made her quite indignant.

As they approached the end of the journey, the man penciled a brief note to her mother on a card, Signed what purported to be his name, and gave it to her. Then he asked if he might get her a carriage provided her uncle, whom she expected, did not meet her, and she assented at once.

When the train arrived in New York, and the conductor came and took her traveling-bag, she was vexed, and protested that the gentleman had promised to look after her. The official told her kindly, but firmly, that her father had put her in his care, and he should not leave her until he had seen her under her uncle's protection or put her in a carriage himself. She turned for appeal to her new acquaintance, but he had vanished.

When she reached home after her visit, and told her experience, and presented the card, her mother said she had never known nor heard of such a man. The stranger had evidently sat within hearing distance of the girl and her schoolmate, and listening to their merry chatter all the way from Boston to Springfield, had given him the clue to names and localities that enabled him to play his sinister game. Only the faithfulness of the wise conductor saved her from possibilities too painful to be recorded here.—Youth's Companion.

$\mathcal{H}$AROLD'S FOOTMAN

"Bob," called Harold to his little brother, who was playing on the back door-step, "trot out to the barn and bring me my saw, will you?"

Bobby left his two pet cats, Topsy and Tiger, on the steps, and ran obediently for the tool. Harold was very busy constructing a hen-coop, and he needed a great deal of assistance.

"Thanks," he said, shortly, as the little boy returned. "Now, where did I put those nails? O, they're on the kitchen table! Hand them out." Bobby produced the nails, and sat down again to watch the work.

"Are you going to finish it today, Hal?" he asked.

"No; haven't time. I am going to the commons in about ten minutes. There is a lacrosse match on; but I want to drive these nails first. O, say, Bob, my lacrosse stick is up in my room! You go and bring it down, I am so awfully busy."

Bobby ran eagerly up the stairs. He always went on errands for his big brother very willingly, but this time he made special haste; for a hope was entering his heart that perhaps Hal would take him to see the match.

"Mother!" he cried, poking his head out to the shady front veranda where his mother and aunt sat sewing, "Hal's going to the commons; may I go too?"

His mother looked up from her sewing rather doubtfully.

"O, I really don't know, dearie!" she began.

"O, let the poor wee man go!" pleaded Aunt Kate, when she saw the look of disappointment on Bobby's round face. "Hal will take care of him."

"Well, keep near Hal, Bobby. I don't like your crossing the rail-road track."

Bobby bounded out to the back yard in high glee, waving the lacrosse stick.

"Mother says I can go, too," he shouted, jumping down the steps in a manner that made Tiger and Topsy rise up indignantly and move to one side.

"O pshaw!" cried his brother, hammering a nail rather viciously. "What do you always want to follow me round for?"

"O, can't I go?" cried the little fellow, in distress. "Aw, Hal, do let me!"

"I can't have a kid like you forever tagging after me. Why can't you play with boys of your own age? You can't come today, that's all about it."

"O Hal! you—you might let me! I won't be a bother!" Bobby's eyes were beginning to brim over with tears. His face wore a look of despair.

"O, cry-baby; of course you must howl! You can stay at home and play with the cats."

And the big brother, whom Bobby had served so willingly all day, shouldered his lacrosse stick and went off whistling.

Harold met his Aunt Kate in the hall.

"Where's your little footman?" she asked gaily. "Isn't he going?"

"Who? Bob? O Aunt Kate, he's too small to go everyvhere with me!"

"Ah!" Aunt Kate looked surprised. "I thought he was quite big enough to be with you when there was work to be done, but I see, a footman is wanted to run errands and do such things."

Harold was not very well acquainted with his aunt, and he was never quite sure whether she was in fun or not. The idea of her saying Bob was his footman! He felt quite indignant.

He had just reached the street when he remembered that he had left his ball where he had been working. He half wished Bobby were with him, so he could send him back for it. And then he felt ashamed when he remembered his aunt's words. Was she right, after all, and did he make use of his little brother, and then thrust him aside when he did not need him?

He did not like the idea of facing Aunt Kate again, so he slipped in through the back gate, and walked quietly around the house. As he approached the house, he heard a voice, and paused a moment, hidden by a lilac bush. Poor, lonely Bobby was sitting on the steps, one hand on Tiger's neck, while the other stroked Topsy. He was pouring out to his two friends all his troubles.

"He doesn't like me, Tops, not one little bit. He never wants me round, only to run and get things for him. You don't be bad to Tops just 'cause she's littler than you, do you, Tiger? But I guess you like Topsy, and Hal don't like me. He don't like me one little teenty bit." Here a sob choked him, and through the green branches Harold could see a big tear-drop upon Topsy's velvet coat.

"I wish I had a brother that liked me." went on the pitiful little voice. "Tom Benson likes Charlie. He likes him an awful lot. And Charlie doesn't do nearly so many things as I do. I guess I oughtn't to tell, Tiger, but you and Tops wouldn't tell tales, so 'tisn't the same as tellin' father, or mother, or Auntie Kate, is it, Tige? But I think he might like me a little wee bit, don't you, Tiger?" And Harold could see the blue blouse sleeve raised to brush away the hot tears.

Harold drew back quietly, and tiptoed down the walk to the street. He had forgotten all about the ball. His eyes were so misty that he did not notice Charlie Benson, waiting for him at the gate, until Tom called:—

"Hello there! I thought you were never coming, What kept you?"

"Say, is Charlie going?" asked Harold, suddenly.

"Of course I am!" cried the little fellow, cutting a caper on the sidewalk.

"Tom said I could. Didn't you, Tom?"

Tom laughed good-naturedly. "He was bound to come," he said. "He won't bother us."

"Well—I—think Bob wants to come, too," said Harold, hesitatingly, "and if
Charlie is going—"

"O, goody!" cried Charlie, who was Bobby's special chum. "Where is he?"

Harold put his fingers to his lips, and uttered two sharp whistles. Bobby understood the signal, and came around the side of the house. He had carefully wiped away his tears, but his voice was rather shaky.

"What d'ye want?" he called. He felt sure Hal had an errand for him.

"Charlie's going to the commons with us," shouted his brother, "so I guess you can come, if you want to."

Bobby came down the path in leaps and bounds.

"I'm going, mother!" he shouted, waving his cap. And away he and Charlie tore down the street ahead of their brothers.

"Hold on, there!" cried Harold, with a laugh. "Don't get crazy! And mind you two keep near us at the track!"

It was about a week later that Aunt Kate laid her hand on Harold's shoulder, and said: "I am afraid I made a mistake the other day, Hal. I believe Bobby's been promoted from the rank of footman to be a brother."—Martha Graham, in the King's Own.

ℰLNATHAN'S GOLD

One morning Christopher Lightenhome, aged sixty-eight, received an unexpected legacy of six hundred dollars. His good old
face betokened no surprise, but it shone with a great joy. "I am
never surprised at the Lord's mercies," he said, reverently. Then,
with a step to which vigor had suddenly returned, he sought out
Elnathan Owsley, aged twelve.

"Elnathan," he said, "I guess I am the oldest man in the poorhouse, but I feel just about your age. Suppose you and I get out
of here."

The boy smiled. He was very old for twelve, even as Christopher Lightenhome was very young for sixty-eight.

"For a poorhouse this is a good place," continued Christopher,
still with that jubilant tone in his voice. "It is well conducted, just
as the county reports say. Still there are other places that suit me
better. You come and live with me, Elnathan. What do you say to
it, boy?"

"Where are you going to live?" asked Elnathan, cautiously.

The old man regarded him approvingly. "You'll never be one
to get out of the frying-pan into the fire, will you?" he said. "But I
know a room. I have had my eye on it. It is big enough to have a
bed, a table, a cook-stove, and three chairs in it, and we could live
there like lords. Like lords, boy! Just think of it! I can get it for two
dollars a month."

"With all these things in it?"

"No, with nothing in it. But I can buy the things, Elnathan, get
them cheap at the second-hand store. And I can cook to beat—well
to beat some women anyway—" He paused to think a moment of
Adelizy, one of the pauper cooks. "Yes," he thought, "Adelizy has
her days. She's systematic. Some days things are all but pickled

in brine, and other days she doesn't put in any salt at all. Some days they're overcooked, and other days it seems as if Adelizy jerked them off the stove before they were heated through." Then he looked eagerly into the unresponsive young face before him. "What's the matter with my plan, Elnathan?" he asked, gravely. "Why don't you fall in with it? I never knew you to hang off like this before."

"I haven't any money," was the slow answer. "I can't do my share toward it. And I'm not going to live off of you. Your money will last you twice as long as if you don't have to keep me. Adelizy says six hundred dollars isn't much, if you do think it is a fortune, and you'll soon run through with it, and be back here again."

For a moment the old man was stung. "I sha'n't spend the most of it for salt to put in my victuals anyway," he said. Then his face cleared, and he laughed. "So you haven't any money, and you won't let me keep you," he continued. "Well, those are pretty honorable objections. I expect to do away with them though, immediately." He drew himself up, and said, impressively: "'That is gold which is worth gold.' You've got the gold all right, Elnathan, or the money, whichever you choose to call it."

Elnathan stared.

"Why, boy, look here!" Mr. Lightenhome exclaimed, as he seized the hard young arm, where much enforced toil had developed good muscle. "There's your gold, in that right arm of yours. What you want to do is to get it out of your arm and into your pocket. I don't need to keep you. You can live with me and keep yourself. What do you say now?"

The boy's face was alight. "Let's go today," he said.

"Not today—tomorrow," decided Mr. Lightenhome, gravely. "When I was young, before misfortune met me and I was cheated out of all I had, I was used to giving spreads. We'll give one tonight to those we used to be fellow paupers with no longer ago than yesterday, and tomorrow we will go. We began this year in the poorhouse; we will end it in our own home. That is one of the bad beginnings that made a good ending, boy. There is more than one of them. Mind that."

The morrow came, and the little home was started. Another morrow followed, and Elnathan began in earnest to try getting the gold out of his arm and into his pocket. He was a dreamy boy, with whom very few had had patience; for nobody, not even himself, knew the resistless energy and dogged perseverance that lay dormant within him. Mr. Lightenhome, however, suspected it. "I believe," he said to himself, "that Elnathan, when he once gets awakened, will be a hustler. But the poorhouse isn't exactly the place to rouse up the ambition of Napoleon Bonaparte in any boy. Having a chance to scold somebody is what Adelizy calls one of the comforts of a home. And she certainly took out her comforts on Elnathan, and all the rest helped her—sort of deadening to him, though. Living here with me and doing for himself is a little more like what's needed in his case."

Slowly Elnathan wakened, and Mr. Lightenhome had patience with him. He earned all he could, and he kept himself from being a burden on his only friend, but he disliked work, and so he lagged over it. He did all that he did well, however, and he was thoroughly trustworthy.

Three years went by. Elnathan was fifteen years old, and Christopher
Lightenhome was seventy-one.

The little room had always been clean. There had been each day enough nourishing food to eat, though the old man, remembering Adelizy's prediction, had set his face like flint against even the slightest indulgence in table luxuries. And, although there had been days when Elnathan had recklessly brought home a ten-cent pie and half a dozen doughnuts from the baker's as his share of provision for their common dinner, Mr. Lightenhome felt that he had managed well. And yet there were only fifty dollars of the original six hundred left, and the poorhouse was looming once more on the old man's sight. He sighed. An expression of patience grew on the kind old face. He felt it to be a great pity that six hundred dollars could not be made to go farther. And there was a wistfulness in the glance he cast upon the boy. Elnathan was, as yet, only half awake. The little room and the taste of honest independence had done their best. Were they to fail?

The old man began to economize. His mittens wore out. He did not buy more. He needed new flannels, but he did not buy them.

Instead he tried to patch the old ones, and Elnathan, coming in suddenly, caught him doing it.

"Why, Uncle Chris!" he exclaimed. "What are you patching those old things for? Why don't you pitch 'em out and get new ones?"

The old man kept silent till he had his needle threaded. Then he said, softly, with a half-apology in his tone, "The money's 'most gone, Elnathan."

The boy started. He knew as well as Mr. Lightenhome that when the last coin was spent, the doors of the poorhouse would open once more to receive his only friend. A thrill of gladness went through Elnathan as he recognized that no such fate awaited him.

He could provide for himself. He need never return. And by that thrill in his own bosom he guessed the feeling of his friend. He could not put what he guessed into words. Nevertheless, he felt sure that the old man would not falter nor complain.

"How much have you?" he asked.

Mr. Lightenhome told him.

Then, without a word, Elnathan got up and went out. His head sunk in thought, and his hands in his trousers' pockets, he sauntered on in the wintry air while he mentally calculated how long Mr. Lightenhome's funds would last. "Not any later than next Christmas he will be in the poorhouse again." He walked only a few steps. Then he stopped. "Will he?" he cried. "Not if I know it."

This was a big resolve for a boy of fifteen, and the next morning Elnathan himself thought so. He thought so even to the extent of considering a retreat from the high task which he had the previous day laid before himself. Then he looked at Mr. Lightenhome, who had aged perceptibly in the last hours. Evidently he had lain awake in the night calculating how long his money would last. The sight of him nerved the boy afresh. "I am not going back on it," he told himself, vigorously. "I am just going to dig out all the gold there is in me. Keeping Uncle Chris out of the poorhouse is worth it."

But he did not confide in the old man. "He would say it was too big a job for me, and talk about how I ought to get some schooling," concluded the boy.

Now it came about that the room, which, while it had not been the habitation of lords, had been the abode of kingly kindness, became a silent place. The anxious old man had no heart to joke. He had been to the poorhouse, and had escaped from it into freedom. His whole nature rebelled at the thought of returning. And yet he tried to school himself to look forward to it bravely. "If it is the Lord's will," he told himself, "I will have to bow to it."

Meanwhile those who employed Elnathan were finding him a very different boy from the slow, lagging Elnathan they had known. If he was sent on an errand, he made speed. "Here! get the gold out of your legs," he would say to himself. If he sprouted potatoes for a grocer in his cellar, "There's gold in your fingers, El," he would say. "Get it out as quick as you can."

He now worked more hours in a day than he had ever worked before, so that he was too tired to talk much at meals, and too sleepy in the evening. But there was a light in his eyes when they rested on Mr. Lightenhome that made the old man's heart thrill.

"Elnathan would stand by me if he could," he would say to himself. "He's a good boy. I must not worry him."

A month after Elnathan had begun his great labor of love, an astonishing thing happened to him. He had a choice of two places offered him as general utility boy in a grocery. Once he would have told Mr. Lightenhome, and asked his advice as to which offer he should take, but he was now carrying his own burdens. He considered carefully, and then he went to Mr. Benson.

"Mr. Benson," he said, "Mr. Dale wants me, too, and both offer the same wages. Now which one of you will give me my groceries reduced as you do your other clerks?"

"I will not," replied Mr. Benson, firmly. "Your demand is ridiculous. You are not a clerk."

The irate Mr. Benson turned on his heel, and Elnathan felt himself dismissed. He then went to Mr. Dale, to whom he honestly related the whole. Mr. Dale laughed. "But you are not a clerk," he said, kindly.

"I know it, but I mean to be, and I mean to do all I can for you, too."

Mr. Dale looked at him, and he liked the bearing of the lad. "Go ahead," he said. "You may have your groceries at the same rate I make clerks."

"Thank you," responded Elnathan, while the gratitude he felt crept into his tones. "For myself," he thought, "I would not have asked for a reduction, but for Uncle Chris I will. I have a big job on hand."

That day he told Mr. Lightenhome that he had secured a place at Mr. Dale's, and that he was to have a reduction on groceries. "Which means, Uncle Chris, that I pay for the groceries for us both, while you do the cooking and pay the rent."

Silently and swiftly Mr. Lightenhome calculated. He saw that if he were saved the buying of the groceries for himself, he could eke out his small hoard till after Christmas. The poorhouse receded a little from the foreground of his vision as he gazed into the eyes of the boy opposite him at the table. He did not know that his own eyes spoke eloquently of his deliverance, but Elnathan choked as he went on eating.

"Now hustle, El!" he commanded one day on his way back to the store. "There's gold in your eyes if you keep them open, and in your tongue if you keep it civil, and in your back and in your wits if they are nimble. All I have to say is, Get it out."

"Get it out," he repeated when he had reached the rear of the store. And he began busily to fill and label kerosene cans, gasoline cans, and molasses jugs. From there he went to the cellar to measure up potatoes.

"Never saw such a fellow!" grumbled his companion utility boy. "You'd think he run the store by the way he steps round with his head up and them sharp eyes of his into everything. 'Hi there!' he said to me. 'Fill that measure of gasoline full before you pour it into the can. Mr. Dale doesn't want the name of giving short measure because you are careless.' Let's do some reporting on him, and get him out of the store," he said. "But there's nothing to report, and there never will be."

But the boy persisted, and very shortly he found himself out of a position.

"You needn't get another boy if you don't want to, Mr. Dale," observed Elnathan, cheerily. "I am so used to the place now that I can do all he did, as well as my own work. And, anyway, I would rather do the extra work than go on watching somebody to keep him from measuring up short or wrong grade on everything he touches." And Elnathan smiled. He had lately discovered that he had ceased to hate work.

Mr. Dale smiled in return. "Very well," he said. "Go ahead and do it all if you want to."

A week he went ahead, and at the end of that time he found, to his delight, that Mr. Dale had increased his wages. "Did you think I would take the work of two boys and pay for the work of one?" asked Mr. Dale.

"I didn't think at all, sir," replied Elnathan, joyously; "but I am the gladdest boy in Kingston to get a raise."

"Uncle Chris," he said that night, "I got a raise today."

Mr. Lightenhome expressed his pleasure, and his sense that the honor was well merited, but Elnathan did not hear a word he said, because he had something more to say himself.

"Uncle Chris," he went on, his face very red, "I have been saving up for some time, and tomorrow's your birthday. Here is a present for you." And he thrust out a ten-dollar piece, with the words, "I never made a present before."

Slowly the old man took the money, and again his eyes outdid his tongue in speaking his gratitude. And there was a great glow in the heart of the boy.

"That's some of the gold I dug out of myself, Uncle Chris," he laughed. "You are the one who first told me it was in me. I do not know whether it came out of my arms or my legs or my head."

"I know where the very best gold there is in you is located, Elna-than," smiled the old man. "It is your heart that is gold, my boy."

Two months later Elnathan was a clerk at twenty-five dollars a month. "Now we're fixed, Uncle Chris!" he cried, when he told the news. "You and I can live forever on twenty-five dollars a month."

"Do you mean it?" asked the old man, tremblingly. "Do you wish to be cumbered with me?"

"No, I do not, Uncle Chris," answered the boy, with a beaming look. "I do not want to be cumbered with you. I just want to go on living here with you."

Then to the old man the poorhouse forever receded from sight. He remembered Adelizy no more, as he looked with pride and tenderness on the boy who stood erect and alert before him, looked again and yet again, for he saw in him the Lord's deliverer, though he knew not that he had been raised up by his own kind hand.—Gulielma Zollinger, in the Wellspring.

ONLY A JACK-KNIFE

When the lamented James A. Garfield was struggling to obtain an education, he supported himself for several years by teaching. His first school was in Muskingum County, Ohio, and the little frame house where he began his work as a teacher, is still standing, while some of the boys and girls who received instruction from him that term are yet alive to testify to his faithfulness as a common-school teacher. He was quite a young man at that time, in fact, he was still in his teens, and it must have been rather embarrassing for him to attempt to teach young men and women, some of them older than himself; but he was honest in his efforts to try to do his best, and, as is always the case under such circumstances, he succeeded admirably.

One day, after repeatedly cautioning a little chap not to hack his desk with the new Barlow in his possession, the young teacher transferred the offending knife to his own pocket, quietly informing the culprit that it should be returned at the close of the afternoon session.

During the afternoon two of the committeemen called to examine the school, and young Garfield was so interested in the special recitations conducted that he let the boy go home in the evening without even mentioning the knife. The subject did not recur to him again until after supper, and perhaps would not have been recalled to him then had not he chanced to put his hand into his pocket for a pencil.

"Look there!" he exclaimed, holding up the knife. "I took it from Sandy Williams, with the promise that it should be returned in the evening, and I have let him go home without it. I must carry it to him at once."

"Never mind, man! Let it stand till morning," urged Mrs. Ross, the motherly woman with whom he boarded.

"I cannot do that," replied Garfield; "the little fellow will think

I am a thief."

"No danger of that, James," insisted the well-meaning woman. "He will know that you forgot it, and all will be well in the morning."

"But, you see, I promised, Mrs. Ross, and a promise is always binding. I must go tonight, and carry it to him," urged the young man, drawing on his coat.

"It is all of two miles to his father's, and just look how dark it is, and raining, too," said the woman, opening the door to convince her boarder that things were as bad as she had represented them.

"I am young and strong, and can make my way quite easily," insisted Garfield. "It is always better to right a wrong as soon as you discover it, and I would rather walk the four miles in the mud and rain than disappoint one of my scholars. Sometimes example is more powerful than precept, and if I am not careful to live an honest life before my pupils, they will not give much heed to what I say on such subjects. There is no rule like the golden rule, but he who teaches it must also live it, if he expects others to follow his teaching."

Mrs. Ross said no more, and James went on, as he had proposed; and before the little boy went to sleep, he was happy again in the possession of his treasure, over which he had been lamenting all the evening. The young teacher declined the hospitality of the family for the night, and walked back in the darkness to his boarding-house, and, as he afterward said, felt all the better for standing up to his principles.—Selected.

𝓐 SPELLING-BEE

"I am going to have a spelling-bee tonight," said Uncle John, "and I will give a pair of skates to the the boy who can spell man best."

The children turned and stared into one another's eyes.

"Spell 'man' best, Uncle John? Why, there is only one way!" they cried.

"There are all sorts of ways," replied Uncle John. "I will leave you to think of it awhile," and he buttoned up his coat and went away.

"What does he mean?" asked Bob.

"I think it is a joke," said Harry, thoughtfully; "and when Uncle John asks me, I am going to say, 'Why, m-a-n, of course.'"

"It is a conundrum, I know," said Joe; and he leaned his head on his hand and settled down to think.

Time went slowly to the puzzled boys, for all their fun that day. It seemed as if "after supper-time" would never come; but it came at last, and Uncle John came, too, with a shiny skate runner peeping out of his coat pocket.

Uncle John did not delay; he sat down and looked straight into Harry's eyes.

"Been a good boy today, Hal?"

"Yes—n-o," said Harry, flushing. "I did something Aunt May told me not to do, because Ned Barnes dared me to. I cannot bear a boy to dare me. What's that got to do with spelling 'man'?" he added, half to himself.

But Uncle John had turned to Bob.

"Had a good day, my boy?"

"Haven't had fun enough," answered Bob, stoutly. "It is all Joe's fault, too. We boys wanted the pond to ourselves for one day, and we made up our minds that when the girls came, we would clear them off But Joe, he——"

"I think this is Joe's to tell," interrupted Uncle John. "How was it, boy?"

"Why," said Joe, "I thought the girls had as much right on the pond as the boys, so I spoke to one or two of the bigger boys, and they thought so, too, and we stopped it all. I thought it was mean to treat the girls that way."

There came a flash from Uncle John's pocket; the next minute the skates were on Joe's knees.

"The spelling-match is over," said Uncle John, "and Joe has won the prize."

Three bewildered faces mutely questioned him.

"Boys," he answered, gravely, "we've been spelling 'man,' not in letters, but in acts. I told you there were different ways, and we have proved it here tonight. Think it over, boys, and see."—Sunday School Evangelist.

JACK'S QUEER WAYS

Everybody liked Jack. He was a pleasant, manly boy, about fourteen years old, a boy who was on friendly terms with the whole world. His father was a physician, and his family lived in a small country town.

Of course Jack went to school. In the afternoon, when school was over, he always ran up to his mother's room to tell her, in his bright, boyish way, how the day had passed, and to see if she had any errands for him to do, always glad to help in any way he could. After this little chat with his mother, he would dash off into the yard to play, or to busy himself in some other way. But he was never far away, ready to be called any moment, and generally where he could be seen from some of the many windows of the big, old-fashioned house.

This had always been his custom until the winter of which I am speaking. This winter Jack seemed to have fallen into queer ways. He came home, to be sure, at the usual time, but, after the little visit with his mother, seemed to disappear entirely. For an hour and a half he positively could not be found. They could not see him, no matter which way they looked, and they could not even make him hear when they called.

This all seemed very strange, but he had always been a trusty boy, and his mother thought little of it at first. Still, as Jack continued to disappear, day after day, at the same hour, for weeks, she thought it best to speak to his father about it.

"How long does he stay out?" asked the doctor.

"Very often till the lamps are lighted," was the answer.

"Have you asked him where he goes?"

"Why, yes," the mother replied; "and that's the strangest part of it all! He seems so confused, and doesn't answer directly, but tries to talk about something else. I cannot understand it, but some way I do not believe he is doing wrong, for he looks right into my eyes, and does not act as if he had anything to be ashamed of."

"It is quite strange," said the doctor. Then he sat quiet for a long time. At last he said, "Well, little mother, I think we will trust the lad awhile longer, and say nothing more to him about it; though it is strange!"

Time passed on, and the mother looked anxious many an evening as she lighted the lamps and her boy was not home yet. And when at last he did come in, flushed and tired, and said not a word as to how he had spent his afternoon, she wondered more than ever.

This kept up all winter. Toward spring the doctor was slowly driving home one day just at twilight, when, as he passed a poor, forlorn cottage, he heard a rap on the window. He stopped his horse at once, got out of his gig, and walked to the door. He knocked, but no one opened, only a voice called, "Come in!"

He entered the shabby room, and found a poor old woman, lying on a miserable bed. The room was bare and cheerless except for the bright fire burning in the small stove, beside which lay a neat pile of wood. The doctor did what he could to ease the poor woman s sufferings, and then asked who lived with her to take care of her.

"Not a soul," she said. "I am all alone. I haven't a chick nor child in all the wide world!"

The doctor looked at the wood near the stove, and wondered to himself how the sick old woman could chop and pile it so nicely; but he said nothing, and she went on sadly:—

"I have had a hard time of it this winter, and I would have died sure if it hadn't been for that blessed boy."

"Why, I thought you lived alone, and had no children!" exclaimed the doctor.

"No more I haven't," she said. "I am all alone by me lone self, as I told ye, but the good Lord has been a-takin' care of me; for a bit of a boy, bless his heart! has been a-comin' here every day this winter for to help me. He chopped the wood the minister sent me, and brought some in here every night, and piled it up like that" (pointing to the sticks in the corner): "and the harder it stormed, the surer he seemed to come. He'd never so much as tell me where he lived, and I only know his name is——"

"Jack?" asked the doctor, with unsteady voice.

"Yes, sir; that's it. Do ye be knowing him, doctor?"

"I think perhaps I do," was the husky answer.

"Well, may the Lord bless him, and may he never be cold himself, the good lad!"

The doctor did not speak for a few moments; then he left, promising to send some one to care for the sick woman that night. He drove home very fast, and a strange dimness came into his eyes every now and then, as he thought it all over.

He went to his wife's room, and began, as usual, to tell her all that had happened during the day. When, at last, he came to his visit at the cottage, he watched his wife's face, as he told of the lonely, sick old woman, the warm fire, and the young chopper.

When he had finished, tears were in her eyes, but she only said, "Dear
Jack!"

Jack's queer ways were explained at last. And "Jack's old woman," as they called her, never wanted from this time for any comfort as long as she lived. So, after all, Jack could not feel so very sorry that his kindness, done in secret, had at last "found him out."—The Round Table.

My Missionary Garden

Some money I desired to earn
 To send to foreign lands,
So mother took some garden seeds
 And placed them in my hands.

Then earnestly I went to work
  With spade and rake and hoe;
I planted every seed I had,
  And wondered if they'd grow.

It wasn't long before I saw
  Some little leaves of green;
I thought they looked more beautiful
  Than any I had seen.

Each day when I came home from school,
  I to my garden went;
In hoeing and in pulling weeds,
  My leisure time I spent.

My mother said to me, "My child,
  You've worked so very well
I'll buy of you, if you desire,
  Whate'er you have to sell."

I never tasted anything
  So tender and so sweet;
I thanked the Lord most heartily
  For all I had to eat.

My mother is so good to me,
  But God is better still;
Whatever I can do for him,
  With all my heart I will.

DORA BRORSEN.

233

WHAT ONE BOY DID

"Don't tell me that boys have no influence," said the dark-eyed lady, with emphasis. "Why, I myself know a boy of twelve whose influence changed the manners of an entire hotel. Tell you about it?—Certainly. It was a family hotel on the seacoast in southern California, and almost all the guests in the house were there for the winter. We had become well acquainted, and—well, lazy I guess is the best word for it. So we decided that it was too much trouble to dress for meals, and dropped into the habit of coming in just as we chanced to be, from lounging in the hammock, or fishing off the pier, or bicycle riding down the beach. Our manners, too, had become about as careless as our dress; we were there for a rest, a good time, and these little things didn't matter, we said.

"One day there was a new arrival. Mrs. Blinn, a young widow, with her little son, Robert, as sturdy, bright-faced a lad of twelve as one often sees. The first time he came into the dining-room, erect, manly, with his tie and collar and dress in perfect order, escorting his mother as if she had been a princess, and standing till not only she, but every lady at the table was seated, we all felt that a breath of new air had come among us, and every one there, I think, straightened up a little. However we looked at one another and nodded our heads, as much as to say, 'He won't keep this up long.' We were strangers, and in the familiarity of every-day life we did not doubt that it would soon wear away.

"But it did not. Rob was full of life, and active and busy as a boy could well be. At the same time, when, twenty minutes before meals, his mother blew a little silver whistle, no matter where he was or what he was doing, everything was dropped, and he ran in to make himself ready. And every time he came to the table, with his clean face and smooth hair and clothes carefully arranged or changed, he was in himself a sermon on neatness and self-respect, which, though none of us said much about it, we felt all the same. Then by and by one and another began to respond to the little silver whistle, as well as Rob. One laid aside a bicycle dress, another a half-invalid negligee, till you could hardly have believed it was the same company of a few weeks before.

"It was the same with manners. Rob's politeness, simple, unaffected, and unfailing, at the table, on the veranda, upon the beach, wherever you met him; his readiness to be helpful; his deference to those older; his thoughtfulness for all, was the best lesson,— that of example. As a consequence, the thoughtless began to remember, and the selfish to feel ashamed, and the careless to keep themselves more in hand.

"And so, as I said in the beginning, in less than a month the whole atmosphere of that hotel had been changed by the influence of one boy; and the only one utterly unconscious of this was Rob himself."

This is truly a pleasing incident. We like to think of this boy who, because he was at heart a true little gentleman, drew what was kindly and courteous and gracious in those about him to the surface as by a magnet. In like manner it is possible for every boy to be so true and kindly and tender, so unselfish of action, so obedient to duty, so responsive to conscience, that, wherever he goes, he shall carry an inspiring atmosphere and influence with him; and whoever he meets shall, because of him, be drawn to better thoughts and nobler living.—Adele E. Thompson.

*H*OW NICK LEARNED MANNERS

"Hallo, Doc! Where'd you get that horse?" called Nick Hammond as he approached his father and Dr. Morris, as they were talking at the gate one evening.

"Why, halloo, little man! I got this horse over the river. Ever see him before?" answered the old doctor, genially, little thinking that he was somewhat to blame for Nick's lack of good manners in thus accosting an older person.

When the doctor had gone, Mr. Hammond called Nick to him and said, "Nick, did not your mother tell you last evening not to say, 'Halloo,' when you meet people?"

Nick's eyes fell, for he remembered, and he said, "Yes, sir."

"Then why did you say it to Dr. Morris this evening?"

"O, I don't think he cares what I say to him!"

"No, I do not suppose he does care; but I do, and I think if your mother had heard you address the doctor as Doc, she would have been very much ashamed; for she has tried very hard to teach you good manners."

"Well, everybody says 'Halloo,' papa, and I can't help it, and I'm sure Mr.
Evans said 'Doc' when he was talking out there this evening."

"It is true that a great many people do use both those words, but that is no reason why you should use them, when you have been told not to do so. There is also some difference, I think, between the age of Mr. Evans and yourself. Men can say things to one another that would be quite improper for a boy to say to a man. Now I want you to be more careful, and speak respectfully to every one you meet."

Nick went to his play, but he took up a string of reasoning like this: "Because I am the only boy mama has set out to make me as good as Mabel, and she doesn't allow me to use slang nor anything of the kind. I know if there were half a dozen boys here, it would be different. I suppose it is all right for girls and women, but, bah! I can't be a goody-goody. I am only a boy. I guess it won't pay to bother about good manners, like a girl. I am too busy these days, when there is no school, to learn manners or anything else, anyway," and he went off with his goat, to forget everything else.

Time after time Nick failed to heed what he had been told, and each time he had to suffer a just penalty; but it seemed as if he never could learn manners. The real reason was that he had no desire to have good manners.

One morning Mrs. Hammond said: "Now, Nick, I am expecting your Aunt Ella and Uncle Alfred today, and I want you to be on your guard while they are here, and not act as if you were a backwoods boy who does not know anything. I especially want you to be gentlemanly; for Uncle Alfred is such a stranger to us yet that he will not understand you, and will think less of your papa and myself for seeing you rude and ill-mannered. You see, you owe it to yourself to make every one like you as much as possible. They live so far away that it may be a long time before they will see you again."

"Well, I should like to see my new Uncle Alf. I hope they won't stay long; for I do hate to be afraid to halloo and do things."

"Now, don't say Uncle Alf, Nick. You know better than that. Say Uncle Alfred, but don't say it too often. As for making a noise, you can relieve yourself when away from the house, but I do not want you to talk when others are talking, and, above all, do not contradict them, no matter what they say."

"All right, mama, I'll try," promised Nick.

But, alas for his promise! It belonged to the large family of promises that Nick had been making for many months. It was as easily broken as a broom straw. Aunt Ella and her husband, who was president of a great Western college, were not long in seeing the worst side of little Nick. He repeatedly did the very things his mama had urged him not to do, and was recklessly disobedient in general.

The last day of the visit was to be spent with some distinguished friends of Uncle Alfred's at the Lake House, nine miles away. Mr. and Mrs. Hammond were going with them, and Nick was determined to go, too. When his mama went to her room to get ready, Nick followed her and begged her to take him. "No, Nick," she said, in a positive way, "I shall not take you anywhere until you learn to behave as a boy of your age should. Go to the dining-room and wait there until we are ready to start, and then you can come down to Grandma Hammond's and stay until four o'clock."

He knew that it was no use to tease, so he went to the couch in the dining-room. He felt very sullen and bitter, and threw himself down on the friendly pillows to indulge in a few tears. In a few moments he heard subdued voices on the veranda just outside the window. Aunt Ella was saying, "I know they would both enjoy the drive this lovely day." "Of course they would," said Uncle Alfred, "and I would like to have them with us, but what would Dr. and Mrs. Watson think of Nick? He surely is the rudest child I have ever known. I am sorry to cheat Mabel out of pleasure, for she is a dear little girl, but really Ella, I should be ashamed of Nick's behavior, shouldn't you?"

Nick waited to hear no more. He slipped out quickly, and said to the cook in the kitchen, "Please tell mama I didn't wait; I've gone to grandma's."

He was so quiet and gentle all day that Grandma Hammond worried a great deal, saying: "I never saw the like of it. The boy is either sick or something is going to happen to him."

That something had already happened to him, but grandma was not aware of it. For the first time in his life, Nick felt ashamed of himself. During that long, long day he made a strong resolution, which he never purposely broke, never to do anything to make himself or anybody else ashamed.—Atwood Miller, in Youth's Evangelist.

* * * * *

"O! There are many actors who can play

Greatly great parts, but rare indeed the soul
Who can be great when cast for some small role;
Yet that is what the world most needs,—big hearts
That will shine forth and glorify poor parts
In this strange drama, Life."

ᵁᵂITHOUT BALLAST

Not many years ago the "Escambia," a British iron steamer, loaded with wheat, weighed anchor and started down the bay of San Francisco. The pilot left her about five miles outside the Golden Gate. Looking back from his pilot-boat a short time after, he saw the vessel stop, drift into the trough of the sea, careen to port, both bulwarks going under water, then suddenly capsize and sink. What was the cause of this sad catastrophe?—A want of ballast.

She came into port from China, a few weeks previous, with a thousand emigrants on board. But she had in her hold immense tanks for what is called water ballast. The captain, wishing to carry all the wheat he could between decks, neglected to fill those tanks. He thought the cargo would steady the ship. But it made it top-heavy, and the first rough sea capsized it.

Here, then, was a vessel, tight and strong, with powerful engines, with a cargo worth one hundred thousand dollars, floundering as soon as she left the harbor, taken down with her crew of forty-five men, because the captain failed to have her properly ballasted. The moment she began to lurch, all the wheat tumbled over to the lower side, and down into the sea she went.

How this wreck of the "Escambia" repeats the trite lesson that so many have tried to teach, and that they who need it most are so slow to learn! Young men starting out in life want to carry as little ballast as possible. They are enterprising, ambitious. They are anxious to go fast, and take as much cargo as they can. Old-fashioned principles are regarded as dead weight. It does not pay to heed them, and they thrown overboard. Good home habits are abandoned in order to be popular with the gay and worldly. The Bible is not read, the Sabbath is not kept holy, prayer is neglected, and lo! some day, when all the sails are spread, a sudden temptation comes that wrecks the character and life.

We cannot urge too strongly upon the young, in these days

of intense activity, the vital importance of ballast. A conscience seems to be an encumbrance—an obstacle to prosperity. But it is a safe thing to have on board. It steadies the soul. It keeps it from careening when the winds drive it into the trough of the sea. If the "Escambia" had taken less wheat and more ballast, it might be afloat today. And this is true of many a man now in prison or in the gutter. The haste to be rich, the impatience of restraint, alas! how their wrecks lie just outside the world's golden gates.—Selected.

Reflex Influence

The artist Hoffmann, it is said, became
In features like the features that he strove
To paint,—those of his Lord. Unconsciously
His thoughts developed in his face that which
He sought upon the canvas to portray;
And with the walls about him covered o'er
With pictures he had made, he toiled and thought
And gave the world his ideal of the Christ,
Becoming more and more like him.

And thus
May we by thinking o'er and o'er again
Christ's thoughts, and dwelling on his love, become
In heart as he, all undefiled and pure,—
Perfect within. The beauty sweet and joy
Of holiness, communion with our God,
The prayer of faith, the song of praise, and all
The peace and uplift grand that Jesus knew
May be our own, our very own, to give
Unto a world made sick and sad by sin.

ELIZA H. MORTON.

INFLUENCE OF A GOOD BOOK

I lost my Christian mother when I was a youth, but not before the instruction I had received from her beloved lips had made a deep impression upon my mind, an impression which I carried with me into a college (Hampden, Sidney), where there was not then one pious student. There I often reflected, when surrounded by young men who scoffed at religion, upon the instruction of my mother, and my conscience was frequently sore distressed. I had no Bible, and dreaded getting one, lest it should be found in my possession.

At last I could stand it no longer, and requested a particular friend, a youth whose parents lived near, and who often went home, to ask his excellent mother to send me some religious books. She sent me "Alleine's Alarm," an old black book, which looked as if it might have been handled by successive generations for a hundred years.

When I received it, I locked my door and sat down to read it, when a student knocked at the door. I gave him no answer, dreading to be found reading such a book, but he continued to knock and beat the door until I had to open it. He came in, and seeing the book lying on the bed, seized it, and examined its title. Then he said, "Why, Hill, do you read such books?"

I hesitated, but God enabled me to be decided, and to tell him boldly, but with much emotion, "Yes, I do."

The young man replied with much agitation: "O Hill, you may obtain religion, but I never can! I came here a professor of religion; but through fear I dissembled it, and have been carried along with the wicked, until I fear there is no hope for me."

He told me that there were two others who he believed were somewhat serious. We agreed to take up the subject of religion in earnest, and seek it together. We invited the other two, and held a prayer-meeting in my room on the next Saturday afternoon. And,

O, what a prayer-meeting! We knew not how to pray, but tried to do it. We sang in a suppressed manner, for we feared the other students. But they found us out, and gathered round the door, and made such a noise that the officers had to disperse them.

So serious was the disturbance that the president, the late excellent Rev. Dr. John B. Smith, investigated the matter at prayers that evening in the chapel hall. When he demanded the reason of the riot, a ringleader in wickedness rose up and stated that it was occasioned by three or four of the boys holding prayer-meetings, and they were determined to have no such doings there. The good president heard the statement with deep emotion, and, looking at the youths charged with the sin of praying, said, with tears in his eyes, "O, is there such a state of things in this college? Then God has come near to us. My dear young friends, you shall hold your next meeting in my parlor." We did hold our next meeting in his parlor, and half the college was there. And there began a glorious revival of religion, which pervaded the college, and spread into the country around.

Many of those students became ministers of the gospel. The youth who brought me "Alleine's Alarm" from his mother was my friend, the Rev. C. Stitt, who is preaching in Virginia. And he who interrupted me in reading the work, my venerable and worthy friend, the Rev. Dr. H., is now president of a college in the West.—Selected.

¶TRAIGHTENING OUT THE FURROWS"

"Boys," he said, "I have been trying every day of my life for the last two years to straighten out furrows, and I cannot do it."

One boy turned his head in surprise toward the captain's neatly kept place.

"O, I do not mean that kind, lad! I do not mean land furrows," continued the captain, so soberly that the attention of the boys became breathless as he went on: "When I was a lad about the age of you boys, I was what they call a 'hard case,' not exactly bad or vicious, but wayward and wild. Well, my dear old mother used to coax, pray, and punish. My father was dead, making it all the harder for her, but she never got impatient. How in the world she bore all my stubborn, vexing ways so patiently will always be to me one of the mysteries of life. I knew it was troubling her, knew it was changing her pretty face, making it look anxious and old. After a while, tired of all restraint, I ran away, went off to sea; and a rough time I had of it at first. Still I liked the water, and I liked journeying around from place to place.

"Then I settled down to business in a foreign land, and soon became prosperous. Now I began sending her something besides empty letters. And such beautiful letters as she always wrote me during those years of absence. At length I noticed how long they grew, longing for the son who used to try her so, and it awoke a corresponding longing in my heart to go back to the clear waiting soul. So when I could stand it no longer, I came back, and such a welcome, and such a surprise!

"My mother is not a very old lady, boys, but the first thing I noticed was the whiteness of her hair and the deep furrows on her brow; and I knew I had helped to blanch that hair to its snowy whiteness and had drawn those lines in that smooth forehead. And those are the furrows I have been trying to straighten out.

"But last night, while mother was asleep in her armchair, I was thinking it all over, and looked to see what progress I had made. Her face was very peaceful, and the expression as contented as possible, but the furrows are still there. I have not succeeded in straightening them out—and—I—never—shall,—never.

"When they lay my mother, my fair old sweetheart, in her casket, there will be furrows on her brow; and I think it a wholesome lesson to teach you, that the neglect you offer your parents' counsel now, and the trouble you cause them, will abide, my lads, it will abide!"

"But," broke in Freddie Hollis, with great, troubled eyes, "I should think if you are so kind and good now, it need not matter so much!"

"Ah, Freddie," said the quavery voice of the strong man, "you cannot undo the past. You may do much to atone for it, do much to make the rough path smooth, but you cannot straighten out the old furrows; remember that."

"Guess I'll go and chop some wood mother spoke of. I had most forgotten," said lively Jimmy Hollis, in a strangely quiet tone for him.

"Yes, and I have some errands to do," suddenly remembered Billy Bowles.

"Touched and taken!" said the kindly captain to himself, as the boys tramped off, keeping step in a soldier-like way.

Mrs. Bowles declared a fortnight afterward that Billy was "really getting to be a comfort!" And Mrs. Hollis, meeting the captain about that time, remarked that Jimmy always meant to be a good boy, but now he was actually being one.

"Guess your stories they like so much have good morals in them now and then," added the gratified mother, with a smile.

As Mrs. Hollis passed, Captain Sam, with folded arms and head bent down, said softly to himself, "Well, I shall be thankful if a word of mine will help the dear boys to keep furrows from their mothers' brows; for, once there, it is a difficult task to straighten them out."—Selected.

* * * * *

"If you were busy being good,
And doing just the best you could,
You'd not have time to blame some man
Who's doing just the best he can.

"If you were busy being true
To what you know you ought to do,
You'd be so busy you'd forget
The blunders of the folks you've met.

"If you were busy being right,
You'd find yourself too busy quite
To criticize your neighbor long
Because he's busy being wrong."

A BOY WHO WAS WANTED

"Well, I have found out one thing," said Jack as, hot, tired, and dusty, he came to his mother.

"What is that?" she asked.

"That there are a great many boys in the world."

"Didn't you know that before?"

"Partly; but I didn't know there were so many more boys than are wanted."

"Why do you think there are more than are wanted?"

"Because I have been 'round and 'round till I am worn out, trying to find a place to work. Wherever I go, there are more boys than places. Doesn't that show that there are too many boys?"

"Not exactly," said his mother, with a smile. "It depends entirely on the kind of boy. A good boy is always wanted somewhere."

"Well, if I am a good boy, I wish that I knew that I was wanted."

"Patience, patience, my boy. In such a great world as this is, with so many places and so many boys, it is no wonder some of them do not find their places at once. But be sure, dear," as she laid a very caressing hand on his arm, "that every boy who wants a chance to do fair, honest work will find it."

"That's the kind of work I want to do," said Jack. "I don't want anybody's money for nothing. Let me see, what have I to offer?— All the schooling and all the wits I have been able to get up in thirteen years; good, stout hands; and a civil tongue."

"And a mind and heart set on doing faithful duty, suggested his mother.

"I hope so," said Jack. "I remember father used to say: Just as soon as you undertake to work for any one, you must bear in mind that you have sold yourself for the given time. Your time, your strength, your energy, are his, and your best efforts to seek his interests in every way are his due.'"

The earnest tone in which the boy spoke seemed to give assurance that he would pay good heed to the words of the father whose counsel could no more reach him.

For two or three days longer Jack had reason to hold his opinion that there were more boys than the world wanted, at the end of which time he met a business man who, questioning him closely, said: "There are a great many applications for the place, but a large number of the boys come and stay a short time, and then leave if they think they can do a little better. When a boy gets used to our route and customers, we want him to stay. If you will agree to stay at least three years, we will agree to pay you three dollars a week as errand boy."

"That is just what I wanted to do, sir," said Jack, eagerly. So he was installed, and proud enough he was to bring his wages home every week, and realize that, small as they were, the regular help was of great value to his mother.

It is not to be wondered at that the faithful carrying out of his father's admonition after a while attracted the attention not only of his employers, but of others with whom he was brought in contact in the pursuit of his duties. One day he was asked into the office of Mr. Lang, a gentleman to whom he frequently carried parcels of value.

"Have you ever thought of changing your situation?" asked Mr. Lang.

"No, sir," said Jack.

"Perhaps you could do better," said the other. "I want a boy who is quick and intelligent, and who can be relied on; and, from what I see of you, I think you are that sort of boy. I want you to drive a delivery wagon, and will pay you five dollars a week."

Jack's eyes opened wide.

"It is wonderfully good pay for a boy like me, I am sure. But I promised to keep on with Mr. Hill for three years, and the second year is only just begun."

"Well, have you signed a regular agreement with Mr. Hill?"

"No, sir; I told him I would stay."

"You have a mother to assist, you told me. Could not you tell Mr. Hill that you feel obliged to do better, when you have a chance?"

"I don't believe I could," said Jack, looking with his straight, frank gaze into the gentleman's face. "You see, sir, if I broke my word with him, I should not be the kind of boy to be relied on that you want."

"I guess you are about right," said Mr. Lang, with a sigh. "Come and see me when your time is out; I dare say I shall want you then."

Jack went home very much stirred by what had been said to him.

After all, could it be wrong to go where he would do so much better? Was it not really his duty to accept the position? He could then drive the wagon instead of trudging wearily along the streets. They had never felt so hot and dusty as they did just now, when he might escape from the tiresome routine. Might, but how?—By the sacrifice of his pledged word; by selling his truth and his honor. So strongly did the reflection force itself upon him that when he told his mother of the offer he had received, he merely added, "It would be a grand good thing if I could take it, wouldn't it, mother?"

"Yes, it would."

"Some boys would change without thinking of letting a promise stand in their way."

"Yes, but that is the kind of boy who, sooner or later, is not wanted. It is because you have not been that sort of boy that you are wanted now."

Jack worked away, doing such good work, as he became more and more accustomed to the situation, that his mother sometimes wondered that Mr. Hill, who seemed always kindly interested in him, never appeared to think of raising his pay. This, however, was not Mr. Hill's way of doing things, even though he showed an increasing disposition to trust Jack with important business.

So the boy trudged through the three years, at the end of them having been trusted far more than is usually the case with errand boys. He had never forgotten the offer made by Mr. Lang, and one day, meeting that gentleman on the street, ventured to remind him that his present engagement was nearly out, adding, "You spoke to me about driving the wagon, sir."

"Ah, so I did; but you are older now and worth more. Call around and see me."

One evening, soon after, Jack lingered in Mr. Hill's office after the other errand boys had been paid and had gone away.

"My three years are up tonight, sir," he said.

"Yes, they are," said Mr. Hill, looking at him as if he had remembered it.

"Will you give me a recommendation to some one else, sir?"

"Well, I will, if you are sure that you want to leave me."

"I did not know that you wanted me to stay, but"—he hesitated, and then went on—"my mother is a widow, and I feel as if I ought to do the best I can for her, and Mr. Lang told me to call on him."

"Has Mr. Lang ever made you an offer?"

Jack told him what Mr. Lang had said nearly two years before.

"Why didn't you go then?" asked Mr. Hill.

"Because I had promised to stay with you; but you wouldn't blame me for trying to better myself now?"

"Not a bit of it. Are you tired of running errands?"

"I'd rather ride than walk," said Jack with a smile.

"I think it is about time you were doing better than either. Perhaps you think that you have been doing this faithful work for me through these years for next to nothing; but if so, you are mistaken. You have been doing better work than merely running errands. You have been serving an apprenticeship to trust and honesty. I know you now to be a straight-forward, reliable boy, and it takes time to learn that. It is your capital, and you ought to begin to realize it. You may talk to Mr. Lang if you wish, but I will give you a place in the office, with a salary of six hundred dollars for the first year, with the prospect of a raise after that."

Jack did not go to see Mr. Lang, but straight to his mother, with a shout and a bound.

"You're right, you're right, mother!" he cried. "No more hard work for you, mother. I'm wanted, you see, wanted enough to get good pay! All the hardest part is over."—Congregationalist.

WANTED: AN EMPLOYER

There was a north-bound car temporarily disabled on Broadway, near Fourth Street, and, in consequence, as far south as the eye could reach stood a row of motionless cars. Also, in consequence, along the curb was ranged a fretting, impatient, helpless crowd, among whom the most anxious was probably Edward Billings Henry.

In stature Edward Billings Henry was briefer than his name would indicate, but to a certain two-room dwelling on Jackson Street he made up in importance what he lacked in height; and it was his overwhelming sense of this importance which made every thin muscle taut and strained every nerve as he stood in the forefront of the crowd, his bare feet planted on the cold asphalt, one hand gripping his remaining stock of papers, the other clutching a nickel.

"I never was in a tearing hurry in my life but that this thing happened!" exploded a man just behind the boy.

Edward Billings Henry turned and looked up. The man was jingling a lot of loose coins in his pocket. The boy looked at his one nickel, and said, with conviction, "You can't need to have 'em go like I do."

The big man stared down at the little man, in surprise, with a gruff "Huh?" but Edward Billings Henry had no time to repeat. His hope had revived. The two men who lay on their backs under the injured car began to crawl out, and the boy rushed forward.

"Will it go now?" he inquired of one of the numerous conductors clustered around.

"Maybe so—in half an hour," replied the conductor, carelessly.

"O," cried the boy, in dismay, "I just can't wait that long!"

"Walk, then!" said the conductor, crossly.

"It's too far," replied the boy, "when you've got a stone toe."

"A what?" ejaculated the conductor; but his voice was lost in the honk! honk! of a big white touring car which pushed slowly through the crowd.

In front of the car Edward Billings Henry raced limpingly on his stone toe back to the curb and to the man jingling the coins in his pocket.

"Just what time is it, please?" he asked.

The man pulled out a watch and showed it to him. Edward Billings Henry heaved a great sigh.

"Half past ten! It'll likely be filled up before I can get there."

"What will be?"

"The place I'm after."

Skilfully he raised the limping foot, laid it across the other leg, and nursed the stone-bruised big toe, his eyes on the automobile, which had halted almost in front of him.

"Halloo, Junius!" a voice in the crowd sang out. "Lucky man you, not to have to depend on street-cars!"

The driver of the car was a young man. That is, Edward Billings Henry judged him to be young by the only feature visible, a flexible, wide mouth, with clean-shaven lips. His eyes were behind goggles, and a cap covered his forehead and ears, meeting the tip of a high collar, which effectually concealed his chin. But the mouth smiled as the goggles turned toward the pavement, the owner answering lightly:—

"Halloo yourself, Dick! Jump in and try my luck."

"Where are you going?"

"Up to Congress Square."

"Well, get along then!" returned the other. "That's no good to me."

Congress Square! What luck! Exactly where Edward Billings Henry wished to go! And here was a rapid-transit vehicle, with room enough for ten such diminutive persons as he! Without loss of time, he limped up on his aching stone toe and jogged the arm of the driver.

Junius looked down at the boy. Edward Billings Henry removed a man's derby from his head and looked out of eyes kindling with hope, as he asked eagerly:—

"Do you suppose you could get me up there inside of twenty-five minutes, mister?"

"What do you mean?" Junius stared hard through his goggles.

"To Congress Square," said Edward Billings Henry, impatiently. "It's business, and if I don't get there I'm out of a job, that's all." The boy mounted the step and clung to the seat, proffering his nickel. "I'll pay just what I'd pay on the car," he argued, "so you'd be making some money as well as giving me a lift."

The goggled eyes looked at the nickel in the dirty hand, and then traveled up and down the small figure back of the hand. The eyes noticed that while those parts of the boy's anatomy which had been exposed all the morning to the city dirt had collected grime, the rims, as it were, of the exposed parts revealed hidden cleanliness.

"Congress Square is an awful way up," urged Edward Billings Henry, "and we mustn't waste much time; for I would like to get that job." The small hand extended the nickel enticingly toward the glove. "You'll be earning as much as the street-car by giving a lift," the boy repeated.

The driver's lips twisted a bit. "That's so," he said. "Huh!" he chuckled, and gracelessly extended his hand for the nickel. "Get in, my man, and I'll give you the lift."

Edward Billings Henry drew a deep sigh of relief dropped the coin into the other's palm, and engulfed himself in the soft front seat.

"Whom have I the honor of giving a lift?" asked Junius, formally, dropping the nickel into a pocket, where it lay alone. After it he sent a curious, lingering smile.

"Edward Billings Henry, Junior," replied the boy.

The lips beneath the goggles smiled. "And where am I lifting you to, may I also ask, Edward Billings?"

"To Mr. Florins's office, where they're going to select an office boy this morning 'tween ten and eleven."

The driver busied himself a moment with the steering-gear as the car passed the crowded mail-wagons behind the post-office building. Then he turned and shot a curious glance at his small companion, asking abruptly:—

"And you think you'll get the job, do you?"

Edward Billings Henry leaned forward as if he could push the machine into a yet faster pace. "I can try for it," he replied. "Father says you never know what you can do unless you try. He's always wanting me to try."

"Yes," muttered Junius, still more interested. "Fathers seem much alike, whether they live up-town or down-town."

"Can't we go faster?" asked Edward Billings Henry, sitting on the edge of the seat.

Junius shook his head. "Too many blue-coats around. But about that job, now—you'll not be the only boy after it. There will probably be dozens older——"

"I'm eleven, if I am small," interrupted the boy.

"And stronger——"

The boy stretched out a thin arm defiantly, and closed his fist. "Just feel!" he cried. "I've got a good muscle, and on my legs it's better yet. Just now I've got a stone-bruise on my big toe, but I tell you I can get round pretty fast just the same. I don't believe Mr. Florins would ever be sorry he took me."

"Yes, I'm inclined to believe that myself," mused the man. "But how are you going to make him believe that in the beginning?"

The boy raised his lame foot and gently rubbed the swollen big toe. "Well," he began, "I'm going to talk up big. Father says you have to sometimes when nobody's round to do it for you, and he says it's all right if you do afterward just as big as you talk."

The driver wagged his head wisely. "That's sound business sense," he agreed, gravely. "You intend to deliver the same goods that you sell. Let's hear what you have to say."

"Well, if you get me there in time to say anything, I'm going to tell Mr. Florins that father went to school a lot when he was young. He went through high school and got all ready to go through college."

Edward Billings emphasized his verbs as if "going through" was solely a physical exercise on the flying-wedge order; and Junius chuckled.

"Then I'll tell him that father stood almost at the head of his class in high school, and he almost took a lot of honors."

"Well," assented Junius, "that 'almost' is a step farther than some of the rest of us got."

"Yes," exulted the boy, "I guess Mr. Florins will say so, too. Then I'll tell him that father taught a lot when he couldn't go through college."

"What next?" inquired Junius.

They were approaching Twelfth Street now, and the car was hardly moving in the press of vehicles.

Edward Billings curled his bare toes under, and unconsciously pushed forward with all his slender might. "Then I'll tell him that father used to read a lot, law books and things, same as he does——"

"But see here!" interrupted Junius. "All this talk will be about your father. What are you going to say about yourself?"

A cloud overspread Edward Billings's face. He raised a pair of troubled eyes to his questioner. "Why, I never stopped to think of that," he began, slowly, all the brightness fading out of his tone. "There's nothing much to say about me. I sell papers and help father——"

"What does your father do?" asked Junius.

The boy hesitated. His face flushed, and he looked up uncertainly at the goggles. "He used to teach, I told you," was the evasive answer, "until his eyes gave out."

"And now?"

Edward Billings Henry wriggled about on the padded leather. "He's always had bad legs,"—the evasion continued,—"but his arms and back are strong, and his legs all right to stand on."

"Yes?" insisted Junius, and waited.

"So he's doing something he ain't going to do if I can get this job. Then I could sell papers after and before office hours, and earn a lot of money." Edward Billings Henry talked rapidly, but the young man beside him was not to be turned from his purpose.

"Then what is it he's not going to do?"

The boy hesitated again. "Father takes in washing," he finally burst out, proudly defiant, "and I help him, and we do it good, I tell you! No one ever complains. Father says if you can't do what you want to, you can try something else, and that was all he could do, so he tried, and found out he could wash and iron good, and a lot of it!"

Junius considerately looked straight ahead of him, not wishing to add to the embarrassment of Edward Billings Henry, Junior, but he could not resist asking, "Are you going to tell this to Mr. Florins?"

"No-sir-ee!" responded the boy, proudly. "Father ain't going to do—washings—any longer if I can get the job."

The car entered Congress Square, drew up in front of an imposing stone building, and stopped. The driver removed his goggles and turned a pair of pleasant gray eyes on the boy.

"Well, Edward Billings, here we are, and you've got the job all right. Can you come in the morning?"

Edward Billings Henry nearly fell off the seat.

"W-hat?" he stammered.

"The job is yours," smiled the young man. "I happen to be that same Mr. Florins who, you have assured me, will never regret employing you. My office is on the second floor here. I did advertise for a boy, but had totally forgotten it." He gave a short laugh. "Report in the morning, please, and we'll see about a suit and some shoes and that stone-bruised toe."

Out of the automobile Edward Billings Henry tumbled in a dazed condition, and stood beside his new employer, looking up speechlessly.

"I'll advance you a car fare on your salary," the young man continued. He carefully avoided the pocket where lay the nickel previously owned by his passenger, and produced the change. "And, Edward Billings, just tell your father from me that his maxims work out so well that I'm thinking of adopting them myself."—Alice Louise Lee, in Youth's Companion, used by permission.

$\mathcal{H}$OW TO STOP SWEARING

When I was out West thirty years ago I was preaching one day in the open air when a man drove up in a fine turnout. After listening for a while he put his whip to his fine-looking steed, and away he went. I did not expect to see him again, but the next night he came back; and he kept on coming regularly night after night.

I said to a gentleman: "Who is that man who drives up here every night? Is he interested?"

"Interested! I should think not. You should have heard the way he talked about you today."

"Well," I said, "that is a sign he is interested."

I asked where he lived, but my friend told me not to go to see him; for he would only curse me. I said, "It takes God to curse a man: man can only bring curses on his own head."

I found out where he lived, and went to see him. He was the wealthiest man within a hundred miles of that place, and had a wife and seven beautiful children. Just as I reached his gate, I saw him coming out of the front door. I stepped up to him, and said:—

"You are Mr. Davis, I believe?"

He said, "Yes, sir, that is my name." Then he asked, "What do you want?"

"Well," I said, "I should like to ask you a question, if you won't be angry."

"Well, what is it?"

"I am told that God has blessed you above all men in this part of the country; that he has given you wealth, a beautiful Christian wife, and seven lovely children. I do not know whether it is true, but I hear that all he gets in return is cursing and blasphemy."

He said, "Come in, come in." I went in. "Now," he said, "what you said out there is true. If any man has a fine wife, I am the man, and I have a lovely family of children, and God has been good to me. But, do you know, we had company here the other night, and I cursed my wife at the table, and did not know it till after the company was gone. I never felt so mean and contemptible in my life as when my wife told me of it. She said she wanted the floor to open and let her down out of her seat. If I have tried once, I have tried a hundred times to stop swearing. You preachers don't know anything about it."

"Yes," I said, "I know all about it; I have been a traveler."

"But," he said, "you don't know anything about a business man's troubles.
When he is harassed and tormented the whole time, he can't help swearing."

"O, yes," I said, "he can. I know something about it. I myself used to swear."

"What! you used to swear?" he asked. "How did you stop?"

"I never stopped."

"Why, you don't swear now, do you?"

"No, I have not sworn for years."

"How did you stop?"

"I never stopped. It stopped itself."

He said, "I don't understand this."

"No," I said, "I know you don't. But I came to talk to you so that you will never want to swear again as long as you live."

I began to tell him about Christ in the heart; how he would take the temptation to swear out of a man.

"Well," he said, "how am I to get Christ?"

"Get right down here and tell him what you want."

"But," he said, "I was never on my knees in my life. I have been cursing all the day, and I don't know how to pray, or what to pray for."

"Well," I said, "it is mortifying to call on God for mercy when you have never used his name except in oaths, but he will not turn you away. Ask God to forgive you, if you want to be forgiven."

He knelt down and prayed, only a few sentences. After he prayed, he rose and said, "What shall I do now?"

I said, "Go down to the church, and tell the people there that you want to be an out-and-out Christian."

"I cannot do that," he said; "I never go to church except to some funeral."

"Then it is high time for you to go for something else," I said.

At the next church meeting the man was there, and I sat right in front of him. He stood up and put his hands on the seat, and he trembled so much that I could feel the seat shake. He said:—

"My friends, you know all about me; if God can save a wretch like me, I want to have you pray for my salvation."

That was thirty years ago. Some time since I was back in that town, but did not see him. But when I was in California, a man asked me to have dinner with him. I told him I could not do so. Then he asked me if I remembered him, and told me his name.

"O!" I exclaimed. "Tell me, have you ever sworn since that night you knelt in your drawing-room, and asked God to help you?"

"No," he replied, "I have never had a desire to swear since then."—D.L. Moody, in "Weighed in the Balances," Published by Morgan &

Scott.

THE CAROLS OF BETHLEHEM CENTER

There might have been no church had not the Rev. James McKenzie come just when it seemed tottering to a fall. There might have been no Sunday-school had not Harold Thornton tended it as carefully as he tended his own orchard. There might have been no class number four had it not been for Gertrude Windsor. But there would have been no glad tidings in one wintry heart save for the voices with which Eddie and the two Willies and Charlie and little Phil sang the carols that morning in the snow; and they came straight from Him who gave the angels the songs of, "On earth peace, good will to men."

At the end of the winter term in Gertrude's junior year the doctor had prescribed a year of rest for her, and she had come to find it with Aunt Mehitable, in the quiet of Bethlehem Center.

On her first Sunday she attended the little Sunday-school, and at the close of service there was an official conference.

"She would be just the one if she would," said the pastor.

"It can't go on as it is," answered the superintendent. "The deacon means well, but he doesn't know boys. There wasn't one here today, and only Eddie last Sunday. I wish she'd be chorister, too," he added. "Did you hear her sing?"

"I doubt if she would do that. I am told she nearly broke down in college, and is here to rest."

"Yes, so Mr. Thompson told me. But we do need her."

"Well, I will call on her, and let you know what I learn."

Gertrude hesitated; for had not the doctor said "It is not so

much college,
Miss Windsor; it is church and Sunday-school and Christian
Endeavor and
Student Volunteer, and all the rest on top of college work that
is breaking
you down, and you must stop it"?

But the wistful face of Harry, who brought their milk, decided
her; and the second Sunday saw her instructing Eddie and little
Phil in the quarterly temperance lesson. It was not until school
was over that she learned the reason of little Phil's conscious
silence; and next day, when she met him with his father on the
street, she tried to atone for her former ignorance.

"Are you Phil's father?" she asked, stepping toward them.

Tim Shartow, who was believed by some to regard neither God,
man, nor the devil, grew strangely embarrassed as he took her
hand, after a hurried inspection of his own.

"Yes'm," he answered.

"I am to be his Sunday-school teacher," she went on; "and of
course I want to know the fathers and mothers of my boys. I hope
Phil can come regularly. We are going to have some very interesting lessons."

"I guess he can come," answered his father. "It's a better place
for him than on the street, anyway."

This was faint praise, but well meant. Gertrude smiled her
appreciation, and in that brief meeting won not only Phil's lifelong regard, but, had she known it, that of his father as well; for
thenceforth Tim Shartow felt that he had two friends in Bethlehem Center of whom he need not be ashamed.

His other friend was the Rev. James McKenzie. The mutu-
al though qualified respect which they felt for each other dated
from their first meeting, when Mr. McKenzie had walked into the
saloon and asked permission to tack up some bills advertising his
revival services.

"I guess you can," the proprietor had answered, standing alertly on his guard.

The bills had been posted, and the unwonted visitor turned to the man behind the bar. They were alone together.

"We should be very glad, Mr. Shartow," he said, "if you would attend some of the meetings."

"It'll be a cold day when I do," answered the saloon-keeper.

Mr. McKenzie did not reply.

"The worst enemies I've got are in that church," added Tim, by way of explanation.

A smile lighted up the pastor's earnest face. "No, Mr. Shartow," he said, "you're wrong. They don't like your business,—I don't like your business,—but you haven't an enemy in our church. And I want to tell you now"—his foot was upon the bar rail, and he was looking straight into the eyes of the man to whom he spoke—"that every night, as I pray that God will remove this saloon, I shall pray that he will bring you to know my Saviour. And if ever you need help that I can give, I want you to feel free to come to me. We are traveling different roads, Mr. Shartow, but we are not enemies; we are friends."

And the pastor departed, leaving Tim, the saloonkeeper, "that shook up," to use his own phrase, that it is doubtful whether he ever entirely regained his former attitude toward "them church folks."

By Gertrude's second Sunday as teacher, the two Willies had come to test the truth of rumors that had reached them. Charlie and Harry came next, and, after Gertrude announced the mid-week class-meetings as a reward for full attendance, not one absence occurred for thirteen weeks.

To Harold Thornton it had the look of a miracle that the class for whom no teacher could be found was as clay in the hands of the potter. There was nothing Gertrude could not do with them. They listened spellbound while she talked, took part in the responsive readings, answered questions, studied their lessons, sat wherever the superintendent wished; they even pocketed their papers without a glance at them until the session was over. And they sang with a wild abandon that was exhilarating to hear. Even Harry, who held throughout the note on which his voice first fastened, never failed to sing; and, though it added little to the harmony, it spoke volumes for the spirit of the school and the devotion to the chorister.

But if Gertrude was doing much for the boys, they were doing much for Gertrude; and in obeying her orders to rest, exercise, and grow strong, she could not have had better helpers. From the time when the first pale blossoms of the bloodroot showed beside the snow, through the seasons of violets and wild strawberries and goldenrod, to the time when the frost had spread the ground with the split shucks of the hickory-nuts, the spoil of all the woodland was brought to her.

Their class-meetings became long tramps, during which Gertrude told them interesting things about insects, birds, and flowers, and they told as much that was strange to her. Every one of them had become a conspirator in the plot to keep her out of doors, away from her books; hardly a day passed that she did not go somewhere with one or more of them. And as the healthy color began to show beneath the tan, as strength came back, and every pulse beat brought the returning joy of life, she often felt that all her work for class number four had been repaid a hundredfold.

It was one mid-August afternoon, when the tasseled corn stood high, and the thistles had begun to take wing and fly away to join the dandelions, that there came the first thoughts of the carols. Harry had to drive cows that day; but the others were with her, and as they came out through Mr. Giertz's woods, and looked down upon the pasture where the sheep were feeding, little Phil began the quaint old version of the shepherd psalm that she had taught them,—

"The Lord is my shepherd;
  I shall not want;
He maketh me down to lie,"—

and, the other boys joining, they sang through to the end.

It was beautiful. She had never realized that they could sing so well, and, suddenly, as she listened, the plan came full-grown into her mind, and she proposed it then and there. The boys were jubilant; for a half-hour they discussed details; and then, "all seated on the ground," like those of whom they sang, she taught them the beginning of, "While shepherds watched their flocks by night."

That was the first of many open-air rehearsals, transferred, when the weather grew colder, to Willie Giertz's, where there were no near neighbors to whom the portentous secret might leak out. There was not one defective voice in the class save Harry's, and he was at first a puzzle; but that difficulty vanished when it was learned that his fondest ambition was satisfied by striking the tuning-fork. Thereafter all went smoothly, with much enthusiasm and a world of mystery.

When the program was complete, they had by heart six songs: "While shepherds watched their flocks by night," "Away in a manger," "We three kings of Orient are," "Hark! the herald angels sing," "There came three kings ere break of day," and last, but best, because it seemed especially made for them, the song that began:—

"O little town of Bethlehem,
  How still we see thee lie!
 Above thy deep and dreamless sleep
  The silent stars go by."

And so at length came Christmas eve. Little eyes were closing tight in determined efforts to force the sleep that would make the time till morning so much shorter. But in Bethlehem Center were six boys who, it is safe to say, were thinking less of the morrow's gifts than of the morning's plan; for preparations for early rising had been as elaborate as if it were fourth of July, and there was a solemn agreement that not one present should be looked at until after their return.

Gertrude had fallen asleep thinking of the letter beneath her pillow, promising her return to college at the beginning of next term; but at the first tinkle of her alarm-clock she was up, and, dressing by candlelight, went softly down the stairs and out into the keen air of the morning. The stars were still bright overhead, and there was no light in the east; but Gertrude Windsor was not the first abroad; for at the gate Eddie, the two Willies, and little Phil stood waiting, and already Harry and Charlie were seen coming at top speed.

"Are we all here?" asked Eddie in a stage whisper; and the other boys huddled close together, and wriggled with suppressed excitement.

"Yes," answered Gertrude. "Which place is first?"

"Mr. McKenzie's," announced Charlie, whose part it was to lay out the route; and, crossing the road, they passed through the parsonage gate. Beneath the study windows, Harry, at a given signal, struck the tuning-fork against his boot heel, Gertrude gave the key, and then, like one, there rose to greet the dawning of another Christmas day those clear young voices:—

"Hark! the herald angels sing,
'Glory to the new-born King;
Peace on earth and mercy mild,
God and sinners reconciled.'"

There were sounds from within before they had finished the first stanza; but when, after the "Amen," the pastor started to open a window, the boys were too quick for him. There was a volley of "Merry Christmas," and his answer reached only the rearguard tumbling over the picket fence.

Beneath the bare apple-tree boughs in Harold Thornton's yard, Charlie, Eddie, and little Phil sang, "We three kings of Orient are," while the others joined in the chorus. At the song's close, the superintendent, swifter of foot than the pastor, overtook them with a great box of candy.

Tears came into the eyes of Mrs. Martin as, watching beside her sick child, she heard again the story of the Babe "away in a manger, no crib for his bed." Old Uncle King forgot for a moment his vexing troubles as he listened to the admonition to "rest beside the weary road and hear the angels sing." Mrs. Fenny cried, as sick people will, when she heard the boys reiterate the sweet, triumphant notes.

So from house to house the singers went, pausing at one because of sickness, at another because those within were lonely, at some for love, as they had serenaded the pastor and the superintendent, and bringing to each some new joy.

The stars were fading out, and they had started to return. On their side of the street was the post-office, and opposite them was the saloon, with its gaudy gilt sign, "Tim's Place." Little Phil was behind Gertrude; and as they passed that building,—it was home to him—his hand just touched her sleeve.

"Do you think," he whispered, and she could see the pitiful quiver of his chin as he spoke—"do you suppose—we could sing one for m' father?"

Tears filled Gertrude's eyes; and had she not known boys so well, she would have stooped and caught him in her arms.

"Why, surely," she answered. "Which one do you think he would like best?"

Phil had shrunk behind her, and beneath the gaze of the other boys his eyes were those of a little hunted animal at bay. "Bethlehem," he said, huskily.

And when Harry had struck the tuning-fork, they began to sing together,—

"O little town of Bethlehem,
  How still we see thee lie!
Above thy deep and dreamless sleep
  The silent stars go by."

The twenty-fourth had been a good day for business in Tim Shartow's place. He had had venison for free lunch; two mandolin and guitar players had been there all the evening; and there was more than two hundred dollars in the till. But now, in the quiet of the early morning, as he sat alone, the reaction had come. He remembered how Rob MacFlynn had had too much, and gone home maudlin to the wife who had toiled all day at the wash-tub. He thought of the fight Joe Frier and Tom Stacey had had. And—he did not drink much himself; he despised a drunkard—and these things disgusted him. There was little Phil, too,—"the saloon-keeper's boy,"—and that cut deep. Wouldn't it pay better, in the long run—and then the music floated softly in.

He did not hear the words at first, but he had a good ear,—it was the singing that had brought him, as a boy, into the beer-gardens,—and, stepping to the window, he listened, all unseen by those without. There the words reached him:—

"How silently, how silently,
  The wondrous gift is given!
So God imparts to human hearts
  The blessings of his heaven.

No ear may hear his coming,
  But in this world of sin
Where meek souls will receive him"—

and until they sang the "Amen," Tim Shartow never stirred from the window.

* * * * *

The storm that had been threatening all day had descended. Without, a blizzard was raging; but within, beside his study fire, the little ones tucked away in bed up-stairs, and a book in his hand, the Reverend McKenzie could laugh at weather. A knock at that hour surprised him; but when he saw who stood upon the threshold, he knew how the saloon-keeper felt when he posted his bills so many months before.

"Good evening, Mr. Shartow," he said. "Won't you come in?"

The face of his visitor was tense and haggard; for the struggle had lasted the day long.

"I've come for help," he answered, shortly. "I guess it's the kind you can give, all right."

For a moment the pastor searched his face. "God bless you!" he exclaimed.
"Come in, come in."

And so was wrought again, before the close of the day that had been ushered in by the singing of the carols, the ever new miracle of Christmas; for God's gift to men had been again accepted, and into another heart made meek and ready to receive him the dear Christ had entered.—Frederick Hall, in Christian Endeavor World.

$TANDING BEAR'S SPEECH

The first time an Indian was permitted to appear in court in this country and have his rights tried, was in the year 1897. Previous to this every Indian in the United States was subject to the orders of the Secretary of the Interior. If he happened to be a man of a tyrannical nature, the Indians fared hard. One Secretary of the Interior at the point of the bayonet had caused all the Poncas Indians to be driven from northern Nebraska down to Indian Territory, depriving them of lands to which they held government deeds. They were left in the new country for months without rations, and more than one third of them died. Among these was the son of Standing Bear. The old chief refused to have the boy buried in the strange country, and, gathering about thirty members of his tribe together, he started for their ancient hunting-grounds, intending to bury his boy where generations of the Poncas chiefs lay.

The Secretary of the Interior heard of the runaways, and through the War Department telegraphed to General Crook, of Omaha, to arrest the Indians, and return them to Indian Territory. So General Crook arrested Standing Bear and his followers, and took them all, with the old wagon that contained the body of the dead boy, down to Omaha.

Standing Bear told his story to the general, who was already familiar with many wrongs that had been committed against the Indians, and who was indignant at their treatment. He detained the Indians at Omaha until he consulted with a Mr. Tibbies, an editor of a newspaper. They agreed to espouse the cause of the Indians, securing to Standing Bear a trial in the United States court. It was the most notable trial ever brought in the West, and, in fact, the scope was as wide as any ever tried in this country; for upon its decision one hundred thousand persons were made citizens.

Mr. Tibbies, who attended every session of the court, describes what took place, in the following words:—

"The court-room was crowded with fashionably dressed women; and the clergy, which had been greatly stirred by the incident, were there in force. Lawyers, every one in Nebraska, and many from the big Eastern cities; business men; General Crook and his staff in their dress uniforms (this was one of the few times in his life that Crook wore full dress in public); and the Indians themselves, in their gaudy colors. The court-room was a galaxy of brilliancy.

"On one side stood the army officers, the brilliantly dressed women, and the white people; on the other was standing Bear, in his official robes as chief of the Poncas, and with him were his leading men. Far back in the audience, shrinking from observation, was an Indian girl, who afterward became famous as a lecturer in England and America. She was later known on both continents by a translation of her Indian name, In-sta-the-am-ba, Bright Eyes.

"Attorney Poppleton's argument was carefully prepared, and consumed sixteen hours in the delivering, occupying the attention of the court for two days. On the third day Mr. Webster spoke for six hours. And during all the proceedings, the court-room was packed with the beauty and culture of the city.

"Toward the close of the trial, the situation became tense. As the wrongs inflicted on the Indians were described by the attorneys, indignation was often at white heat, and the judge made no attempt to suppress the applause which broke out from time to time. For the department, Mr. Lambertson made a short address, but was listened to in complete silence.

"It was late in the afternoon when the trial drew to a close. The excitement had been increasing, but it reached a height not before attained when Judge Dundy announced that Chief Standing Bear would be allowed to make a speech in his own behalf. Not one in the audience besides the army officers and Mr. Tibbies had ever heard an oration by an Indian. All of them had read of the eloquence of Red Jacket and Logan, and they sat there wondering if the mild-looking old man, with the lines of suffering and sorrow on his brow and cheek, dressed in the full robes of an Indian chief, could make a speech at all. It happened that there was a good interpreter present—one who was used to 'chief talk.'

"Standing Bear arose. Half facing the audience, he held out

his right hand, and stood motionless so long that the stillness of death which had settled down on the audience, became almost unbearable. At last, looking up at the judge, he said:—

"'That hand is not the color of yours, but if I prick it, the blood will flow, and I shall feel pain. The blood is of the same color as yours. God made me, and I am a man. I never committed any crime. If I had, I would not stand here to make a defense. I would suffer the punishment and make no complaint.'

"Still standing half facing the audience, he looked past the judge, out of the window, as if gazing upon something far in the distance, and continued:—

"'I seem to be standing on a high bank of a great river, with my wife and little girl at my side. I cannot cross the river, and impassable cliffs arise behind me. I hear the noise of great waters; I look, and see a flood coming. The waters rise to our feet, and then to our knees. My little girl stretches her hands toward me and says, "Save me." I stand where no member of my race ever stood before. There is no tradition to guide me. The chiefs who preceded me knew nothing of the circumstances that surround me. I hear only my little girl say, "Save me." In despair I look toward the cliffs behind me, and I seem to see a dim trail that may lead to a way of life. But no Indian ever passed over that trail. It looks to be impassable. I make the attempt.'

"'I take my child by the hand, and my wife follows after me. Our hands and our feet are torn by the sharp rocks, and our trail is marked by our blood. At last I see a rift in the rocks. A little way beyond there are green prairies. The swift-running water, the Niobrara, pours down between the green hills. There are the graves of my fathers. There again we will pitch our teepee and build our fires. I see the light of the world and of liberty just ahead.'

"The old chief became silent again, and, after an appreciable pause, he turned toward the judge with such a look of pathos and suffering on his face that none who saw it will forget it, and said:—

"'But in the center of the path there stands a man. Behind him I see soldiers in number like the leaves of the trees. If that man gives me the permission, I may pass on to life and liberty. If he refuses, I must go back and sink beneath the flood.'

"Then, in a lower tone, 'You are that man.'

"There was silence in the court as the old chief sat down. Tears ran down over the judge's face. General Crook leaned forward and covered his face with his hands. Some of the ladies sobbed.

"All at once that audience, by one common impulse, rose to its feet, and such a shout went up as was never heard in a Nebraska court-room. No one heard Judge Dundy say, 'Court is dismissed.' There was a rush for Standing Bear. The first to reach him was General Crook. I was second. The ladies flocked around him, and for an hour Standing Bear had a reception."

A few days afterward Judge Dundy handed down his famous decision, in which he announced that an Indian was a "person," and was entitled to the protection of the law. Standing Bear and his followers were set free; and, with his old wagon and the body of the dead child, he went back to the hunting-grounds of his fathers, and buried the body with tribal honors. —Indian Journal.

Some Things We Need

> The courage born of God, not man,
>   The truth to speak, cost what it may;
> The patience to endure the trials
>   That form a part of every day;
> The purpose firm, the will to do
>   The right, wherever we may be;
> The wisdom to reprove the faults
>   That in our loved ones we may see,—
> Reprove in tone and spirit sweet,
>   And ne'er in temper's eloquence;
> The heart to love the ones in wrong,
>   While wrong we hate in every sense;
> The strength to do our daily task
>   As unto God,—for we're his own,—
> To seek his approbation sweet,
>   And not men's praise, fame, or renown,—
> These, these, and more, are things we need
>   If Christ we'd represent indeed.

C. C. ROBERTS

$\mathcal{M}$ABEL ASHTON'S DREAM

As the guests came together in the brilliantly lighted parlors at the home of Mabel Ashton that crisp winter evening, there was nothing unusual in the appearance of the rooms to indicate that the party to which they had been invited was to be in any respect different from the round of gaiety to which they had been devoting themselves for the greater part of the winter. Some of the guests, as they greeted their young hostess, noticed an unusual degree of nervousness in her manner, but, attributing it to the excitement of preparation and anticipation, thought no more of it, and all were soon engaged in conversation.

The musicians were in their places, and the young people were beginning to wonder why the signal was not given for the orchestra to strike up, when Mabel Ashton, her sweet face flushed and pale by turns, took her stand near the musicians. After closing her eyes for a moment, during which the room became perfectly still, in a voice at first trembling, but clear and steady, she said:—

"Friends, I know you will think me very queer; but before we do anything else, I must tell you a little story.

"I had a dream last night, which has made such an impression on my mind and heart that I must tell it to you. I dreamed that tonight had arrived, and you had all assembled in these rooms, when there came to the door, and was ushered in, a guest who seemed strangely familiar, and yet whom I could not recognize. He had a rare face, peaceful, yet a little sad in its expression, and his eyes were more penetrating than any that I had ever before seen. He was dressed in neat yet very plain clothing, but there was something in his appearance which marked him as no ordinary man.

"While I was trying to think where I had seen him, he advanced to me, took my hand, and said, gently, 'You do not recognize me, Mabel?' Surprised at such a form of salutation from a stranger, I could only say, 'Your face, sir, seems familiar, yet I cannot recall your name.'

"'Yet I am one whom you have invited here this evening, or, I should rather say, one to whom both you and your parents have extended many invitations to be present here whenever I am able to come. You have even invited me to make my home here; and I have come tonight to join your little company.'

"'I beg a thousand pardons,' I replied, 'but you mystify me all the more, and I beg you will relieve me by telling me whom I have the pleasure of greeting.'

"Then he offered to my view the palms of his hands, in which were scars as of nail wounds, and looked me through and through with those piercing yet tender eyes; and I did not need that he should say to me, 'I am Jesus Christ, your Lord.'

"To say that I was startled would be to express only a very small part of my feelings. For a moment I stood still, not knowing what to do or say. Why could I not fall at his feet and say with all my heart, 'I am filled with joy at seeing you here, Lord Jesus'?

"With those eyes looking into mine, I could not say it; for it was not true. For some reason, on the instant only half comprehended by myself, I was sorry he had come. It was an awful thought, to be glad to have all the rest of you here, yet sorry to see my Saviour! Could it be that I was ashamed of him, or was I ashamed of something in myself?

"At length I recovered myself in a degree, and said, 'You wish to speak to my parents, I am sure.'

"'Yes, Mabel,' as he accompanied me to where my mother and father sat gazing in surprise at my evident confusion in greeting an unexpected guest; 'but I came this evening chiefly to be with you and your young friends; for I have often heard you speak enthusiastically in your young people's meetings about how delightful it would be if you could have me visibly present with you.'

"Again the blush came to my cheeks as the thought flashed through my mind, Tomorrow night is prayer-meeting night; I should have been delighted to see him then. But why not tonight, on this pleasant occasion? I led him to my parents, and, in a somewhat shamefaced fashion, introduced him.

"They both gave a start of amazed surprise, but, convinced by his appearance that there was no mistake, my father recovered a degree of self-possession, and bade him welcome, as he offered him a seat, remarking that this was an unexpected pleasure. After a somewhat lengthy pause, he explained to Jesus that his daughter Mabel, being very closely occupied with her studies, and having little variety in life, had been allowed to invite a few friends in for a social evening, with a little quiet dancing by way of healthful exercise. Her friends were all of the very choicest, and he felt that this was a harmless amusement, which the church had come to look upon in a somewhat different light from that in which it was viewed forty years ago. Removing the objectionable feature of bad company, had made this pleasant pastime a safe indulgence.

"As my father stammered out, in the presence of Jesus, these words of apology, which had fallen from my own lips, I felt myself flush crimson with shame both for my dear father and for myself. Why should he apologize at all for what he considered unquestionably right? How hollow it all sounded there in the presence of the Lord! Did not Jesus know that my studies were not so pressing but that I could keep late hours, sometimes several nights in the week, at parties?

"Then father, anxious to relieve my evident embarrassment, said, 'I am sure we can leave these young people safely to themselves, and nothing would please me so well as to take you, my Lord Jesus, off into my study for a talk.'

"'No,' said Jesus, 'Mabel has often invited me, and I came tonight especially to be with her. Will you introduce me to your friends, Mabel? Some of them I know, but some I do not know.'

"Of course, all this time you, friends, were looking much in our direction, wondering at our embarrassment, and perhaps guessing that we had been made uncomfortable by the arrival of a not altogether welcome guest. I led him first to some of the church-members among you, and there was not one of you who looked so comfortable after the introduction as before.

"As it became known who the guest was, faces changed color, and some of you looked very much as if you would like to leave the room. It really seemed as if the church-members were quite as unwilling to meet Jesus as those who were not Christians.

"One of you came up quietly and whispered to me, 'Shall I tell the musicians not to play the dance music, but to look up some sacred pieces?' Jesus caught the question, and, looking us both squarely in the face, he simply asked, 'Why should you?' and we could not answer. Some one else suggested that we could have a very pleasant and profitable evening if we should change our original plans, and invite Jesus to talk to us. And he also was met with that searching question, 'Why should my presence change your plans?'

"After I had introduced the Lord Jesus to you all, and no one knew what to do next, Jesus turned to me and said: 'You were planning for dancing, were you not? It is high time you began, or you cannot complete your program before daylight. Will you not give the word to the musicians, Mabel?'

"I was much embarrassed. If my original plan was all right, his presence ought only to add joy to the occasion; yet here were all my guests, as well as myself, made wretchedly uncomfortable by the presence of him whom most of us called our best Friend. Determined to throw off this feeling and be myself, at his word I ordered the musicians to play for the first dance.

"The young man with whom I was engaged for that dance did not come to claim me, and no one went upon the floor. This was still worse embarrassment. The orchestra played once more, and two or three couples, more to relieve me than for any other reason, began to dance in a rather formal fashion. I was almost beside myself with shame and confusion, when the Lord Jesus turned to me and said: 'Mabel, your guests do not seem at ease. Why do you not, as their hostess, relieve their embarrassment by dancing, yourself? Would it help you any if I should offer to dance with you?'

"My confusion gave way to an expression almost of horror, as I looked into those tenderly sad eyes and cried, 'You dance! You cannot mean it!'

278

"'Why not, Mabel? If my disciples may dance, may not I? Did you think all this winter, when you and others of my disciples have gathered for the dance, or the card-party, or at the theater, that you left me at home or in the church? You prayed for my presence in the prayer-meeting; you did not quite want it here; but why not, my dear child? Why have you not welcomed me tonight, Mabel? Why has my presence spoiled your pleasure? Though I am "a Man of sorrows, and acquainted with grief," yet I delight to share and increase all the pure joys of my disciples. Is it possible that you leave me out of any of your pleasures, Mabel? If so, is it not because you feel that they do not help you to become like me and to glorify me; that they take your time and strength and thought to such an extent that you have less delight in my Word and in communion with me? You have been asking, "What's the harm?" Have you asked, "What is the gain?" Have you done these things for the glory of God?'

"It was plain to me now. Overcome with self-reproach and profound sorrow, I threw myself on the floor at his feet, and sobbed out my repentance.

"With a, 'Daughter, go in peace; thy sins be forgiven thee,' he was gone. I awoke and found that it was all a dream. And now I want to ask you, my friends, shall we go on with the program tonight, or shall we take these lists which we have prepared, and discuss for a time with our partners the question, 'What can young people do to make the world better for their having lived in it'?"

As the vote was unanimous in favor of the latter plan, which was followed by other wholesome recreations, and as the social evening was declared the most delightful of the winter, it is safe to say that the Lord Jesus had sent that dream for others besides Mabel Ashton.—Presbyterian Journal.

A SAD BUT TRUE STORY

It was in the large parlors of a mansion in Missouri, where, on a pleasant October evening, ten or twelve young people were gathered from the wealthiest homes of the elite of the city. Among them was a young woman who, though always genial and social with the young, was ever clad in mourning garb, and bore the name of Mara, chosen by herself to express the grief and bitterness of her life, since the time when she, seven or eight years before, had been bereft of all her family.

The pleasant hours flew fast till about half past ten in the evening, when one of the company pulled out a pack of cards and flung it on the table where Mara Moor was sitting. The effect was startling. Her face took on a deathly pallor; she trembled, arose from her seat, staggered across the room, and took a chair in the remotest corner. So great was her agitation that every one saw it, but none was aware of the cause.

One of the party, who had been reading law for some time, not imagining the seriousness of her anguish, went to her, and in a bantering way threatened her with a legal prosecution before an impaneled jury in case she refused to return to her place at the table, and submit to the regulations of the evening. While the lawyer was urging her to this, a thoughtless young man of the company stepped up to them and placed a few cards in her hand. She jerked her hand away, and gave it a sling as if to rid it of the contaminating filth of the cards; and, with an agonizing scream, she began weeping and sobbing as if her heart would break.

Surprised at this new outburst, the lawyer sought to soothe the wounded spirit; and when she had become somewhat quiet, he, with the rest, entreated her to give them the reason for her terrible agitation. This she at first refused to do, but being urged very strongly by all the company, she at length consented. At the first word a shudder passed over her whole frame; but pausing to regain her self-control, she began:—

"When I was nineteen years old, I was living in an Eastern city, in one of the happiest homes within its limits. A rich and tender father, with a loving and gentle mother, and as bright and true a brother as ever a sister could want, were my companions in the delightful home of my childhood. Wealth and comfort smiled upon us, and prophesied of future happiness, until, with my own hand, I plucked down upon us all the greatest curse imaginable.

"Two of our cousins, a brother and sister, came to visit us, and we spent the evening in pleasant conversation, as we did this evening; and just as those cards were thrown upon the table, and at about the same hour, my parents having retired, our cousin threw a deck upon our table. They two and I sat down to play, while my dear and tenderly loved brother, not liking the idea of playing cards, turned to his music, which he was composing as a graduating exercise for examination day, and went to work at that. We three needed a fourth one to make the game go properly, and we began trying to persuade my brother to come and take part with us; but he declared he thought it was not right to spend time in card-playing—that it was an amusement of the lowest character, and he did not want to get into it.

"After using all our arguments to induce him to assist us, but to no purpose, I went to him, put my arm around his neck, and told him that I was a Christian, and was trying to get to heaven, and thought it no harm to play cards just for amusement; that I thought he ought to lay aside his scruples, and come and help us, as we could have no fun without his nelp; that he was too fastidious, anyway. With this he arose from his seat very reluctantly, and came, protesting that he knew nothing about it. We told him he could soon learn, and he did, only too quickly; for, in a little time, he was enough for any of us; and when we three had become tired of the sport, he was so delighted with it that he sat for an hour studying the cards and shuffling them.

"We laughed heartily at him for his interest in the matter, and finally retired for the night, leaving him with the cards. Next morning he took them up again, and tried to induce us to play with him; but our cousins had to go home, and soon left us, taking the deck with them. But the fatal act had been done. That night my brother was in the city until a late hour, which was a thing that had never occurred before. When he came home, he seemed morose; and to our inquiries for the cause, his replies were evasive.

"The next night he was out again; and this continued for some nights, until his money—two hundred dollars—was all gone. He then went to father for more, and, as he had unbounded confidence in my brother, father very readily gave him quite a little sum, without asking what he was going to do with it. This was soon gone. When he asked for more, father desired him to tell what he was doing with so much money. Not receiving a direct answer, father gave him a small sum, and told him he could get no more unless he would give a clear report of the use he made of his money. This money was soon spent, and when he went for more, but was unwilling to account for what he had received, father refused to give him more. With this refusal he became angry, and told father he would make him willing to let him have the money. My brother then went into the city again, and, as usual, into a gambling-den, where he managed to get money for gaming, or sat and looked on. He was absent for nearly a week.

"During this time my mother neither ate nor slept, as I might say; and when my brother was brought home drunk, she took her bed, and never got up again, but died of a broken heart, within a few days.

"We hoped this would stop my brother's course, but it did so only for a short time. He soon began gambling and drinking again; and, being young and rather delicate, it was not long until he was brought home in delirium tremens. Upon this father took his bed, languished, sank, and died, leaving myself and my brother alone in the world. O, how I wished I could die, too! But it seemed that God determined that I should see the end of my work in wrecking our family, and I was compelled to still remain, and reap the harvest of my own doings.

"Every influence that could be brought to bear on my poor brother I made use of, but to no avail; and, O, how I prayed for him! But it was of no use! He went even more rapidly down the way of ruin, now that father was dead and out of his way. Only a few weeks after I had followed my father to his resting-place in the silent grave, my brother was brought home with delirium tremens again, and, after suffering for a short time the most terrible agony, the poor boy died, and was laid in a drunkard's grave. O my God! why was I ever born? Why cannot I die, too? But what will my eternity be for having thus ruined my own brother, the bright and beautiful boy? This is why I spell my name Mara."

Soon after the lady commenced her sad story, the ladies in the company began weeping; and when it was finished, they were all sobbing as if their hearts would break; and the eyes of the men also were moist. The cards had disappeared, and vows were solemnly expressed by the entire company that never again would one of them be guilty of engaging in that sport, but that they would ever do their best to endeavor to put the practise out of society.—Selected.

Sowing to the Flesh

Are you sowing to the flesh, O youth?
Have you turned your back upon the truth?
Are you scattering seeds of evil
From the garner of the devil?
Are you thinking of the harvest
   By and by?
Soon will spring and summer pass,
Brown and sere will grow the grass;
No time then for good seed-sowing:
   You and I
Must gather what we've sown, forsooth.
Are you sowing to the flesh, O youth?

Are you sowing to the flesh, O maid?
Can you think of the harvest unafraid?
Is this world your only treasure?
This life all your joy and pleasure?
Are you laying up no portion
   In the sky?
He that soweth to the wind
Shall a whirlwind's harvest find,
And he'll see himself a pauper
   By and by.
We must reap of what we sow, it is said:
Are you sowing to the flesh, O maid?

ELIZABETH ROSSER.

"THE MAN THAT DIED FOR ME"

For many years I wanted to go as a foreign missionary, but my way seemed hedged about. At last I went to live in California. Life was rough in the mining country where I lived, with my husband and little boys.

While there I heard of a man who lived over the hills and was dying of consumption. The men said: "He is so vile that no one can stay with him; so we place some food near him, and leave him for twenty-four hours. We will find him dead sometime, and the sooner the better. Never had a relative, I guess."

This pitiful story haunted me as I went about my work. For three days I tried to get some one to go to see him and find out if he was in need of better care. As I turned from the last man, vexed with his indifference, the thought came to me: "Why not go yourself? Here is missionary work, if you want it."

I will not tell how I weighed the probable uselessness of my going, nor how
I shrank from one so vile as he. It was not the kind of work I wanted.

But at last one day I went over the hills to the little abode. It was a mud cabin, containing but one room. The door stood open. In one corner, on some straw and colored blankets, I found the dying man. Sin had left awful marks on his face, and if I had not heard that he could not move, I should have retreated. As my shadow fell over the floor, he looked up and greeted me with an oath. I stepped forward a little, and again he swore.

"Don't speak so, my friend," I said.

"I ain't your friend. I ain't got any friends," he said.

"Well, I am your friend, and—"

But the oaths came quickly, and he said: "You ain't my friend. I never had any friends, and I don't want any now."

I reached out, at arm's length, the fruit I had brought for him, and stepping back to the doorway, asked if he remembered his mother, hoping to find a tender place in his heart; but he cursed her. I spoke of God, and he cursed him. I tried to speak of Jesus and his death for us, but he stopped me with his oaths, and said: "That's all a lie. Nobody ever died for others."

I went away discouraged, saying to myself that I knew it was of no use. But the next day I went again, and every day for two weeks. He did not show the gratitude of a dog, and at the end of that time I said that I was not going any more. That night as I was putting my little boy to bed, I did not pray for the miner. My little boy noticed it and said:—

"Mama, you did not pray for the bad man."

"No," I answered, with a sigh.

"Have you given him up, mama?"

"Yes, I guess so."

"Has God given him up, mama? Ought you to give him up till God does?"

I could not sleep that night. I thought of the dying man, so vile, and with no one to care! I rose and went away by myself to pray; but the moment that I knelt, I was overpowered by the sense of how little meaning there had been to my prayers. I had had no faith, and I had not really cared, beyond a kind of half-hearted sentiment. I had not claimed his soul for God. O, the shame of such missionary zeal! I fell on my face literally, as I cried, "O Christ, give me a little glimpse of the worth of a human soul!" Did you, Christian, ever ask that and mean it? Do not do it unless you are willing to give up ease and selfish pleasure; for life will be a different thing to you after this revelation.

I remained on my knees until Calvary became a reality to me. I cannot describe those hours. They came and went unheeded; but I learned that night what I had never known before, what it was to travail for a human soul. I saw my Lord as I had never seen him before. I knelt there till the answer came.

As I went back to my room, my husband said:—

"How about your miner?"

"He is going to be saved."

"How are you going to do it? he asked.

"The Lord is going to save him; and I do not know that I shall do anything about it," I replied.

The next morning brought a lesson in Christian work which I had never learned before. I had waited on other days until afternoon, when, my work being over, I could change my dress, put on my gloves, and take a walk while the shadows were on the hillsides. That day, the moment my little boys went to school, I left my work, and, without waiting for gloves or shadows, hurried over the hills, not to see "that vile wretch," but to win a soul. I thought the man might die.

As I passed on, a neighbor came out of her cabin, and said, "I will go over the hills with you."

I did not want her to go, but it was another lesson for me. God could plan better than I could. She had her little girl with her, and as we reached the cabin, she said, "I will wait out here."

I do not know what I expected, but the man greeted me with an awful oath. Still it did not hurt; for I was behind Christ, and I stayed there; and I could bear what struck him first.

While I was changing the basin of water and towel for him, things which I had done every day, but which he had never thanked me for, the clear laugh of the little girl rang out upon the air.

"What's that?" said the man eagerly.

"It's a little girl outside waiting for me."

"Would you mind letting her come in?" said he, in a different tone from any
I had heard before.

Stepping to the door, I beckoned to her; then, taking her hand, said, "Come in and see the sick man, Mamie." She shrank back as she saw his face, but I assured her with, "Poor sick man! He can't get up; he wants to see you."

She looked like an angel, her bright face framed in golden curls and her eyes tender and pitiful. In her hands she held the flowers that she had picked from the purple sage, and, bending toward him, she said: "I'm sorry for 'ou, sick man. Will 'ou have a posy?"

He laid his great, bony hand beyond the flowers, on the plump hand of the child, and tears came to his eyes, as he said: "I had a little girl once. Her name was Mamie. She cared for me. Nobody else did. Guess I'd been different if she'd lived. I've hated everybody since she died."

I knew at once that I had the key to the man's heart. The thought came quickly, born of that midnight prayer service, and I said, "When I spoke of your mother and your wife, you cursed them; I know now that they were not good women, or you could not have done it."

"Good women! O, you don't know nothin' 'bout that kind of woman! You can't think what they was!"

"Well, if your little girl had lived and grown up with them, wouldn't she have been like them? Would you have liked to have her live for that?"

He evidently had never thought of that, and his great eyes looked off for a full minute. As they came back to mine, he cried: "O God, no! I'd killed her first. I'm glad she died."

Reaching out and taking the poor hand, I said, "The dear Lord didn't want her to be like them. He loved her even better than you did, so he took her away. He is keeping her for you. Don't you want to see her again?"

"O, I'd be willing to be burned alive a thousand times over if I could just see my little girl once more, my little Mamie!"

O friends, you know what a blessed story I had to tell that hour, and I had been so close to Calvary that night that I could tell it in earnest! The poor face grew ashy pale as I talked, and the man threw up his arms as if his agony was mastering him. Two or three times he gasped, as if losing his breath. Then, clutching me, he said, "What's that you said t'other day 'bout talkin' to some one out o' sight?"

"It is praying. I tell Him what I want."

"Pray now, quick. Tell him I want my little girl again. Tell him anything you want to."

I took the hands of the child, and placed them on the trembling hands of the man. Then, dropping on my knees, with the child in front of me, I bade her pray for the man who had lost his little Mamie, and wanted to see her again. As nearly as I remember, this was Mamie's prayer:—

"Dear Jesus, this man is sick. He has lost his little girl, and he feels bad about it. I'm so sorry for him, and he's sorry, too. Won't you help him, and show him how to find his little girl? Do, please. Amen."

Heaven seemed to open before us, and there stood One with the prints of the nails in his hands and the wound in his side.

Mamie slipped away soon, and the man kept saying: "Tell him more about it. Tell him everything. But, O, you don't know!" Then he poured out such a torrent of confession that I could not have borne it but for One who was close to us at that hour.

By and by the poor man grasped the strong hand. It was the third day when the poor, tired soul turned from everything to him, the Mighty to save, "the Man that died for me." He lived on for weeks, as if God would show how real was the change. I had been telling him one day about a meeting, when he said, "I'd like to go to a meetin' once."

So we planned a meeting, and the men from the mills and the mines came and filled the room.

"Now, boys," said he, "get down on your knees, while she tells about that
 Man that died for me."

I had been brought up to believe that a woman should not speak in meeting, but I found myself talking, and I tried to tell the simple story of the cross. After a while he said:—

"Boys, you don't half believe it, or you'd cry; you couldn't help it. Raise me up. I'd like to tell it once."

So they raised him up, and, between his short breathing and coughing, he told the story. He had to use the language he knew.

"Boys," he said, "you know how the water runs down the sluice-boxes and carries off the dirt and leaves the gold behind. Well, the blood of that Man she tells about went right over me just like that. It carried off about everything; but it left enough for me to see Mamie, and to see the Man that died for me. O boys, can't you love him?"

Some days after, there came a look into his face which told that the end had come. I had to leave him, and I said, "What shall I say tonight, Jack?"

"Just good night," he said.

"What will you say to me when we meet again?"

"I'll say, 'Good morning,' over there."

The next morning the door was closed, and I found two men sitting silently by a board stretched across two stools. They turned back the sheet from the dead, and I looked on the face, which seemed to have come back nearer to the image of God.

"I wish you could have seen him when he went," they said.

"Tell me about it."

"Well, all at once he brightened up, 'bout midnight, an' smilin', said: 'I'm goin', boys. Tell her I'm going to see the Man that died for me;' an' he was gone."

Kneeling there with my hands over those poor, cold ones, which had been stained with human blood, I asked that I might understand more and more the worth of a human soul, and be drawn into a deeper sympathy with Christ's yearning compassion, "not willing that any should perish."—Mrs. J. K. Barney.

How Wonderful!

He answered all my prayer abundantly,
And crowned the work that to his feet I brought,
With blessing more than I had asked or thought,—
A blessing undisguised, and fair, and free.
I stood amazed, and whispered, "Can it be
That he hath granted all the boon I sought?
How wonderful that he for me hath wrought!
How wonderful that he hath answered me!"
O faithless heart! He said that he would hear
And answer thy poor prayer, and he hath heard
And proved his promise. Wherefore didst thou fear?
Why marvel that thy Lord hath kept his word?
More wonderful if he should fail to bless
Expectant faith and prayer with good success!

—F. R. Havergal.

OUR GRASS RUG AND—OTHER THINGS

Our house isn't so very nice. We own it, of course, and that is a great deal, as mother has often reminded us when we grumbled. But we girls always thought there were some drawbacks even to that, because we couldn't ask a landlord for new paper or fresh paint, and as for us—we never had money to spare for such superfluities.

There are only four of us,—mother and Jack, Rose and me. We children have been busy all our lives trying to get educated, so we could keep mother in luxury after a while. In the meantime, she had done with bare necessities, for the life-insurance father left wasn't large enough to take any liberty with. Mother has things spick and span. No palace could be more beautifully kept than our home, but the furnishing is nothing whatever to boast of.

Our room was almost the worst of all, with its odds and ends of things. "Other girls have silver-backed hair-brushes!" wailed Rose one night, regarding her old one with a scornful glance.

"Yes, and chairs that don't tip one over," I added, as I managed to save myself from a fall.

"Isn't it horrid to be poor, Meta?" said Rose.

"It's no joke." I was very grim because I had bruised my hand on the rickety chair, and tomorrow was music-lesson day, as I remembered.

It was then and there we rebelled. Not so mother could hear us—we weren't mean enough for that! She'd have been only too glad to help matters if she could. So we had our indignation meeting by our two selves. We said we'd had enough of old furniture and cheap sash curtains, and we decided it was time to act.

Having reached this decision, we proceeded to carry it out,

and we surprised ourselves with the speed of our achievements. My hope lay in music, Rose's in arithmetic. I trailed around the neighborhood, next day, looking for scholars, and Rose betook herself straight down to the Cowans, who had been hunting for a "coach" for their twins. We had discussed the Cowan possibility some time before, but Rose declared then that she couldn't spare a minute from the demands of her studies, while I knew it would keep me busy to be graduated on schedule time without doing anything outside.

It makes a difference when you get interested in something for yourself. As soon as ever we girls viewed these occupations in the light of furnishings for our room, we felt sure we could squeeze them in—and we did. I got six beginners, and Rose captured the Cowans, root and branch—four instead of two; for it seemed they were not proficient in mathematical pursuits, and their mother was delighted to get them off her distracted hands. All our friends know that Rose adores sums and problems, and she didn't need any other recommendation.

Well, we did it! It wasn't easy, either. If my half-dozen aspirants for fame escaped shaking till their teeth chattered, it wasn't because I didn't ache to administer it. And Rose feared her hair would be white before the end of the term. You see, when there's a certain amount of housework you feel obliged to do, and when your studies fairly clamor for attention the rest of the time, it sets your nerves all awry to keep the tempo for clumsy fingers that go just half as fast as they should; or to teach over and over again that four times five are always twenty.

But I suppose all these trials helped us to appreciate our possessions when we did get them. They were just as sweet and dainty as we had hoped. We got two single beds—white enamel with brass trimmings—and a pretty mirror in a neat frame. Our old dressing-table looked like new with fresh drapery, and there were full-length curtains to match. Two cunning white rockers, two other chairs, and a little round stand made us feel simply blissful. We painted our book-shelves with white enamel paint, and did our woodwork ourselves. Jack painted the floor a soft gray that would blend with anything, and after it was dry we laid on it one of our chief treasures. It was a grass rug, in two shades of green, with a stenciled border and a general air of elegance that almost overpowered us. It was large enough almost to cover the floor, and we stenciled green borders on our curtains and drapery in the same Grecian pattern.

It seemed too good to be true as we stood in the door and viewed the landscape o'er after we had it done. "It isn't often that our dreams come true!" sighed Rose.

"But this one has," I assured her.

She nodded happily. "Yes, and it's just as nice as we thought it would be!"

"Won't it do our hearts good to 'give notice,' as the cooks say?"

"I can hardly wait to tell those awful Cowans that they may get along as best they can. I'm so tired of them, Meta!"

"I know you are. I wouldn't mind the music so much if I had time. But it's dreadful when your own studies drag like millstones about your neck. I'm not clever at learning as you are, Rose. I have to work for what I get. So I shall tell them, next Tuesday, that I've decided not to teach any more till school's out."

Jack stopped on his way down the hall to look over our shoulders. "Huh!" he said, if you know what that means.

"Doesn't it look lovely?" asked Rose, her face all full of dimples. Rose is as pretty as a picture, anyway, and when she smiles, you can't help smiling back. Jack patted her cheek, and said, "It certainly does," and then he passed on abruptly.

"Something doesn't suit him!" I declared as he shut his room door behind him. "I can't imagine what it is, and it's of no earthly use to ask him." It wouldn't have been. You can't worm a thing out of that boy till he gets ready to tell.

Mother came up the stairs just then waving a note in her hand. "It's from Helen Hunt!" she announced joyfully. "She is going to spend a day and a night with us next week on her way to Grovesport. I shall be so glad to see her." Mrs. Hunt and mother have been friends more years than Rose and I have lived, and they very seldom meet any more. So we girls were almost as glad as mother was, because that dear woman doesn't have as many pleasures, as she deserves.

After we went to bed that night, we planned the surprise. The visitor should have our lovely new nest, and we'd go and camp in the shabby old guest-room. We knew it would please mother, for she hadn't had so pretty a place to entertain Mrs. Hunt in for many years. It did please her, too, so much that she almost cried, and she hugged us and thanked us till we felt very happy and self-satisfied. Jack was standing by, and he said "Huh!" again, in that same queer tone. Then mother turned and hugged him, and Rose and I said to each other how strange it was that Jack should be jealous of his own sisters.

It shone the day she came—the room, I mean, though the sun was on duty. too. Mother went to the station to meet her, and, as she started out, she called back, "Children, if any of you have occasion to go into my room while I'm gone, be sure to shut the door when you come out!"

We answered "All right!" all three at once, and then Rose said, "How funny!
What do you suppose made her tell us to do that?"

"I can't imagine," I replied, and then Jack smiled. If it had been anybody but our jolly old Jack, I'd have said his smile was sarcastic; but no one ever accused that boy of anything so ill-natured. Then he said in a quiet, even voice: "It doesn't take a Solon to see through that. She wants to make sure that Mrs. Hunt doesn't see the contrast between her room and the one across the hall. She might not understand—or approve."

And with that he took his cap and went out.

Stunned? I guess we were! Rose and I stared at each other as if we'd seen a ghost. Then we put our arms around each other and went up-stairs without a word. It was mother's door we opened, and we stood there and gazed as if we'd never seen that room before. She had been darning her carpet again. We could see the careful stitches and the frayed edges her art couldn't quite conceal. "She has polished her furniture, too! See how it shines, Meta. She tried to make it look its best." Rose's voice was mournful, so I tried to speak up cheerfully.

"To be sure she did, and succeeded!" Then we turned, and both of us choked back a sob at what we saw. She had taken our discarded dressing-table drapery, cut out the best portions, ruffled it daintily, pressed it neatly, and put it on her own bureau. Our worn-out sash curtains, nicely laundered, veiled her book-rack.

"Meta, our mother—our precious jewel of a mother! We've taken everything for ourselves and left her the rags!"

Rose had her head on my shoulder, and by that time I was crying as hard as she was.

"No wonder Jack was dissatisfied!" I sobbed. "Rose, why didn't he tell us?"

"O Meta, why did we need telling? That's what breaks my heart. Even our rickety chair fixed up and set back in the shadow! O, I can't stand it!"

"We've got to!" I stiffened up grimly. "We've got to stand it, and it serves us right. But we'll make it up to her as soon as Mrs. Hunt is gone!"

"Yes, if we can live till then!"

"I think we'll manage to. Mortification won't kill us in twenty-four hours. We'll make her sleep in there tonight, and they can have one cozy visit in suitable quarters. Monsters!"

Rose didn't resent the epithet. She knew it was appropriate.

We did some thinking that night. I never felt so utterly insignificant in my life. We realized at last that there are other ways to show love than letting its object do all the sacrificing, all the giving and enduring, while the one who bestows it revels in selfishness. We didn't say anything then, but mother wasn't allowed to touch that supper, only the portion of it that filled her own plate, and she didn't wash a dish after it, either! If Rose and I sat over our books an hour after our usual bedtime, in consequence, it hurt no one but ourselves, and we deserved it.

They had a lovely time together. We could hear their soft voices rise and fall, with once in a while a ripple of laughter, till we dropped off to sleep. The next night, mother went back to her own room. We didn't say a word to prevent it, though it hurt us to think of our old duds in there for mother to use.

Next day the early morning post brought a note from Mrs. Hall, an old neighbor, urging mother to meet her down-town at ten o'clock. There was some important shopping on hand, and mother's advice was indispensable. The dear thing didn't suspect that her daughters had frantically besought Mrs. Hall the day before to concoct some scheme that would clear the coast at home. "All day, Mrs. Hall!" we pleaded. "We've planned a surprise for her, and it will take a good while to arrange it."

Mother didn't see how she could be spared to go, but we assured her that since we'd be at home, she wasn't needed at all. If this struck her as a most unusual state of affairs, she was too polite to say so, and, true to her habit of helpfulness, she dressed and went to Mrs. Hall's rescue.

We didn't waste any time, I assure you. We couldn't paint her floor then, but Jack stained it around the edges where it wouldn't have to be walked on, and the grass rug covered the rest. We burned the made-over rags. It did our hearts good to see them crisp and turn to ashes.

Into the attic went the ugly old things, and across the hall came the pretty new ones,—curtains, dressing-table, chairs, every single dainty belonging, even the drapery from our book-shelves. Teddy Ward came in and helped carry things, and Jack worked like a beaver. He didn't need any urging, either. If ever a boy's face shone like a full moon, Jack's did that happy day, though he stopped at least a dozen times to hug his sisters. "What a beast I was to think you could be as selfish as all that!" he exclaimed once, "I ought to have known better!"

"But we were just that selfish, Jacky," we told him. We didn't mean to sail under false colors. "We'd never have thought, if it hadn't been for you."

"Yes, you would. The first jolt would have waked you up. Lend a hand here,
Meta!"

It was done at last, all cozy and fresh. Rose stopped in the door. "It looks like mother," she said, and her voice was husky. "It's pure and sweet like her!"

"The other one looks pretty forlorn, girls. What are you going to do about it?" Jack had a hand on our shoulders as he spoke, and we felt his sympathy.

"Do?" we chirped up as brisk as millionaires. "Why, furnish it, of course."

"We have one bed to start on," Rose reminded him. "That's a big help, and the floor and woodwork are still painted. How are we to do it? Lessons, to be sure. Cowans and scales!"

"Thought you wanted to quit." Our brother looked troubled, for all his satisfaction.

"My son, we have changed our minds. Our most ardent desire now is to keep on," I told him. Rose smiled drolly. "I am seriously considering refurnishing the entire domicile," she remarked. "The Cowans are good for the next twenty years, judging from their present attainments, and it's fine practise for me!"

We didn't give mother a hint till after supper. It was hard to wait, but we made ourselves do it so everything would come about quite naturally. She took her bonnet and wrap up to put them away, and we three tagged, as softly as if we had pads on our feet, like cats. She opened her door and gave one bewildered glance, then she turned and saw us. "It's yours, Lovey, every bit!" we told her.

"Darlings, I couldn't!" she said. "Your hard work—your dear new treasures! I couldn't permit such a sacrifice, my darlings!" We just would not cry, though the lumps in our throats made our voices sound as if they belonged to some other family.

"They aren't our new treasures, they're yours."

"Who has been making sacrifices all our lives?"

"We love you so—you couldn't hurt us by refusing, Lovey!"

"There is no question of refusing." Rose spoke with great emphasis. "This room is hers, once for all, and there is no more to be said about it."

We tucked her into her pretty white bed that night, and we kissed the dear face on the ruffled pillow. Jack came in for his good night, too, and we all stood looking down at her, so happy we couldn't talk. She lifted her arms—those arms that had worked so hard for us—and gathered the three of us to her at once. "My darlings!" was all she said, and we crept out softly, knowing we had received her benediction.

Yes, we are getting our second collection of furniture into shape slowly but surely. But we have learned that there are more precious things to be had in homes than beds and chairs, or even green grass rugs. We have them—the precious things—so, now that mother's room is accomplished, we can wait very happily for the beds and chairs—Rose, and Jack, and I.—Elisabeth Price, in St. Nicholas, copyrighted by the Century Company, 1913.

* * * * *

"The tender words unspoken,
  The letters never sent,
The long-forgotten messages,
  The wealth of love unspent,—
For these some hearts are breaking,
  For these some loved ones wait;
Show them that you care for them
  Before it is too late."